W9-CQL-977

Critics Give Rave Reviews
to Simon Brett:

"An exploration of the public and private side of evil every bit as horrifying as that classic dark tale by Robert Louis Stevenson, *The Strange Case of Dr. Jekyll and Mr. Hyde.*"
—*Sun-Times* (Chicago)

"A swift, expertly developed novel."
—*Publishers Weekly*

"Fascinating . . . a tribute to Brett's cleverness as a writer."
—*Newsday*

"Brett is an ingenious entertainer. . . . We may applaud his wit, invention, and keen eye for character."
—*The San Diego Union*

"A marvelously wry tale."
—*UPI*

"Chilling . . . a compellingly tense departure for the talented Brett."
—*The Detroit News*

"There's a neat twist at the end and a surprising amount of suspense in the telling, as well as a sharply drawn portrait of the generation that came of age in the '60s and entered middle age in the '80s." —*The Denver Post*

By the same author:

CAST, IN ORDER OF DISAPPEARANCE
SO MUCH BLOOD
STAR TRAP
AN AMATEUR CORPSE
A COMEDIAN DIES
THE DEAD SIDE OF THE MIKE
SITUATION TRAGEDY
MURDER UNPROMPTED
MURDER IN THE TITLE
NOT DEAD, ONLY RESTING

A SHOCK TO THE SYSTEM

SIMON BRETT

A DELL BOOK

Published by
Dell Publishing Co., Inc.
1 Dag Hammarskjold Plaza
New York, New York 10017

First published in the United States by Charles Scribner's Sons 1985.

Dell ® TM 681510, Dell Publishing Co., Inc.

ISBN: 0-440-18200-X

Reprinted by arrangement with Charles Scribner's Sons

Printed in the United States of America

January 1987

10 9 8 7 6 5 4 3 2 1

WFH

To Larry,
who understands the system

CHAPTER ONE

The first murder was almost accidental. Indeed, if it had ever gone to court the charge would probably have been manslaughter.

But the legal difference between the two crimes can be one of intention, and there is no doubt that at the moment he hit the old man, Graham Marshall intended to kill him.

And that was his first taste of the power of death.

But murder can also be reduced to manslaughter by provocation, and there was no doubt in Graham Marshall's mind that at the moment he killed the old man, he was provoked beyond human endurance.

Not provoked so much by the importuning of his victim, as by the entire forty-one years of his life. It had been a life, it seemed to Graham, of false promise and false promises; a life of carrots dangled, prizes offered, a long sequence of incentives to lure him along a road which he had only recently discovered to be a dead end.

That the realisation had taken so long to come only made it the more bitter. Like the victim of an elaborate confidence trick, he had contributed to his own deception, and was that much more reluctant to accept the real facts. For a long time he had refused to believe that he was up against a blank wall, convincing himself that the way out was merely hidden, and that finding it was another challenge to his proven intelligence and acknowledged ingenuity.

But the events of the Thursday in March 1981 that led up to the old man's death left him no further excuse for self-deception.

He was sealed off in a dead end, too far along the road to turn back and make a new start. And the gold for which he had spent forty-one years prospecting was fool's gold.

His life up until that point had been a series of competitions, and the only thing they had in common was the fact that he had won them all. With his new cynicism, he could see that the competitions had been limited in scope, his aspirations prudently pitched at his own level of ability, but he had not realised this at the time, and had faced each new test with regenerated enthusiasm and the determination to pass, to come out on top.

His parents had set the competitive tone of his life. For their son, subsequently to prove their only child, conceived in 1939 and born into a Britain at war, they had wanted the best, better at least than the hard road they had travelled through the privations of the 'Twenties and 'Thirties. Graham's father, who had worked himself up from a local government office in Rotherham to clerical eminence in the Ministry of Agriculture and Fisheries, saw daily the easier advance of colleagues with public school and university backgrounds, and determined that his son should have these advantages. Economy came naturally to Eric Marshall, and he forced it on his wife. Economy was the reason they restricted their family to one child. Any parsimony in the small semi in Mitcham, where they moved after the war, was justified if it contributed to Graham's education. 'Public school and university,' Mr. Marshall kept saying, 'they're the keys to the system – got to have those if you're going to get anywhere, Graham.'

A prep-school was the first essential. Graham probably never knew his parents' tension as they presented their son to the ex-Harrovian headmaster of a minor establishment in Streatham. Nor their relief when he passed this, the first of his public tests.

The school's attitude mirrored his parents'. Weekly progress reports, and a seating plan regularly reorganised according to academic achievement, encouraged Graham's competitive

8

nature. And the fact that he was rarely out of the top three desks gratified both pupil and parents. Meanwhile, he shed their Northern vowels and adopted the speech patterns of the other boys at the school.

Common Entrance was Graham's next public assessment and again he was not found wanting. A day-school in New Malden, whose headmaster attended the all-important conference which justified the name of 'public school', welcomed the aspirant with arms wide enough to include a small scholarship.

Once there, when the run-up to O-levels demanded that the pupils specialise, Graham followed his father's advice, based on the observation that 'there'll always be jobs for teachers', and concentrated on languages, intensifying his studies of French and adding German.

These disciplines, in which words corresponded with other words, and answers were either right or wrong, suited the analytical turn of his mind, and he easily cleared the next hurdles of good marks in O-levels, A-levels, and finally – a peak hitherto unscaled in the Marshall family – entrance with a much-prized 'State Scholarship' to the University of Leeds where he was to read French and German (and, incidentally, just miss National Service).

The cynicism of forty-one years diminished these achievements in retrospect.

Post-war stringencies had made the prep-school desperate for pupils; the public school had been an extremely minor one; and Leeds University was not Oxbridge. But at the time they had been important milestones on the road to being a 'success'. Indeed, Graham became accustomed to hearing the word 'success' associated with his name. His parents and their friends used it often; even some of his fellow students used it, not without ambivalence, but still with admiration for his quick intelligence and dedication.

But achievement in examinations, where the rules were simple and unvarying, did not inevitably mean success in 'the outside world', an expression he heard increasingly during his

9

final year at Leeds. 'The outside world' was full of achievers of different backgrounds, making their own rules. To earn the title of 'a success', Graham knew he had to contend with, and beat, this new competition.

It was therefore regarded as a significant – indeed, huge – triumph, when he won, against a reputed opposition of six hundred applicants, one of six Management Traineeships with the British subsidiary of the international oil company, Crasoco. The achievement was the greater because the opposition was not made up exclusively of university graduates, but included applicants who had been through National Service and older men from other oil companies, candidates with long experience of 'the outside world'.

For Graham's parents the appointment was a vindication of the long years of abstinence. Their investment had paid off. Their pride in their son knew no bounds. But with the pride came a certain distance, a recognition that Graham had now achieved that step-up into another earnings-bracket – potentially even another class – for which they had so ardently worked. And that his experiences in life would have a decreasing amount in common with their own.

So when, during the two years of his traineeship, he came back to Mitcham with stories of flying to the Middle East to inspect oil wells, of staying in the best hotels on company expenses, they regarded him with something approaching awe.

And when he moved into a flat in Kensington with three other young men, one of whom had been to Eton, the awe increased. As it did when he spoke casually of dinners eaten out in Chelsea bistros, of sports cars bought and sold, or of foreign holidays.

So far as his parents were concerned, there was no doubt of Graham Marshall's right to the title of 'a success'.

And, within Crasoco, it seemed to be increasingly applicable. After his two years' induction Graham confounded the expectation that he would use his language degree in a foreign posting by opting for administration. He applied for, and

10

obtained, a staff appointment in the Personnel Department, where he quickly demonstrated an unsuspected talent for management, his quick intelligence and sufficient personal charm steering him fluently through the intricacies of meetings and committees.

The move to Personnel was unpredictable but shrewd, a calculated step sideways which could in time place him higher on the management ladder than a more obvious, but more directly competitive, career pattern. Personnel was an area where a bright newcomer could make a mark more quickly than in the departments which were more glamorous, but in which bright newcomers were ten a penny. As in many large organisations, the Personnel Department of Crasoco was something of an elephant's graveyard. It contained its share of staffing and welfare specialists, earnestly flaunting their third-class degrees in Psychology, but too many of the senior posts went to staff with long service records who had been proved inadequate in other fields. Failed General Managers, pushed sideways from foreign postings which they couldn't quite handle, spiralled down to retirement finding accommodation for expatriate staff. There hung about the Department an air of resigned insufficiency, a tendency to live in a past which had never quite delivered its promise.

While some young men would have found this atmosphere depressing, Graham recognised how well it suited his talents. He would have little intellectual competition, and his achievements would shine more brightly in a prevailing atmosphere of defeat. It was an ideal position from which he could play the system, from which he could continue to be 'a success'.

His age was also on his side, at a time when youth was becoming fashionable. Rationed straight-talking and studied casualness of dress fostered for him an image amongst senior management of something between *enfant terrible* and whizz-kid, a phenomenon which was impressive, even to those who distrusted it.

As a result, he collected special commendations and increments, and achieved his first promotion, to Assistant

Personnel Officer, after only four years with the company, in the process leap-frogging other contenders over ten years his senior. His rise did not always make him friends, but none could deny his intelligence and skill in the complex board-game of company politics.

By the age of twenty-five he was earning more than his father and had the money to enjoy the much-discussed excitements of 'Swinging London'. Though almost too old for the 'Beatles generation', he participated in the clubs, parties and pop concerts with his customary controlled abandon. He started to shop in Carnaby Street, finding the gaudy expanse of a flowered tie or the ill-disguised evidence of beads about his neck more valuable counters in the game of confusing his superiors.

He also took some advantage of the supposedly new sexual licence, though not as much as he liked to imply to older colleagues. One or two mini-skirted dolly-birds came back to his flat (he was by now buying one of his own in a modern block in Chelsea), but these random couplings were not as guilt-free as he would have wished. A Calvinist streak, inherited from his parents and inspired by their unimpeachable example, left him with the unfashionable conviction that sex should be allied to marriage.

But marriage, when it came in 1967, continued the image of 'a success'. In the June of that year, when Procol Harum topped the charts with the moody pretentiousness of 'A Whiter Shade of Pale', Graham met at a party Merrily Hinchcliffe, the beautiful waiflike daughter of television actress Lilian Hinchcliffe and sister of pop journalist, Charmian Hinchcliffe. By the beginning of September, when Scott McKenzie, from every juke-box and radio, urged visitors to San Francisco to wear some flowers in their hair, he had married her.

At the wedding, held in Chelsea Register Office, Merrily obeyed the musical injunction and was crowned with a garland of Michaelmas daisies. Her dress, of plain white Indian muslin, left no doubt that she wore no brassière.

Graham, for his part, had on a see-through patterned shirt beneath a gold-frogged guardsman's jacket and, around his neck, a small brass temple bell.

They made a fine couple – Graham nearly six foot, dark-haired and handsome to those who did not look too closely at the narrowness of his eyes, Merrily a blonde wisp of thistledown on his arm. So they figured in the wedding photographs, kept framed and fading through the years ahead.

Graham's parents, stiff respectively in three-piece and two-piece suits of the sort people they knew wore to weddings, gaped throughout the proceedings. The presence at the reception of Lilian Hinchcliffe, informally famous in a turquoise kaftan, and Charmian, in a totally transparent blouse, urging a tame pop group to yet another chorus of 'All You Need Is Love', left them in no doubt that their son had arrived socially. They talked a little to some of his (also three-piece-suited) Crasoco colleagues, such as his immediate boss, George Brewer, but generally found the occasion bewildering. When Graham and Merrily set off in his latest car, a Mini-Moke, for what they called 'four weeks of love and freedom on the Continent', Mr. and Mrs. Marshall returned to Mitcham, doubting whether they would ever see their son again.

Graham and Merrily, after a wedding which was a hymn against materialism, had their month of 'dropping out', mostly on the Greek island of Mykonos (which had yet to go completely gay), and returned, she to the expensive flat in Chelsea and he to his well-paid job at Crasoco.

A year later they sold the flat at a handsome profit and moved to a three-bedroomed house in Barnes. Within another year they had a son, Henry, and in 1970 Merrily gave birth to a daughter, Emma. By that time they had also accumulated a colour television, a hi-fi, a washing-machine and a dish-washer, and changed the Mini-Moke (whose unworldly zip-on top leaked rather badly in the rain) for a Citroen DS.

Through the 'Seventies, which coincided exactly with his thirties, Graham Marshall's main concern was work. Deploying his old skills with a new toughness born of experience, he continued to climb up the Crasoco management ladder from his unchallenged outpost in Personnel. Promotions and increments rippled along in a predictable sequence. He kept his finger on the company's pulse, noting whose opinions carried weight and whose were ignored. He went on management training courses, where he demonstrated great aptitude for the sterile exercises which were then fashionable. He was offered the chance of going on computer courses, but turned them down on the grounds that 'some gnome could always be summoned from the computer room to produce the figures'.

In this opinion he echoed George Brewer. Indeed, he kept very close to George Brewer and made himself an indispensable assistant when his mentor was elevated to the post of Head of Personnel. It meant rather more sessions than Graham might have wished of drinking in the company bar, lighting his boss's nasty little cigarettes, helping out with *The Times* crossword and agreeing with George's plans for Crasoco's future, but Graham knew it was worth it. The occasional insincerity could only strengthen his position in the system.

He did not agree with all of George Brewer's opinions, but usually kept his own counsel. George was a businessman of the old school, who constantly bemoaned the dearth of 'gentlemen' in the oil industry. He liked to conduct his affairs over lavish lunches and to spend the mimimum of time in the office. Though always ready with an 'Old boy' and bonhomous arm clapped around the shoulders, he was less good at the minutiae of grading systems, budgeting and job evaluation. Increasingly he was grateful to Graham for taking the burden of some of these tedious details off his shoulders.

George's antipathy to computers was almost Luddite in its intensity. They represented to him the threat of the unknown, and he was constantly heard to remark, 'I'm glad I'll have retired before the bloody things take over completely.' The whole Operations Research Department (or O.R.), computers and those who tended them alike, he dismissed under the derisive soubriquet of 'Space Invaders'.

In the early 'Seventies, under George's predecessor, most of

14

the Personnel Records had been put on to computer, a proceeding which George regarded as 'more trouble than it was worth'. There was a feeling in certain areas of the company that the system was now outdated and should be replaced with something more modern, but George resisted the change. 'Over my dead body,' he would splutter after a few whiskies in the bar. 'Not while I'm in charge. I don't care what they do after I've gone.'

And Graham Marshall, the Head of Personnel's customary companion, would nod agreement while he made his plans for what *would* happen after George had gone. The system would be modernised. Though he knew nothing of their technicalities, Graham recognised the power that computers could bestow. And it was a power he intended to harness when he was in a position to do so.

Because there was little doubt by the end of the 'Seventies in the Department, or elsewhere in the company, that Graham Marshall was poised to take over George Brewer's job (and the five-thousand-pound increase in salary it entailed), when the incumbent reached retirement age in 1982.

That prospect paid for the years of nodding and curbing his true opinions, for the long and, since George's wife had died, increasingly difficult business of getting away from his boss in the evenings. It would all have been worthwhile when Graham was appointed Head of Personnel.

Since George had not reached this eminence until the age of fifty-three, and Graham would be only forty-two when he achieved it, there seemed little doubt that he was destined for even higher reaches of management.

On the strength of these expectations, early in 1980, Graham and Merrily Marshall took out a thirty-thousand-pound endowment mortgage on a much grander, though rather dilapidated, house in Boileau Avenue, Barnes. It would mean a couple of years of economy, but when he got the new job, things would ease considerably.

There was no doubt that Graham Marshall would continue to be, in his parents' oft-repeated words, 'a success'.

CHAPTER TWO

It was after the move into the Boileau Avenue house that things began to change. Whether the change was for good or for bad was not at first clear – certainly there was no sense of things 'going wrong', but events of the ensuing six months produced a marked difference in Graham's attitude to his life and circumstances.

First, there was money. He had, needless to say, done his sums carefully and knew that the house was a good long-term investment. But the property market was sluggish. There seemed to be no immediate sign that prices would rise, as they had done so gratifyingly over the previous decade.

And the outgoings on the new house were considerable. The Marshalls had dispensed with a private pre-purchase survey. Graham, in unconscious echo of his father's manner, had announced that, since the building society was prepared to lend so much money on the property, there couldn't be much wrong with it. This economy was rewarded by a sudden bill for woodworm treatment, which ate up what was left of their savings after the expenses of the move.

Graham and Merrily had prepared theoretically for certain retrenchments after they moved, but they found their reality unpalatable. Ten years of living above their income had nourished habits of extravagance which they found hard to break. The spectre of worrying about money, which had loomed over Graham's childhood but been exorcised in his early twenties by success at Crasoco, threatened to rise again.

Their altered circumstances were reflected in that year's

holiday. Instead of the customary fortnight in Cyprus, they decided to economise by renting a cottage in South Wales. Appalling weather ensured that the holiday was a disaster and necessitated long drives to find diversions for the children, which made the whole exercise almost as expensive as going abroad.

The children did not enjoy it and were not of an age to disguise their disappointment. Graham found he spent much of the holiday shouting at them. They had lost the charm which smallness had imparted, and their physical development presaged worse problems ahead. Henry already had the downy lip, swelling nose and moody secrets of adolescence. Emma, though only eleven, had lost her spontaneity of affection and replaced it with a kind of mannered coquettishness, which augured badly for the future.

Also, they were getting expensive. Both went to private schools and, apart from the inevitable cost of replacing the clothes they outgrew with such rapidity, they were getting to the age of costly entertainments. Graham found himself sounding more and more like his father as he grudgingly paid out for school trips or cinema seats or the hire of tennis courts. They seemed incapable of doing anything that didn't cost money.

And, as they grew more expensive, so he seemed to get less out of them. They were just two young people who happened to be growing up in his house, and at his expense. When he looked at them objectively he realised they held no interest for him whatever.

The habit of objectivity, or even remoteness, increasingly coloured his view of his wife, too. Having not thought about her much for some years, he now found he was looking at her as an outsider might.

And what did the outsider see? A thin, materialistic, rather silly woman of nearly forty.

The waiflike beauty which had been crowned with flowers at their wedding had hardened into angularity. Childbearing had deflated the breasts and spread the hips. And the waiflike

17

charm which went with the appearance had degenerated into empty mannerism.

There was no split in the marriage. They were faithful to each other, and still made love at least once a week, murmuring apposite endearments as they did so. But love-making had become routine for both of them, almost a chore, better than stacking the dishwasher, but less exciting than having a gin and tonic.

As he had with his children, Graham now looked increasingly at his wife with detachment. He realised, with only the mildest of shocks, that she meant nothing to him.

And she did bring with her positive disadvantages, mostly in the form of her mother. Initially, Graham had got on well with Lilian Hinchcliffe. He enjoyed the reflection of her fame as an actress, and the studied bohemianism of her lifestyle contrasted favourably with his own parents' mouselike reticence. Visits to Lilian's cottage near Abingdon ensured varied – sometimes eminent – company, plentiful alcohol and occasional cannabis. Her extravagant personality and his limited connection, through her, with the unconventional world of show business gave him an extra dimension to his colleagues. He could still hold attention in the Crasoco canteen with accounts of her outrageousness, of her much-vaunted affairs, of the fifteen-year marriage to Charmian and Merrily's playwright father (long vanished into alcoholism and death), and, more significantly, of the supposed early liaison with the internationally known and fabulously wealthy film actor, William Essex. All these details gave Graham's mother-in-law very positive advantages.

But Lilian changed as she grew older. Her youthful looks, skilfully maintained into her sixties, suddenly gave way, and cosmetic attempts to repair them made her grotesque. Round the same period, acting work seemed to dry up, and her long-term live-in lover, a costume designer, suddenly dropped dead of a heart attack. The extravagance of her character, so charming in company, curdled, with loneliness, into resentment and contrivance. She made increasing emotional demands

18

on her two daughters, particularly Merrily. Charmian, having broken off an unsatisfactory marriage, lived a career girl existence on the fringes of journalism. Lilian blamed her for not producing a nice set of grandchildren like Merrily, who, as a result, had the dubious privilege of being the favoured daughter.

The climax of Lilian's emotional demands came in September 1980, with a suicide attempt. It was hopelessly inept. She left a blackmailing note and she tried to kill herself by swallowing paint stripper, of all things, though the small amount she took exposed the true nature of the gesture.

As a cry for help, however, it worked; it was agreed that she was too isolated out in Abingdon, and she was moved into a flat in Barnes to be nearer her daughters (or, more strictly, her younger daughter, since Charmian lived in Islington).

This made Lilian a semi-permanent fixture round the Boileau Avenue house. Graham didn't mind that, so much as the fact that he seemed to have to keep subsidising her. She had had money in her time, but spent it all with a ready prodigality. Now she always seemed to be hard-up, and Merrily was constantly asking Graham for small sums to help her mother out.

He resented it. But more than the fact that she was poor, he resented the fact that she was not rich. Though appreciating the advantages his parents had given him by education, he could not help noticing, as he felt his financial circumstances straiten, the even greater advantages enjoyed by contemporaries who had inherited, or stood to inherit, money.

The biggest blow of a bad six months came at the end of November when Graham's father and mother were both killed in a car crash.

Though he had not of latter years seen them that often, and though his relationship with them was not a particularly affectionate one, he felt the shock profoundly.

First, there was just the shock of a disaster, an intensified form of that experienced on passing a road accident or hearing news of a plane crash.

19

This was followed by a feeling of anger, almost contempt, towards his father. For Eric Marshall and his wife's deaths seemed to cast doubt on the principles of economy by which they had run their entire lives. The accident, Graham discovered from the police, need not have happened. His father, for whom saving money became an obsession as he grew older, had insisted on doing his own car maintenance. It was his inefficiency, in failing to tighten the wheel nuts adequately after a tyre-change, which had led to the fatal crash. For Graham, this knowledge diminished his father's memory.

All of Eric Marshall's dicta now seemed suspect. The old line that 'there'll always be jobs for teachers' took on a new irony with the growing recession, and the much-vaunted economy was also shown to be based on a false premise. A lifetime's scrimping had produced virtually nothing to pass on to the next generation. Eric Marshall left no will (another supposed economy) and so legal fees took a large bite from the proceeds of the Mitcham house sale.

But the greatest shock was the slowest to come. Since he had seen so little of his parents, and felt so little for them, it took Graham a long time to define the void that their deaths left in him.

Slowly he realised that what he had lost with them was a point of reference for his achievements. From his earliest recollection, he had performed for *them*. Even in latter years he had rung them from time to time when he had news of some promotion or other triumph. And they had always responded.

It had been their valuation that had given him the definition of 'a success', which he so readily accepted. He did not realise how much he had been cushioned by their unfailing response to his achievements.

With them gone, he could now only be assessed by the harsher standards of 'the outside world'.

At work, the second half of 1980 also proved a sticky period, though Graham Marshall did not feel his own position was challenged. There was just a general malaise throughout the company.

Partly, it was financial. The recession was well-established and, though the oil companies suffered less than other industries, wage rises were curbed and the national unemployment figures made everyone twitchy about their job security.

The situation was not improved by the fact that Crasoco had recently employed a firm of Management Consultants to assess the company from top to bottom. This had an unsettling effect, there was much talk of the likelihood of redundancies following their report. Graham, who had seen a few such investigations come and go without making more than cosmetic changes, remained unworried.

He had his problems, but he managed them with his customary skill. He was busy with commitments to an increasing number of meetings and other responsibilities that George Brewer now shirked, and he found that the whole business of moving house had taken more of his energy than he would have anticipated. He got very tired, but he coped.

Also, increasingly, he had the challenge of bumptious underlings to deal with. One of the effects of the recession had been to restrict job movement in the more obvious channels of promotion, so more young men had followed his course into the Personnel Department. It was inevitable that these were people with similar skills and ambitions to his own. And inevitable that they would try, as he had done, to outmanoeuvre their superiors. At forty, Graham found he had a whole pack of men ten years younger snapping at his heels.

But he felt confident that he was wilier than they were. Most would burn themselves out, lower their sights and settle at their present level. A few would achieve promotion.

The most promising of them was called Robert Benham. He had joined Crasoco three years previously from an American-based oil company. Before that he had worked for an electronics firm and he had a background of computer training. He was bright and ambitious, though he lacked

George and Graham's public-school finish. He spoke with a flat Midland accent and lacked humour. But to everything he did he brought great application and aggression. He played squash on the company court every Tuesday lunchtime and apparently sailed in his spare time.

A good Personnel Officer, Robert Benham might, Graham reckoned, in ten years or so, be in line for his job as Assistant Head of Department. For that reason, he sponsored and encouraged the younger man. When he took over as Head of Personnel, Graham knew that he would need the support of such protégés. And when he masterminded the changeover to the new computer system, he would require specialist help.

Early in 1981 the Management Consultants' report was submitted to the Board of Directors.

Its main criticisms were that the British division of Crasoco was too insular in outlook, insufficiently aware of the oil industry's world picture, and overstaffed at some levels.

To the surprise of all, and the consternation of many, it became clear within a month that this time the consultants' recommendations were going to be heeded. The report, coinciding with the recession, made the company determined to trim down their staff. In spite of rearguard action by the unions and the staff association, there would be redundancies and early retirements.

Anxious weeks followed this announcement, but still Graham Marshall did not worry. He was confident of his abilities and knew his value to the company. He was the best Assistant Head of Department they had had for years.

His confidence proved justified. As ever, because they were closest to the decision-making, the management side suffered least in the cuts.

The only major casualty in the department was George Brewer, who was asked (though the question was not one which would accept any answer but yes) to take an early retirement.

Graham Marshall breathed more easily. The delays of the last few months were over and the continuing road to success lay open before him. He would get the job a year earlier than he had anticipated.

In March George Brewer's post was duly advertised, and Graham duly submitted his application. There were other candidates, but all younger and less experienced, with less years of service to the company. George Brewer was on the selection board, and at the interview virtually said that Graham was the obvious man for the job. David Birdham, the Managing Director, asked some searching questions about the Personnel Department's future, and Graham's answers, without overt disloyalty to George, implied that he was prepared to make substantial changes. He left the boardroom after much bonhomous smiling and handshaking.

He felt as if he had just been admitted to the company's most exclusive club, and, although he had never doubted it, knew that the job was his.

CHAPTER THREE

So when, on the Thursday after the board he received a call from George Brewer's secretary, Stella Davies, to pop up for a drink before lunch, Graham had little doubt what the summons was about.

He entered the outer office confidently and exchanged a little banter with Stella. She was particularly forthcoming that morning. Attractive divorcée in her forties, Graham found himself wondering – not for the first time – if she went with the job. And how far she went with the job.

His confidence was, as ever, increased by the sight of his boss. George had been ageing fast in the last few years, as the precipice of retirement drew nearer. The recent decision, which had brought him so suddenly to its brink, had had a devastating effect. He looked an old man, confused and afraid, as he sat in his swivel chair and fiddled with a paper knife. His lapels were sprinkled with ash from his constant stream of cheap cigarettes. Graham felt the atavistic surge of superiority that youth will always feel as age withdraws from the contest.

George acceded to Graham's offer to get the drinks. His confused state, and the eagerness with which he put the proffered Scotch to his lips, suggested that it was not his first of the morning.

Hmm, Graham found himself reflecting, if old George is hitting the bottle, the sooner he's moved on and I take over, the better.

'Cheers,' he said.

George Brewer echoed the toast, belatedly, since half his

drink was already gone. He reached in his pocket for a cigarette and placed it sadly in his mouth. Graham leaned forward and lit it with his gold lighter, which bore the initials G.M. (an atypically expensive twenty-first birthday present from his parents).

'Good of you to come up, Graham.'

'No problem.'

'No.' George swayed restlessly in his chair. Cigarette ash dropped unnoticed on to his lap.

'You know, Graham, I don't mind telling you, I don't like the way the company's going. Don't know what management's up to.'

'I agree they've given you a pretty shabby deal, but . . .'

'Oh, me,' George shrugged, as if dismissing a cause beyond redemption. 'I'm not talking about me. I'm talking about everything . . . No, from my point of view, I'm glad to be getting out. Don't like the look of the future. The oil won't last much longer, apart from anything else.'

'There's still a bit,' Graham consoled. 'And the company's putting a lot of money and research into alternative fuels.'

'Yes, yes, I suppose so . . .'

George seemed very low. Retirement was frightening him sick. Since the death of his wife, he seemed to have no resources outside his work. One of those who could be dead within a year from sheer inactivity, Graham reflected. He was quite fond of old George, but the thought didn't shock him. Since his parents' deaths, he had been increasingly conscious of how expendable people were.

'Look, Graham,' George began again unnecessarily loudly, to shake himself out of his mood, 'you know I've always had the highest respect for your abilities . . .'

'Thank you.'

'And I've always hoped, when the time came for me to go . . .' His bottom lip, slightly misshaven, quivered. 'Not that I thought I would be going so soon . . .'

'Nor did any of us,' Graham supplied loyally. Oh, get on with it, George, get on with it.

'I always hoped that you'd take over from me. I think we see eye to eye on the important issues in this company. Both want to keep out the bloody Space Invaders, eh?'

'Yes.' Graham laughed loyally at the recurrent joke.

'And I like to think that, with you sitting in this seat, my policies would be continued – at least in outline.'

That's all you know, thought Graham. But he nodded and said, 'Of course, George.'

'So I've always wanted you to take over this job.'

Graham nodded again. He was having difficulty in controlling a little smile at the corners of his lips.

'Unfortunately the rest of the selection board didn't agree with me.'

So total was the surprise of these words that Graham could not for a moment take them in.

'I think it's just faddishness,' George continued petulantly. 'They're all so twitchy after that damned Management Consultants' report, they just want change for change's sake. Won't go for the obvious candidate for the very reason that he is obvious.'

'I'm sorry?' Graham managed to say. 'Are you telling me I haven't got the job?'

'Yes, of course I am,' George replied testily.

Graham's first thought was that George must have got it wrong. He was so confused these days, possibly so drunk, that he'd got the wrong end of the stick.

'Are you sure, George? I mean, I thought –'

'So did I, Graham. And, had it been in my gift, you'd have . . .' The stubbly lower lip trembled again. 'Maybe it's my support that's dished you. Now I'm completely discredited in the company, maybe it's . . . Maybe they don't *want* my policies continued . . .'

But I wouldn't continue them, Graham wanted desperately to say. Wanted to be back before the selection board and say it to them. Good God, had he been backing the wrong horse all these years? Had all those tedious sessions of agreeing with George been wasted?

26

'Don't think they *do* want my policies continued,' the old man went on truculently. 'Said they wanted a "new broom".'

'And who . . .' asked Graham thickly, 'who is the new broom?'

'Robert Benham.'

'Robert Benham! As Head of Personnel!'

'Yes.'

'But he's only thirty-four!'

'That, to the rest of the board, seemed to be a point in his favour.'

'And he's only been with Crasoco three years.'

'That, too. It's the Management Consultants' jibe about our being *insular*. Benham's worked for American companies, he's been all over the place.' George Brewer shrugged hopelessly. 'Graham, there's nothing I can do. I've been overruled – yet again – and Robert Benham is to be the next Head of Department.'

Graham Marshall took a deep breath. 'Does he know yet?'

'No. I must tell him now. I thought the least I could do for you was to let you know first.'

'Thank you.'

'I trust your discretion, of course.'

'Of course.'

George looked at him with old, watery eyes.

'I'm sorry, Graham. I'm afraid we're both in the same boat.'

'And both sold up the same river.'

'Yes.'

Betrayed, totally betrayed. Graham Marshall could feel the fury building inside him. For nearly twenty years he'd played the company game. And now, just when a major prize was within his reach, the rules had been arbitrarily changed.

That evening, when he joined George Brewer and Robert Benham for a celebratory drink in the company bar, Graham found the bitter truth of Oscar Wilde's dictum, that "anyone can sympathise with the sufferings of a friend, but it requires a very fine nature to sympathise with a friend's success".

His nature was not particularly fine, nor was it practised in that kind of sympathy. Nor, come to that, was Robert Benham a friend. Through the afternoon following Graham's announcement, Graham kept coming back to the realisation that this was the first public competition he had failed, and the habits of success were hard to break.

Robert Benham was very cool about his elevation. He could afford to be. Graham, from his own experience, knew how easy it was to avoid brashness and show sympathy in a moment of triumph. The winner always has time to be magnanimous; it is the also-rans following him in who are left breathless and unprepared to comment on their failure.

So Robert Benham, short, dark, and – to Graham's mind – sloppily dressed in a leather-patched tweed jacket, had no difficulty in appearing diffident and modest. He was more relaxed than Graham had ever seen him; the constant aggression he showed at all other times was now curbed. Having achieved his ambition, he didn't need it for a while. Again, from his own experience, Graham could recognise this unassailable calm.

And he could almost recognise his own words when Robert Benham murmured to him, in his flat Midland voice, 'Never had a bigger surprise in my life, Graham. I was convinced you were going to get the job. Hope management know what they're playing at.'

What was more, he could recognise how insincere the words were. Of course Robert Benham hadn't been surprised. The appointment had merely confirmed his own opinion of himself.

Just as it would have confirmed Graham's self-image . . . had he got it.

Had he got it. He was still having difficulty in assimilating the idea of failure. He had lived so long with the conviction of taking over from George that it would take some time to dismantle the superstructure of consequences that had been built on to that fantasy.

28

But at the same time he knew how total the failure was. Forty-one was young for someone to become Head of Department; it was much older for someone to fail to become Head of Department. The stigma would stay. For the first time, Graham realised how his concentration on the one particular job had disqualified him from others. The shrewd thing would have been to have spent the last ten years moving around, going to other departments, even other companies.

As Robert Benham had.

What had Robert Benham got that he hadn't? Nothing, Graham decided, just the same qualities in greater concentration.

And youth. And no wife and children and massive mortgage to slow him down.

Background?

Not as good as Graham's. State education, primary and comprehensive. Out of school at sixteen and into a job. Then, in his early twenties an external degree, and subsequently business school. No public-school gloss.

The rules had certainly changed. Once again, Graham felt contempt for his father's memory. 'Public school and university, they're the keys to the system – got to have those if you're going to get anywhere, Graham.'

Untrue. A deception. All the miserable years of penny-pinching in Mitcham had been unnecessary. Like his car maintenance, like his savings policy, Eric Marshall's plan of education had been simply incompetent.

'Fact is, I'll be making some changes when I take over,' Robert Benham confided, after George had nipped out to the Gents for the second time in an hour's drinking. Really, the old man seemed to be falling apart.

'For a start, Graham, I'm going to see that everyone works a lot harder. Hell of a lot of slackness has crept into the Department while George has been in charge.'

He hastened to qualify this. 'Not you, of course, Graham. Always had great respect for your application and sheer bloody graft.'

Patronising, almost like a school report. *Makes the most of his limited abilities*. Again, Graham knew he had said the same to candidates he had beaten in previous contests.

'But what I want to do is get a new attitude going, really shake people up a bit. Stop them thinking they're on to a cushy number and can just wind down to retirement. Get some concept of *productivity* into the Department.'

'Yes. Sure,' Graham agreed enthusiastically. Just as enthusiastically as he had endorsed George's plans in the past.

Robert reached into his pocket for a box of small cigars and proffered them. Graham refused. Robert took one and replaced the box. Instinctively Graham found the gold lighter in his hand, cocked and ready. God, so quickly he was slipping into a subservient role to his new boss. He hated himself for it.

'Won't necessarily be popular, what I'm suggesting, Graham, so I'm going to need a lot of support. And advice. Lots of areas of the company I know nothing about, so I'm going to be relying on your experience, consulting you a lot.' A pause. 'If I may, Graham.'

So ingenuous. So magnanimous. So humble.

Just as he would have been, if he had got the job.

'Of course,' said Graham. 'Anything I can do to help, Robert.'

The drinking session went on for a long time and it was half past eleven when Graham lurched off the Tube at Hammersmith.

He was, he realised, very drunk. Fiercely he clutched his umbrella's ridged handle. His briefcase had been left in the office. Graham had been intending to take some work home that evening, but it was too late for that. Anyway, what was the point of doing extra work now he wasn't going to become Head of Department?

What was the point of anything?

The injustice of Robert Benham's appointment rose like vomit in his throat as he went through the barrier, with a reflex flick of his season to the ticket-collector.

There were few people about. It was chilly. Rain fell outside the station. He crossed automatically to the subway that led to Hammersmith Bridge and Boileau Avenue.

Rain had trickled down the steps, forming wide puddles, which he sidestepped with the rigid concentration of the very drunk.

The old man was slumped against the tiled wall at the foot of the steps leading up to the pavement.

Graham Marshall hardly noticed the shapeless figure. There were often down-and-outs in the subway. His own thoughts were too turbulent for him to be aware of anything else.

As Graham drew alongside, the old man straightened up.

'Spare us a quid, guv.'

Graham caught a sour whiff of stained clothes on unwashed flesh as he continued on his way up the steps. He felt the rain as he emerged, but did not put up his umbrella. The handle remained clenched rigidly in his hand.

He was some way along Hammersmith Bridge Road before he realised the old man was following him. There was a peculiar slap-slap of feet in ill-fitting shoes on the wet pavement.

Graham lengthened his stride. Headlights of the occasional car crossing the bridge laid ribbons of white on the shining black road. Traffic hummed and swished on the flyover above, eliminating the slapping sound of the feet.

'Hey! Guv!'

He strode on, unaware of the rain or his legs automatically tracing their daily route home. In spite of its fierce tension, his body felt weak and out of control.

He was past the pub and on to the bridge before he realised that the old man was still following.

'Guv!'

The closeness of the voice was a shock and he gave an involuntary half-turn before striding on. He had an impression of a fuzzed outline of rags.

Next there was an arm on his sleeve. Graham swung round

31

in fury. The lights of Hammersmith were behind the old man. He was still just an outline and a smell. Nothing.

Graham felt huge, unfocused by the alcohol, a cartoonlike bulk looming over the stooped figure.

'Guv, can you spare us a quid? Please. I made a mess of my life. But I only have to look at you to see you're a success.'

Had he chosen any other word, the old man would have lived.

But suddenly he was everyone who had ever deceived Graham Marshall. He was Eric Marshall, he was George Brewer, he was Robert Benham. He was provocation beyond human endurance. And he had to be obliterated, removed from the face of the earth.

All the fury of Graham's disappointment, of his forty-one wasted years, went into the blow, as the ridged umbrella handle smashed down on the faceless head.

With no sound but a little glug like a cork coming out of a bottle, the old man crumpled to the ground.

Graham looked round. There was no one on the bridge and, for the moment, there were no cars.

He looked at the umbrella handle, fearing the viscous gleam of blood. But the overhead lights caught only on the ridges of polished wood. It was unmarked.

Instinctively, Graham bent down and, without feeling the body's weight, picked it up and tipped it over the parapet of the bridge.

He was walking again before the small splash sounded.

He was inside the house before the realisation of what had happened hit him.

In the bathroom, as he raised the toothbrush to his lips, he suddenly knew he had committed murder.

He doubled up, vomiting into the basin.

'Oh God,' Merrily's little voice drawled behind him. 'Have you had too much to drink?'

32

CHAPTER FOUR

Graham Marshall passed a terrible night. The alcohol put him off to sleep quickly, but he awoke within an hour, sweat prickling along his hairline and soon drenching his nightshirt. The duvet pressed down damply as if to smother him, and the undersheet ruckled into torturing ridges. His arms started to tremble uncontrollably.

Merrily slept on beside him, unperturbed, the evenness of her breathing a continuing reproach. 'The sleep of the just.' The phrase came jaggedly into his mind – the sleep enjoyed by the righteous, by those good citizens who were not murderers.

His teeth started to chatter. He twitched noisily out of bed. Part of him wanted to wake Merrily, not to tell her what had happened, but just to have some reaction, some comment on his nervous collapse. The rhythm of her breathing broke, but settled almost immediately back to its infuriating regularity.

He looked at her outline, padded by the duvet, and felt unreasoning hatred. 'The sleep of the just' – again the phrase gatecrashed his mind. But it was the injustice of her sleep that hurt him. She had not had to suffer the provocation that he had. She had not had to murder an old man.

He lurched out of the bedroom. The skin felt tight and tingled on his scalp; he had a clear image of his brain drying up, shrivelling, sucking the flesh inward.

He went downstairs to the sitting-room and had a large Scotch, which he knew was a bad idea, but at least controlled the shaking for a moment.

All too quickly the thoughts returned.

He had committed murder.

A new inward trembling started, sending out fierce little shudders from his stomach, as the reality took hold of him.

What he felt was simply fear. There was no remorse – certainly no guilt – for what he had done. The old man had insufficient identity for him to feel such personal emotions.

And certainly Graham's agony had no moral cause. Abstract morality played no part in his scheme of things. Abstract thought of any kind was alien to him. If he had stopped to examine his motives – which he never did – he would have found their sole impetus had always been the pursuit of success without social indiscretion. This had led him to a pattern of behaviour which was, from the outside, often indistinguishable from that of a moral person. But its imperatives were always those of expediency; they were not dictated by any system of belief. He believed in nothing except his own ability to recognise the next move required and to make it.

But the events of the day had given that belief a hammering. His failure to get George Brewer's job had written off his life. The murder, and his subsequent arrest, would just be public recognition of that fact.

Fear of discovery was the only cause of his nervous collapse.

And, even through the paralysis of fear, he felt anger, fury at the injustice that had subjected him to the old man's provocation. He regarded the murder as his misfortune, but not his fault.

He had to sleep. Alcohol wasn't going to do the trick. There must be something else in the house. Wasn't there some draught Merrily had given the children when they were wakeful? The stuff hadn't been used for years, but it might still be around.

His angry scrabbling in the bathroom cupboard woke Merrily. She appeared again, bleary in the doorway. 'What are you looking for?' the little voice asked.

'That stuff you used to give the kids. I can't sleep.'

'Oh, the Phenergan. I chucked it out before we moved.'

34

'Damn.'

'Why can't you sleep?'

'I don't know. Why can't one sleep?'

'Are you worried about the job?'

'Job?'

'George's job. Have you heard anything about the board?'

It was absolutely instinctive, but Graham didn't know why he said no.

He had a triple hangover on the Friday morning – first, from the alcohol; second, from the loss of George's job; and, third, from the knowledge of the murder.

He couldn't eat any breakfast; Merrily and the children seemed more alien than ever; so he mumbled something about having to be in early, and left at about quarter to eight.

He was almost on Hammersmith Bridge before he thought about the route he was taking. A panic seized him. He felt he should run away and hide. There would be a little crowd of policemen in the middle of the bridge, questioning the passers-by, waiting for him. His step faltered.

But logic stopped his flight. His only chance lay in behaving normally, doing exactly as he had always done, exactly as he had done before he was a murderer.

He dared to look ahead. There were no policemen on the bridge; only the usual trail of pedestrian commuters moving faster than the solid mass of cars on their way into London.

With a great effort, he didn't break step when he reached the scene of the crime. He flashed a look at the damp pavement, fearing bloodstains.

There was nothing.

The parapet too looked unmarked.

As he walked along he looked down at the Thames beneath. The tide was high, its level increased by the recent rains. The dull water flowed on strongly, its surface broken only by slow-turning driftwood and high-riding plastic containers.

For the first time, Graham Marshall almost believed the murder hadn't happened.

*

Any serenity he experienced was short-lived. As he approached the office, again he faltered, convinced that there would be a policeman waiting inside for him. And again he managed to damp the panic down. His only hope was to behave naturally. The day before no one had thought of him as a murderer; he must act exactly as he had the day before.

Inside the building the commissionaire gave the usual respectful greeting as Graham flashed his identity card. George Brewer's Stella was getting in the lift. It was early yet; just the two of them travelled up to the fifth floor.

'I'm very sorry about the job,' said Stella.

'Oh. Thank you.' To his amazement, his voice sounded normal. Or if it was a little thicker than usual, that could be put down to disappointment about the job. To people who didn't know about the murder, there would always be an alternative explanation.

'I was flabbergasted,' she went on. 'I'm not sure whether I'll enjoy working with young Mr. Benham.'

He looked at her. He'd always rather fancied her in a resigned way, though never really contemplated being unfaithful to Merrily.

And now . . . For a man who had committed murder and was shortly to be arrested, for someone like that even to fancy a woman was ridiculous.

On the other hand . . . To his surprise, the thought came into his mind that any other transgression was meaninglessly trivial compared to the crime of taking human life.

'I didn't realise,' he said, 'that you went with the job.'

'Oh yes. The desk, the chair, the fitted carpet, rubber plant, and me.'

'Oh dear. That makes not getting it all the more disappointing.'

She smiled at him.

He smiled back. But he wasn't really smiling at her; he was smiling at the incongruity of anyone framing pretty compliments only ten hours after murdering an old man.

There was no policeman waiting for him in his office, but Robert Benham was there, poring over some files on his desk.

The Head of Personnel Designate looked up without apology. 'I've been in for an hour or so checking through some stuff.'

'Ah.'

'That report you did for George on Human Resources, you know, staffing in the 'Eighties . . .'

'Oh yes.'

'His copy's locked in his files, so I'm checking yours.'

'Fine.'

'Disagree with your conclusion that the size of Department's right. There are a lot of idle buggers who don't pull their weight.'

'I know that, Robert, but George was very keen to maintain the Department at its present size.'

'So you came up with the conclusions he wanted?'

Graham shrugged. Robert Benham nodded brusquely and closed the file. 'Of course. As I've said, I'm more concerned with productivity than maintaining the *status quo*.'

'Yes.'

'We must have a long talk about it. No time in ordinary office hours. You come down to my cottage at Stoughton one weekend. It's near Chichester. We'll fix a date.'

'Oh, but I –'

'But what?'

But what indeed? Graham didn't continue the sentence he'd been framing about Merrily and the children and trying to keep the weekends free as far as possible. He couldn't pretend he enjoyed Saturdays and Sundays *en famille*. Anyway, for a man shortly to be arrested for murder, what did it matter whether or not he fulfilled his family responsibilities?

'Nothing. No, I'll look forward to that. Any weekend'll be fine.'

At that moment George Brewer's harassed face appeared around the door. 'Oh, er, Robert, I was looking for you.

I . . . er–'

'I'll be along in a moment.' Robert Benham gestured his boss away without finesse, almost snapping his fingers at him. George's head withdrew.

When Robert had gone, Graham had another attack of the shakes. They hadn't found the body yet; it had been swept along by the river.

But they would find it soon.

And then they'd come and get him.

'More sherry, Lilian?'

He knew the answer. He had never known his mother-in-law to refuse. Since she had moved to Barnes, they'd got through a lot more sherry. At least he'd managed to wean her off the Tio Pepe and on to a cheaper brand. But it was still expensive.

He always had money to worry about in the rare moments of not worrying about being arrested.

Three days had passed, three days of nausea, broken by brief intervals of calm. The calm only came with oblivion, often after a few drinks, when he could forget about the old man, wipe the whole episode from his mind, pretend it hadn't happened. But these moments did not last; soon his thoughts would be invaded by another image of the murder, or a recollection of having lost the job he'd hoped for.

The two injustices had by now become inextricably entwined in his mind. If he hadn't been cheated of his job, he wouldn't have had to kill the old man. The murder was Robert Benham's fault, George Brewer's fault for not standing up for his protégé; anyone's fault but Graham Marshall's.

The killing itself had elaborated in his imagination. Though the reality of the episode had lasted less than half a minute, in his mind it had spread into a slow-motion horror film, with the sickening crunch of the blow to the victim's skull, an endless dying gurgle, and long sprawling fall down to the dark water of the Thames.

The old man had assumed a face, too. It was the face of

Graham's father.

These were the images that kept the metallic taste of vomit in his mouth. But between the nausea and the snatched moments of calm, there were other thoughts, thoughts he could not yet fully define, but whose shadows were not displeasing.

Lilian Hinchcliffe let out an operatic sigh as her son-in-law recharged her sherry glass. It was more than her usual call for attention. On this particular day she had some substance on which she could build her performance, a dramatic theme round which she could improvise with increasing elaboration. The previous evening's television news had announced the death in Switzerland of the distinguished film actor, William Essex. He had been found by his companion of many years, a considerably less distinguished actor.

To Graham, who watched bulletins in terror for announcements of bodies discovered or police investigations launched, the news had meant little. To Lilian it had been a licence to stage a major production of sentiment, nostalgia and meretricious grief. The climax of this performance had been reached the night before, but the sobs were reminders, after-echoes, each one requesting enquiry and solicitude.

Graham wilfully withheld both. A side-effect of his recent shock had been to liberate him from the need for pretence. He could now recognise, without guilt, the irrelevance of things that did not interest him.

'Sherry, darling?'

Merrily had just come into the room from putting the kids to bed.

'Thank you, darling.'

The 'darlings' were as automatic as a sailor's obscenities. And as meaningless.

Merrily sank into an armchair. 'Oooh, they've been wearing today.'

'Poor you. I remember just what you and Charmian were like at the same age.' Perhaps because of her background as an actress, Lilian Hinchcliffe could not avoid bringing every

39

observation back to herself. Her sympathy for Merrily demanded, however retrospectively, sympathy for herself.

'Where is Charmian, anyway? I thought she was meant to be coming this evening.' She made her elder daughter's absence sound like a personal affront, a particularly vicious affront in the circumstances, following the death of Lilian's alleged lover.

'She'll be along soon,' said Merrily. 'I told Emma, if she's here by nine, Charmian'd read her a story.'

'Emma used always to want *me* to read her stories.'

'Yes, Mummy, but she doesn't see as much of Charmian these days as she does of you.'

Lilian Hinchcliffe swept her hair back with a petulant gesture. 'Familiarity, no doubt, breeding contempt.'

Having given his women their sherry, Graham poured himself another large Scotch and took a long swallow. There was no doubt that drink helped. He felt steadier, the taste in his mouth less bitter.

The calm he felt now was subtly different. For the first time it came not from blotting out the murder, but from the tiny hope that it might never be discovered.

The doorbell rang, strangling the new idea at birth.

'I'll go.' As he rose, the nausea and the terrible interior trembling returned. There would be a policeman at the door; the moment had finally come.

It was Charmian. He kissed his sister-in-law perfunctorily and she ran upstairs to see the children. Henry and Emma got on very well with her, better than they did with their parents or grandmother. She had the glamour of a career, of having no children, and of treating them like adults.

She seemed to love them too, something Graham found inconceivable. No doubt it was easier when they weren't your own.

His calm was broken again and another large Scotch didn't mend it. There is no way you can get away with murder. It was only a matter of time before they caught up with him.

Charmian came down. He equipped her with a gin and

tonic and refilled the glasses of the other two, emptying the sherry bottle. God, have to buy more.

'Jesus, they were playing a horrible game when I went up there,' said Charmian.

'What?' Merrily drawled, putting into the monosyllable a reminder that she had been putting up with her children's 'horrible games' ever since they came back from school, and indeed for years before that, while her sister only swanned in every now and then, so it was hardly surprising that she had novelty value for them. Merrily got more like her mother daily.

'Henry said he was the Yorkshire Ripper and Emma was one of his victims.'

'How revolting,' Lilian emoted emptily.

Merrily shrugged. 'It's not surprising. There was so much in the papers, on the radio, television.'

'There'll be more when the trial starts,' Lilian contributed gloomily.

'Do you think he is the right bloke – the one they've got?'

'Oh yes,' said Charmian, with the authority of her Fleet Street connections.

Merrily shuddered. 'Quite horrible, the whole business.'

Lilian wasn't going to be emotionally outdone by her daughter. 'Quite, quite horrible. What makes someone do something like that, to kill just for . . . ugh, it's beyond belief.'

You'd be surprised, thought Graham. People will kill for strange reasons. Because they've lost a job, maybe.

For the first time, his secret seemed valuable. He didn't want to be identified with the Yorkshire Ripper; their crimes had nothing in common. And yet there was something, an exclusivity almost, in being a murderer.

'Did you see that film on the box last night,' Charmian began, 'about a mass murderer? God, it was terrible. Some awful 'Fifties B-feature. Bad script. Terrible acting.' She paused before the afterthought and sting of her statement. 'It was the one they showed as a "tribute" to William Essex.'

The remark was aimed straight at Lilian, another salvo in

41

the strange warfare that was their relationship. With absolute predictability, she rose to her daughter's slight.

'William Essex was one of the finest actors of his generation.'

'Richest, maybe. Most exposed, perhaps. But, if you're talking about talent, he wasn't even on the map.'

'Now listen, Charmian!' Lilian screeched. 'You don't know what you're talking about! When William and I were lovers . . .'

And so on. The same tired old stories. The same justifications. The same recriminations and tears. The same eternal sparring between mother and daughter.

Graham felt weary. He narrowed his eyes and sighted his mother-in-law along his toecap. From an early age, long before the Bond films had popularised such gadgetry, he'd had a fantasy of a machine-gun along the sole of his shoe. You point it at someone, press down with your toe, and . . . bang, bang, bang. The person vanishes, obliterated, gone for ever.

A childish fantasy.

Except, of course, now he had taken one step nearer to realising that sort of fantasy.

Graham Marshall smiled.

CHAPTER FIVE

Death is the only power that actually stops time. Love and fear can suspend it; intense concentration or pleasure can make people unaware of it; but only death can stop it.

And since Graham Marshall didn't die, time passed for him. It didn't pass quickly, or comfortably, but it passed. He weathered an agonising weekend, and soon a whole week had gone by since the murder. Still there had been no policeman at the front door, no discreet but firm detective to greet him in the office.

Gradually the intervals of sanity between the panics grew longer. An attractive new logic crept into his thinking. There had been no witnesses to the murder. Even when the body was found, there might well be nothing to connect the death with him. Surely immersion of any length in the Thames would make accurate forensic examination difficult.

And, as for marks on his own clothing and the murder weapon . . . well, he'd inspected them himself and seen nothing. But to be on the safe side, he had had the suit cleaned (a regular procedure which would not raise any suspicion). And, though it showed no apparent signs of its unconventional employment, he had contrived to leave his umbrella on the Piccadilly Line (again something he had done more than once before, guaranteed to prompt the not-quite-teasing comment from Merrily that he was getting old).

Given the circumstances of the death, the police were going to be hard put to it to point the finger at Graham Marshall. And since the victim was presumably a homeless vagrant,

43

they weren't going to make their investigations too exhaustive.

That was even assuming that they found the body. Graham remembered reading stories of corpses long submerged, clichés about rivers being 'slow to give up their secrets'. Every day that passed with the body undiscovered would make more difficult the identification of the victim, and certainly of his murderer.

At times Graham's calm was coloured by a sort of humour. If you're going to murder someone, he thought wryly, choose a victim you have never met – it's so much safer.

But such thoughts only came when he was at his most relaxed. And, though the intervals of calm were increasing, nausea and panic still stalked him and would pounce suddenly. And because he had dared to hope they might be gone for ever, each new attack seemed to come with increased force.

He had committed murder, and there was no way he could get away with it.

The worst attack of panic came on the Thursday morning of the week after the old man's death. Graham had woken feeling moderately human and, while Merrily refereed the children's breakfast in the kitchen, had taken his toast and coffee through to the sitting-room for a leisurely riffle through the papers.

Sunlight streaked in at the tall windows and what he could see of the garden suggested spring. For almost the first time, he saw the benefits of the new house, space and a bit of elegance. And an investment. Oh, there was a lot that still needed doing to it, but somehow they'd manage. Even without George's job there'd still be the odd increment and pay settlement.

The loss of the job didn't at that moment seem too appalling. Graham knew so much about the Department that Robert Benham was constantly asking him for information. And controlling the flow of that information gave Graham a kind of power. Besides, Robert's urgency for change might make him too unpopular to stay long as Head of Personnel.

Graham had seen other bright young men overreach themselves.

His own rôle was clear – to wait in the wings, giving Robert Benham apparent, but limited, support, until something, as it inevitably must, went wrong. He certainly did not intend to tie his career so closely to that of the new Head as he had to the old.

He took a sip of coffee and glanced at the papers. *The Daily Telegraph* and, being Thursday, *The Barnes and Mortlake Times*. They only really had the local paper for cinema times and property prices; its news content of restaurant licences refused, under-13 swimming galas and resistance to ring-road schemes was less than fascinating.

But out of habit, he glanced down the columns.

There it was – at the bottom of the front page:

BODY FOUND
The body of an elderly man was found in the Thames near Putney Bridge on Saturday. He has not yet been identified, but is described as being in his late sixties and shabbily dressed.

Saturday. Only two days after the killing. That didn't give long for the water to remove any clues as to how he died.

The happy vision, that the murder might never be discovered, shattered. The police had had five days to investigate. It wouldn't be long now.

Graham was seized by a trembling so strong that he had to put down his coffee cup to avoid spilling it.

At that moment Merrily came into the room. She was wearing one of her fluffy lace dressing-gowns. When she had been young and waiflike, they had made her look like a fledgling in a downy nest; Graham had even used the image in the early days of their marriage. Now they only emphasised her angularity and the scrawniness of her neck; if any bird came to mind, it was a plucked chicken.

She looked down at the sun marking parallelograms on the

floor. 'This carpet,' she observed, 'rather belongs to the bear called Frederick.'

Graham was in no mood to sort out one of her precious remarks. 'What?'

'Fred Bear. Threadbare, darling.'

'Oh.'

'We'll have to get a new one. Apparently there's a sale at Allied Carpets . . .'

Graham rose jerkily, upsetting his plate. The remaining slice of toast flopped on to the floor, marmalade-side down.

'Oh, daaarling.' Merrily had her mother's knack of extending vowels beyond their natural span. And of infusing them with reproach. 'Now we'll *have* to get a new carpet.'

'I must go,' he blurted out. The trembling was worse.

Merrily looked at him, concern emphasising the wrinkles of her tight little face. 'Are you all right, darling?'

'Yes, I . . .' He reached down to the local paper and roughly folded it so that the front page was hidden.

'Graham, is there something . . . ?' Merrily laid a thin hand on his sleeve.

He twitched his arm away as if she had been a nettle.

His mood at the office was subtly different, the panic dulled to a kind of acceptance. The bright image of 'getting away with it' had been shown up as a fantasy. Doggedly, like a condemned man, he went through his work, wondering how long he had got, waiting for the summons.

But the only summons came from Robert Benham, who asked him to go up to George Brewer's office. Once inside, Graham was waved to a chair by his prospective boss, casual in a faded blue Levi sweatshirt.

'I told George to take the day off. He's looking pretty washed out and, quite honestly, he's just a nuisance round the office these days, fussing like an old woman every time I want to look at a file.'

'He is still Head of Personnel,' Graham felt bound to say.

Robert read no reproach into this remark. 'Yes, damn it.

Still got a couple of months to go. Last few weeks, though, he'll be kept out of mischief with company cocktail parties. But it means it'll be some time before I can get down to any *proper* work.'

'Look, wanted to say – about this weekend down at the cottage to talk through things . . .'

'Oh yes.'

'Got one of the directors coming down this weekend, next one I'm going to Miami . . .'

'Business?'

'No, I just need a break. I'll be reading reports and things, of course . . .'

'So how about the one after?'

'Sounds fine.' Graham remembered that that was yet another weekend that Lilian was coming to stay. Which made it sound even finer.

He assimilated Robert's news about the weekend in Miami. It was the sort of flamboyant gesture he might have made a few years back. When he'd had the money. A move designed to impress and confuse his colleagues.

With difficulty, Graham resisted the temptation to be impressed and confused.

In the Levi sweatshirt, too, he could recognise his own style. He had worn his flowered ties for the same purpose (though he liked to think he'd never looked quite that *scruffy*). Nowadays, like George Brewer, he favoured suits.

No, Robert Benham was using all Graham's old tricks, so Graham would have to beat him at his own game. Because there was no doubt, one way or the other, he was going to beat him. He'd lost the latest round due to carelessness, but now he had the measure of his opponent, he was not going to be caught napping again.

Suddenly, Graham remembered that he was about to be arrested for murder, and the incongruity of any future planning seemed laughable. He felt a surge of almost manic irresponsibility.

As he left George's office, he asked Stella if she'd like to meet for a drink after work.

Travelling home on the Tube, he thought about Stella. Talking to her had taken him back into a world from which he had long been unwittingly banished.

First it had been, albeit mildly, a sexual encounter. No physical contact had been made, no suggestions voiced, but the circumstances, a man inviting a woman to have a drink with him *à deux*, had sexual overtones. And the automatic way in which Stella walked with him out of the building to a wine bar rather than turning right by the lifts to the company bar, showed that she recognised this.

Graham also found, to his surprise, that he slipped easily into the observances of 'chatting up'. It was a style of speech which he had not practised for over fifteen years, but it seemed to come back. Again, it was very mild, just small-talk, but relaxing. It was so long since he had spoken to a woman he did not know to the point of tedium, or about topics of mutual interest, rather than mutual responsibility.

The second difference he felt with Stella was that between their worlds. She had been divorced nearly as long as he'd been married and was childless, so her preoccupations were totally unlike his. For her, spare time was for entertainment, not for maintaining houses, tolerating mothers-in-law, and marshalling unresponsive children. She spoke of films she had seen, theatres, exhibitions. For Stella, London was a huge complex of varied entertainments to be explored and tasted; whereas, for Graham, it was somewhere he lived so that he had a less intolerable journey to work.

Her need to fill spare time so avidly was perhaps born of the single person's obsessive fear of loneliness, but to Graham it seemed an ideal of freedom. It joined with Robert Benham's trip to Miami in an image of a world he had once known, and might still know, if he hadn't taken another course.

Since the reasons he had taken that other course – wife and children – now meant nothing to him, he felt unjustly excluded from the free world, in which people did what they

48

wanted to when they wanted to without committee decisions and unwelcome company.

He wanted to be shot of his family.

It was because he was a murderer that he could feel so irresponsible. Once again he thought how trivial other lapses were when compared to the crime of taking human life.

'Where have you been?'

Merrily looked wan and weepy when he got home. It was not late, still daylight, so he felt annoyed by her demand.

'Why?' Answer a question with a question, the resource of the devious in all walks of life.

'It's awful, Graham. I've had a shock.'

She started crying and came forward into his arms. He clasped them automatically and held her, murmuring apposite reassurance. But he felt for her no more than he would for the unknown victim of a car accident.

'What do you mean – shock? What happened?'

'Electric shock. I was changing a light bulb in the utility room and –'

'Show me.'

She led him through. The row of square white appliances watched impassively as he reached up towards the old brass light-fitting.

He stopped. 'Did you switch off the power?'

'What?' Merrily's voice was even smaller with self-pity.

'The mains – did you switch them off?'

'No, of course I didn't, Graham. I just had a horrid shock.'

'I know, but to avoid getting another shock – indeed, to avoid me or the children getting a shock – you should have switched the electricity off at the mains.'

'And am I expected to know where the mains are?'

'Yes, you bloody are. This house is in both our names and you should be responsible for it just as much as I am.'

'Well, I don't understand about electricity and *things like that*.'

The petulant contempt she put into the last three words

49

made it hard to remember that her lack of practicality had once been part of Merrily's winsome charm. It was an attitude her mother had encouraged through childhood; Lilian had always worked on the principle that, whatever went wrong technically, there would always be some ardent young actor around to fix it. The trouble was, the supply of ardent young actors had dried up, leaving Graham to deal with all the dripping taps, 'funny bonking in the hot-water pipes' and 'silly little red lights that keep coming on in the car' for his mother-in-law. And for her equally useless daughter.

Merrily, he had recently decided, was not even a very good housewife. The house always looked faintly messy and, though she often averred that this was a matter of policy, a determination not to be obsessed by cleaning and polishing like the older generation, Graham suspected it was just old-fashioned inefficiency. And when Merrily did do a major cleaning project, it was never simply in the cause of hygiene; it was an accusation, some subtly charged probe to make him feel guilty or to let him know she wanted something. Merrily's methods were very like her mother's.

He switched off the electricity, got a torch and climbed a ladder to inspect the defective fitting.

It didn't take more than a glance to see what was wrong. The positive and negative wires were red and black, the old system. Old enough for the insulating rubber to have perished. He could see where the shiny exposed wire touched the brass bulb-holder. The whole fitting was live.

He fetched a screwdriver to take it off. Have to buy a replacement. As he pulled the wire free, he saw that even more of the rubber was perished. Presumably that meant the whole electrical system was the same. The house had never been properly rewired; the old round-pin plugs had just been replaced with square-pins. Have to get an electrician to look at it. Damn, that was bound to mean more expense.

While he was perched on the ladder, separating the wires so that they didn't fuse everything when the power came back, Merrily's little voice floated plaintively up to him.

'Who were you with?'

'What?'

'This evening – who were you with?'

'Eh?'

He pointed the torch down, bleaching her little face. She blinked, but pressed on. 'Graham – are you having an affair with someone?'

'What!' He almost laughed at the incongruity of the question. God knows, he hadn't done anything with Stella. But had Merrily got some amazing radar that could pick up the fact that he'd invited the girl out for a drink?

He came down the ladder. 'What on earth are you talking about?'

'Well, there's something funny going on, Graham. You've been so twitchy the last week. You leap up every time the 'phone goes – or the front doorbell. You're acting exactly as if you'd done something you shouldn't.'

He almost laughed. 'And you think the thing I shouldn't have done is to sleep with another woman?'

'Yes.'

'Well, it isn't. No, the thing I shouldn't have done . . .' he continued nonchalantly.

'Is what?'

The words were out before he had time to think. 'Oh, just murdering someone.'

But the confession only got a 'Ha, bloody ha' from Merrily. The humour of the situation hit Graham and he giggled uncontrollably.

'What is it, Graham? Is it another woman?'

'No, it's not.' As he got control of himself he started to regret the mention of the murder. Better feed her a bit of truth before she started to think about it. 'No, it's George's job.'

'Oh, of course. Have you heard yet?'

'Yes.'

'Oh, good.'

'Not good. I haven't got it.'

'What!'

He shone the torch again in Merrily's face and saw there some of the disappointment and betrayal which he had felt when he heard the news.

Her disappointment, however, was purely materialistic.

'But we need the money, Graham. There are lots of things that need doing to the house, and I haven't got a stitch to wear.'

Merrily was very put out for the rest of the evening. She made no secret of the fact that she felt her husband had let her down.

Simply to get her off that subject, Graham again raised the question of his having an affair. He denied it, with perhaps a little too much vehemence. And in bed he made love to her to convince her of his fidelity.

Again, perhaps with a little too much vehemence.

The events of the evening had suspended his fears about the murder, but they came back when he woke sweating at three in the morning. He soon gave up the hope of further sleep, and walked round the house to control the trembling of his body.

To give himself something to do, he looked at other electrical fittings and found what he had feared, the same old wiring with its perished insulation.

That added a new panic. He tried to recapture the nonchalance that being a murderer had sometimes given and ask himself how potentially lethal wiring could matter to a man who had taken the life of another, but it didn't work. He switched off the mains.

At eight-thirty, having shouted down the rest of the family's moans about the lack of light, radios, hot water and hot food, he rang an electrician, asking him to come round and say how serious the danger was.

The post then arrived, bearing a letter from his bank manager, complaining about the abuse of the Marshalls' overdraft 'facility' and demanding a 'remittance'.

While he was recovering from this blow, Lilian Hinchcliffe rang to say her little Fiat had a flat tyre. Would Graham be an angel and come round and fiddle with whatever needed fiddling with?

No, he bloody wouldn't. He curbed this response before he voiced it, but said unfortunately he couldn't because he was waiting in for the electrician, Lilian would have to get in touch with a tyre place and get the thing mended herself (like ordinary bloody people did). But they charged so much, Lilian whined, surely it wasn't a lot to ask for Graham to just come and have a little *look* at it. Very well, he'd see if he could get over later.

Merrily, who had gone up after their cold breakfast to dress, came down in the ragged T-shirt and patched jeans she wore for painting. Since they weren't ever going to have any money ever again, she announced, she'd better get used to their new style of life. The gesture was characteristic, particularly in its totally inappropriate timing.

As if this weren't enough, Emma, about to leave for school, said she felt funny, and turned out, on examination by Merrily, to have started, at the tender age of eleven, her first period.

Henry, uninformed by his father – or indeed anyone else – about such matters, did not understand and made some inapposite remark, which sent the two women (as they both now were) into floods of tears.

At this moment the doorbell rang. Graham would almost have welcomed a policeman come to arrest him, but it turned out to be the electrician.

Tight-lipped, Graham showed him round the house. The electrician fingered the odd wire that all too easily came out of the wall, tapped a few plugs and tutted over junction boxes. Then, with the understanding gravity of a cancer surgeon, he said the house was a deathtrap, and it would need complete rewiring, at a cost of one thousand four hundred pounds. Excluding V.A.T.

What about switching the power back on – would it be safe? The electrician shook his head dubiously. Well, he wouldn't like to be responsible. Still, have to take the risk till it was all properly done. What? No, he couldn't think about doing it for three weeks. Up to here he was. Oh yes, but no question it was urgent. Very urgent.

Graham Marshall thought of Stella with her little flat and no more weighty decision than which cinema to go to that evening.

He thought of Robert Benham, with his potential Head of Personnel's salary and his weekend trip to Miami.

He thought of himself, who, on top of everything else, was a murderer.

And he thought that at least, when you're in prison for life, you don't have any responsibilities.

CHAPTER SIX

Time continued to pass and for Graham Marshall the balance between peace and fear slowly changed. The panics still came, terrors could still clutch at him when least expected, but they did not come so often and they did not stay so long.

Murder, he began to think in moments of detachment, was like any other new experience. Like sex, maybe. The first time it seemed all-important, as if it would dominate the rest of one's life, but gradually it came to be accepted, even taken for granted. How many married men, he wondered, questioned on their way to work, could remember whether or not they'd made love to their wives the night before.

Sex only became an obsession when the impulse was unnaturally strong or when it was infected with guilt.

Continuing his analogy, he found that his impulse to murder was not unnaturally strong. Nor did he feel any guilt about the one that he had committed.

He sometimes wondered idly whether he'd feel any different if the victim were someone he knew.

Of course, the big distinction between sex and murder was that one wanted to make a habit of the first, and probably not of the second.

Graham Marshall certainly didn't. Three weeks after the event he still found the shock was sufficient to last him for a lifetime. And he would do anything to avoid the paralysing fear of discovery.

But that fear was receding. Increasingly logic told him he was going to get away with it.

Committing the murder had been a stroke of bad luck; getting arrested for it would be really appalling luck.

And, as the fear left him, his attitude to the crime changed. Previously he had not dared to examine his feelings, but now he found he kept coming back to the incident with something approaching relish.

It was not everyone who had committed a murder.

He began to feel a certain exclusivity. The crime gave his life an unpredictable dimension. It filled the void the loss of George Brewer's job had left in him.

The feeling was comparable to that he had felt in the old days at work when talking about Lilian's show-business friends or when unconventionally dressed: that there was more to Graham Marshall than met the eye.

Except, of course, he couldn't really tell his colleagues about the murder. It had to be his secret.

But it was a secret from which he drew strength. When Robert Benham was at his most patronising, when Merrily at her most precious, or Lilian at her most demanding, Graham Marshall would say to himself: 'What you don't realise is that I am a murderer, that I have taken human life.'

And the thought gave him a sense of power.

CHAPTER SEVEN

'And I bought the paddock too, because you could easily land a helicopter there.'

Graham laughed indulgently at the fancy, then realised from his host's face that Robert Benham wasn't joking. He didn't joke. When he said he'd bought the paddock adjacent to his cottage as a helipad, that was exactly why he had bought it. And for someone who had become Head of Personnel at Crasoco by the age of thirty-four, the idea of owning a helicopter was not fanciful.

With sudden clarity Graham realised the truth that had only been hinted at hitherto – that Robert Benham's ambition and potential did not stop at Crasoco, that Head of Personnel there was only another step on a staircase that would lead through many companies, ever onward and upward. Robert Benham was destined to lead the sort of life in which helicopters were necessary, the life of a real 'success'. Even in ambition his new boss outstripped him. Graham felt diminished and parochial.

He searched for some comfort, as he always did when threatened, in his opponent's failings. Everyone has an Achilles' heel – a flaw of character, an awkward mannerism, a past failure, an ill-chosen mate, an unsuitable home – that can alleviate the pang of envy.

But in the case of Robert Benham, Graham could not find it. Certainly, judged on an absolute scale, the young man had moral shortcomings, but these were not of a kind to solace his rival. Rather the reverse, for Graham recognised his own qualities of efficiency and ruthlessness reflected with more intense concentration. Robert Benham shared his approach to life, but was better at it.

Benham's mannerisms, too, were hard to fault. The inadequacies which Graham had immediately identified on their first encounter had been proved by success to be more than adequate to the challenges they faced. What Eric Marshall would have described as 'a common accent' and 'lack of social graces' had proved positive advantages. Benham had been preferred over Graham for being, amongst other things, 'more in touch with the work force'. And Robert's strong regional identity only increased the sense of rootlessness Graham had felt since his parents' deaths.

As to past failures, there seemed unfortunately to be no blots on the Benham *curriculum vitae*.

Nor did his choice of accommodation let him down. Graham was prepared to take the Dolphin Square flat on trust; though he had not seen it, the address was sufficient to make him bitterly nostalgic for his own lost life in Kensington and Chelsea.

And what he was seeing at Stoughton denied him the opportunity of superiority. As the weekend approached, he had prepared a small armoury of pejoratives to describe the cottage. 'Pokey', 'run-down', 'draughty', 'primitive' and 'damp' vied with 'tarted-up', 'precious', 'chocolate-box' and 'poncy' as his imagination shifted.

But the reality of the place blunted his weapons. The thatched roof, neat white paint and Tudor beams seen as Robert's Scirocco drew up outside on the Friday evening had given hope for 'chocolate-box', but this had been denied by the building's imposing proportions. 'Primitive' was rendered inapplicable by the neat Calor gas tank and the bright blue burglar alarm affixed under the eaves. Though its size and condition ruled out 'pokey' and 'run-down', as they entered the cottage Graham thought 'draughty' might still be in with a chance, but this hope was quickly dashed by the blast of central heating and open fire that welcomed them. He toyed momentarily with 'overheated' and 'smoky', but was forced to reject them as inappropriate. 'Tarted-up', 'precious' and 'poncy' met the same fate. It was just a very nice cottage, practical, skilfully modernised, well-equipped. Above reproach, even for such a skilled practitioner of reproach as Graham Marshall.

And any hope that Robert Benham's image might be shattered by a grotesquely unsuitable partner was dispelled as a girl issued from the kitchen to greet them.

Before he met her, Graham knew her primary attraction – that she was a girlfriend rather than a wife. The more he saw of Robert's life, the more he blamed the unfavourable comparison of his own on his ill-considered and premature marriage to Merrily. She was his handicap; she was the obstacle to the full realisation of his potential.

He felt this with redoubled force when he saw how beautiful the girlfriend was. Not only beautiful, but *famously* beautiful. He recognised her face from his television screen. The pale blue eyes and black hair identified Tara Liston, an English actress who had made it in the States and been reimported to her own country in an internationally successful detective series.

And Robert Benham actually possessed this creature who peopled the wet-dreams of the world. His recent weekend trip to Miami fell into place.

And Graham's last hope of comfort fell into oblivion.

What was more, Tara Liston proved to be charming. His defensive wishful thinking that she might turn out to be a bitch, might even give Robert a hard time, dissipated through the evening. She was delightful, entertaining and apparently deeply in love.

Graham made the mistake at one point of mentioning his mother-in-law's name, brandishing it as if to show his own association with the glamour of show business, in the way that had proved so successful in his early days at Crasoco. Tara was of course charming about it and, jutting out a dubious lower lip, said yes, she was sure she had heard the *name*. But

Graham felt deflated and shabby, like a man name-dropping in a pub.

The dinner she cooked for them the first evening revealed no shortcoming in domestic skills, and an imagination that contrasted with Merrily's predictable offerings from the Corden Bleu partwork.

Neither Tara nor Robert could have been nicer to him. To compound his malaise, Graham had the knowledge that it all came from within himself.

At the end of the meal, the talk moved to drugs and he brightened at the prospect of showing his cosmopolitan insouciance on the subject. Those rare and over-dramatised puffs of pot taken in Lilian's Abingdon cottage would now stand him in good stead. Even though it was a good ten years since he had smoked, he spoke of cannabis with familiarity and enthusiasm.

As Tara produced the little bag of cocaine, he realised his mistake, but he had already said too much. His refusal to participate, a reflex born of Calvinist upbringing and the fear of doing it wrong, left him feeling gauche and immature.

He watched the others covertly, but it was Tara who held his gaze for the rest of the evening. He stared, with fascinated envy, at the neat, practised way in which she snorted the white powder and, later, the unambiguous intent with which she led Robert off to their bedroom.

As he lay awake in his single bed, Graham's mind lubriciously translated every creak of the old cottage to his own disparagement.

And, once again, as was increasingly the case, the only thought that gave him strength and identity was the knowledge that he was a murderer.

He was woken on the Saturday morning by more creaking. It was probably just the complaint of old beams at the impertinence of central heating, but again he provided an alternative, diminishing interpretation.

The envy he felt was, however, qualified. He did not wish he had Merrily with him, her angular body by his side to be rolled over and enjoyed with comatose morning compliance. It was a pleasure to be on his own. No wife, no squabbling children to force him out of bed on some expensive errand of ferrying.

And no responsibility for the attractive surroundings in which he found himself. The guest bedroom had been recently decorated. The straight lines of white gloss on the window-frames gleamed. The wallpaper clung close and lovingly round the contours of old plaster. The white emulsion on the ceiling and brick chimneybreast was immaculately even. It was the work of a professional, another sign of the financial latitude that bachelordom allowed. Graham contrasted it with the hasty do-it-yourself efforts of his own home, the slight mismatches of wallpaper patterns, the brushstroke whorls on surfaces that should have had another coat, the scalloped outlines of windowframes that Merrily had attacked with her usual imprecision.

The guest-room's one flaw, a breadcrumb edging of unpainted plaster around the washbasin, offered Graham no chance of ascendancy over his host. The basin was obviously such a recent addition that its installation was not complete; it was just a matter of time before 'the little man', obedient to Robert Benham's dictates, finished the job.

The cottage had ceased to creak. Either its beams had adjusted to the change in temperature or the passions in the other bedroom had been sated, and Graham felt a kind of peace. This was the life for him . . . other people to do everything, their services adequately remunerated, every offloaded responsibility a financial transaction rather than a tangled mess of duty, bargaining and blackmail. He needed to live on his own. A service flat was the answer, with 'little men' responsible for the tedious functions of cleaning, decorating and repairs, little men who could be bawled out for any deficiencies in their contractual obligations. The excessive responsibilities of family life might perhaps be justified, speciously, by love; but when love had gone, they became no more than a form of exploitation.

Being away from Merrily and the children crystallised the thought that had been forming slowly over months or maybe years – that he had outgrown them, that mentally he had set them aside from his life, that they were not included in any projections he made of his future.

Recognising this fact gave him a sense of relief, the feeling of a decision reached.

But his repose was disconcerted by a flutter of fear. It was not the thought of the murder, whose shadow seemed now a source of strength rather than of panic, but the question of why Robert Benham had summoned him for the weekend.

The reason given had been for an opportunity to talk about work, specifically about departmental staffing and the rival claims of maintaining the existing establishment and making cuts in the cause of efficiency. But Graham understood Robert well enough to suspect a deeper motive. The Head of Personnel Designate had had ample opportunity – which he had used – to check the relevant files, and Graham did not flatter himself that his own opinions on the subject were going to change Robert's intentions. No, there was another purpose in the invitation.

And though he could not yet define that purpose, the knowledge of its existence made Graham feel on his guard. He was not there to be consulted, but, in some obscure way, tested.

The nature of the test did not become clearer as the weekend progressed. Everything seemed very leisurely, Robert's office abrasiveness smoothed. As a pressured executive should, he took the opportunity to relax. And though this, like all his actions, was a conscious decision, it did not seem forced. Graham, for whom constant comparison with his rival was becoming a habit, felt himself by contrast tense and unnatural.

The communal day began round ten with a large breakfast. The time Tara spent in America showed in the frizzled bacon, pancakes and scalding black coffee.

Then came the brief tour of the estate, including the

identification of the paddock as a potential helipad. Work was not mentioned, though Robert had to take a couple of calls which obviously concerned the affairs of Crasoco. One of the calls involved his checking some facts stored on the office computer and Graham tried to keep his mouth from gaping as Robert produced a small briefcase, dialled through on the telephone, set the receiver on two rubber pads and had the information printed out. 'Bit of a lash-up,' the younger man apologised when the transaction was complete. 'I'm going to get a proper terminal rigged up when I have a moment.'

Graham gave what he hoped was a knowing nod. Then there was a call from Tara's London agent.

After that, Robert switched on the Ansaphone and drove them down to the local pub. 'Feel lost if I don't get my Saturday lunchtime drinking,' he announced as they set off. It seemed out of character, an unexpected heartiness; maybe, Graham hoped maliciously, an overconscious attempt at being a man of the people.

But no. At the pub Robert was obviously well-known, more than a weekender imposing himself on a rural community. He seemed to have a social mix of friends, with whom three rounds of drinks were consumed. Graham, having missed earlier cues, offered to buy the fourth round, insisting that he felt like another. Few of the group wanted more, but having made his statement, he felt obliged to buy himself a fourth pint, along with the couple of halves that were all the others demanded.

Four pints were more than he was accustomed to and more than he wanted, but he had committed himself. Half-way through the fourth he had to go and pee, which felt like another admission of failure.

When they left the pub, Robert, who seemed unaffected by the alcohol, said they'd drop Tara off at the cottage. 'She'd better start cooking. Doing her Chinese number for us tonight.'

They, meanwhile, would go down to Bosham and have a look at 'the boat'.

When Tara was dropped, Graham felt obliged to go into the

cottage for another pee, and had to ask his driver to stop twice more on the way down to the boat's mooring so that he could relieve himself by the roadside. Robert made no comment, but Graham had a feeling of points lost.

There was no *nouveau riche* hesitancy about Robert's dealings with the boat. He clearly knew about sailing and the knowledge was not a recent acquisition.

First they went to the quay and got into a rubber dinghy, which Robert rowed expertly round to the mooring. The slapping of water gave Graham an unpleasant queasiness in the stomach.

Robert kept up a flow of sailing information to which his guest only half listened. He knew nothing about boats and had never had much interest in them.

'Hope to get a deep water mooring in time,' the expert confided. 'Have to watch the tides here, she's grounded when it's low.'

Graham nodded.

'Tide's ebbing now, so we can't take her out. Have to wait too long to get back on the mooring. We'd miss Tara's Chinese magic. Sorry.'

Graham, in whom the queasiness was shifting over to nausea, said he didn't mind.

'Tomorrow morning, though, with a bit of luck. If we make an early start. I just wanted to come down today and check everything's shipshape. Boatyard had her out for an overhaul.'

'Ah.'

'Not that these fibreglass hulls need much maintenance. Just needed a bit of refitting.'

'Oh.'

'There she is.'

He pointed ahead. The boat was called *Tara's Dream*. Robert provided a lot of statistics and details, but all Graham took in was that she was about twenty foot long, had four berths, but was 'quite a nippy little mover'.

Neatly Robert rowed up to the stern. 'You hang on, make

her fast, I'll just open up.'

He leapt nimbly from the dinghy into the well of the boat, while Graham clung to the transom. The combined motion of the two vessels compounded his queasiness. Water splashed up in little spouts between them. Graham struggled to bend and tie the stiff nylon painter round a rail.

Robert, steadying himself against the lashed boom, moved forward to the cabin entrance. He reached into his pocket for a bunch of keys, selected the right one and opened the padlock. With a flourish, he pushed against the top hatch, which rattled on rails away from him, opening a little cockpit. Then he lifted out the vertical board and entered the cabin to stow it.

His torso emerged from the opening and he waved.

'Come and have a look at her.'

Graham didn't enjoy the leap and scrambled into the boat. He felt absurdly unstable standing up in the dinghy, and not much better on the boards of *Tara's Dream*.

'Surprisingly roomy, isn't she?' said Robert as his guest lurched into the cabin.

It didn't look roomy to Graham. Claustrophobia added to his unease. In the forepart four bunks were somehow crammed, shut off 'when required for privacy' by a thick curtain. The rest of the space, barely enough, Graham thought, for the two of them to turn around in, was 'galley, dining area, everything else'. He was shown folding tables, seats that doubled as storage lockers, more overhead stowage and neat double gas rings behind a curtain recess. 'Calor,' said Robert, revealing the blue cylinder. 'Hope the boatyard checked it was full. Tara's cooked some wonderful meals here, you know.'

Graham gave yet another nod and grunt of apparent interest. He didn't like it at all. The cramped conditions reminded him of a holiday with his parents when they'd rented a caravan near Hunstanton. He had been in his teens, too large for such enforced proximity. The holiday had been another example of Eric Marshall's penny-pinching, and

Graham remembered he had made a vow at the time that, when he had the freedom to choose, all his holidays would be in luxury hotels.

But the caravan hadn't suffered from this awful rolling motion. With shame, he realised he was desperate to pee again, and had to disturb Robert, who was checking the free-running of a halyard, to ask what he should do about it.

'Head's in there.' Robert pointed to what looked like a cupboard. 'Easier if you just go over the side. Not into the wind, though, or you'll get your own back.' He laughed coarsely.

Graham felt exposed and ridiculous as he faced the picturesque frontage of Bosham and peed. The beautiful row of houses looked somehow formal and disapproving. No doubt full of retired admirals and other sailing hearties armed with binoculars. A huge picture window on the end house seemed to gaze at him with particular disapprobation. When he had finished, he slunk back into the cabin, hearing Robert's feet booming overhead as their owner went through an interminable sequence of checks on the deck.

Graham looked out dismally at the shifting rectangle of daylight visible through the hatch. The tiny high windows of the cabin were curtained and let in little light. The rigging chattered incessantly. The boat creaked and lurched in its endless irregular rhythm. He looked up at the grooves along which the top hatch ran, and longed for it to be closed. He looked at the Robson's padlock on the vertical board and longed for it be locked up again. He longed to be on shore.

Eventually Robert Benham's grinning face appeared at the opening. 'They've done a good job. Usually do, but I have to check. Have to rely on the boatyard more than I'd like to. Don't have the time myself.'

And at last the words Graham had been longing for. 'O.K., let's be on our way.'

The sensation of incipient nausea stayed with him through the evening, which was a pity, because Tara's Chinese cookery

66

matched her other accomplishments. Graham could not do justice to the perfect Peking duck or its spicy accessories, though he managed to keep up consumption of the excellent red wine Robert had produced.

He also had a couple of brandies, refusing Robert's offer of a small cigar. 'I enjoy one every now and then,' his host asserted, as usual making his habits sound definitively correct. When the cocaine was again produced, Graham said he felt tired and went up to bed. Under the duvet, his last thought was of being threatened. There had still been no talk of work.

He was in a deep sleep before any creaking the others might set up could disturb him, but he woke at three with the sour taste of vomit in his mouth. He wasn't actually sick and gradually the nausea passed, but he was left with that naked wakefulness that offers no hope of real rest for the remainder of the night. His mind became a corridor for a cavalcade of unwelcome thoughts.

He must have slept again eventually, because he was woken by a hearty Aran-sweatered Robert at seven. They needed an early start, the guest was reminded, because of the tides, and because Tara had a plane to catch in the afternoon; so if they were to get any time on the boat, they'd better move.

To Graham's surprise, the actual sailing was enjoyable. Robert displayed no impatience with his guest's ignorance of the sport; indeed he showed great generosity, constantly offering the tiller, flicking loose sheets which his guest had jammed, or calling warnings as the boom swung across. There was no attempt to score points or to crow about his and Tara's practised expertise. Graham almost wished there had been. Cockiness from Robert would have given him a moral lever; generosity left him completely unmanned.

Tara had provided a picnic up to her usual standards and Robert supplied two bottles of crisp Sancerre from the cool-box. They finished up with coffee made on the little gas ring. The early April day showed promise of summer and his idyllic surroundings only made the meanness of Graham's thoughts

67

seem the more reprehensible.

Back to the cottage by three. Miraculously the other two had already packed and had to wait while Graham snatched his belongings together.

Then in the Scirocco fast but safely to Gatwick. Tara had contrived to compress everything into hand-luggage, and they arrived just as her flight was called. She kissed Robert in a casual way that implied deep trust, and disappeared, turning a few heads of television enthusiasts, through the departure gate.

Robert and Graham walked back to the car, parked illegally but unmolested, on double yellow lines. Now, thought Graham, now it comes. Now we get on to work, now I find out the purpose of the weekend.

But it didn't come. Robert talked affably of irrelevancies, showing interest in Graham's life, asking about his house, his family. Graham answered warily, waiting for the bite.

There was no bite. Robert parked the Scirocco outside the house in Boileau Avenue just before seven and refused the invitation to come in for a drink. 'No, no, I'll leave you to your family,' he said, making the word sound subtly like an unfortunate physical handicap.

Graham stood on the kerb, suitcase in hand.

'Well, um, thank you for . . .' No, he mustn't say 'having me', that sounded too like a schoolboy.

Absurdly, he felt as if Robert was about to tip him, with an avuncular wink to shove a fiver into his hand. 'Thank you for a great weekend.'

'My pleasure. You must come again.'

And the Scirocco was gone.

Confused, Graham walked slowly towards his front door. He felt obscurely shamed. Patronised. Put in his place.

And as he unwillingly reached for his keys, he realised that making him feel like that had been the object of the exercise.

CHAPTER EIGHT

Four unwelcome surprises were waiting for Graham as he entered the house.

The first was the sound of a female row issuing from the sitting-room. The second was the absence of response when he switched on the hall light. The darkness delayed impact on him of the third and fourth, which lay in envelopes on the hall table.

Since the raised voices from the sitting-room continued uninterrupted, he reckoned they hadn't heard him come in. He couldn't face all that yet, so started towards the stairs and the inadequate refuge of his 'study', a room optimistically described on the estate agent's details as 'fifth bedroom/dressing-room' and currently filled with lumber. At least it contained his swivel chair where he could sit for a while and make the adjustment from the conflicting emotions the weekend had stirred in him and the more predictable ones his family would arouse.

But that idea was scotched when he tried to switch on the landing light. Nothing. So it wasn't just the bulb gone in the hall. A power-cut? He looked hopefully out of the semi-circle of coloured glass over the front door, but the glow of lights opposite told him only his house was affected. Something else wrong with the wiring, no doubt.

Sanctuary denied, he dropped his overnight case heavily on the hall floor to announce his arrival, and pushed open the sitting-room door.

There were no lights in there either, though unlit candles

stood on the mantelpiece and shelves, suggesting the power failure had happened at least twenty-four hours earlier. But the curtains had not been drawn and the room was lit by the orange spillage from a street light. The effect was theatrical, something Lilian Hinchcliffe managed to achieve in most of her scenes.

For, though she was shrinking in an armchair in her 'poor little widow' pose, there was no doubt that it was Lilian's scene. Her two daughters stood either side of her, tense as cats over a mousehole. The atmosphere in the room combined with the evidence of the unlit candles to suggest the row had been going on for some time.

And the antagonism between Lilian and Charmian had reached such a pitch that Graham's entrance did not immediately stop their bitter hostilities.

'. . . how you have the nerve to call your own mother selfish –'

'Very easily. All my life I have never once seen you think of another person!'

'How you can say that! Do you know what it's like to hear that from a child you have looked after, brought up –'

'Fucked up, more likely.'

'Now don't use that language to me. Anyway, if we're talking about selfishness, what about you?'

(Graham recognised one of his mother-in-law's favourite ploys. If Lilian was criticised, she immediately referred the criticism to her attacker; if someone was commended, she immediately brought the commendation round to herself. For Lilian Hinchcliffe nothing existed in its own right, nothing was granted life except in a comparison which included her.)

'What about you, Charmian?' she repeated.

'O.K. I know I'm selfish in some ways, but at least I don't pretend otherwise. I don't pretend to be loving and caring –'

'Pretend! How little you understand!' Lilian appeared now to be auditioning for *Mother Courage*.

'Just because you have never known the love that a mother feels for a child. Merrily and I at least have that in common,

70

whereas you —'

This was another favourite Lilian Hinchcliffe tactic — bring in whoever else was present, assume their support by a subtly inexact identification of their feelings with her own.

Merrily acknowledged the reference with a little shrug, which managed to combine smugness at the commendation and dissociation from her mother's words. Her eye caught Graham's with what, in another marriage, would have been complicity.

He decided maybe it was time to intervene, but he had not reckoned with the speed or vehemence of Charmian's reaction.

'Don't you throw that in my face, you fucking cow! Just because I haven't had any children, don't think that—'

'I'm sorry.' Lilian was now using her noble suffering voice. 'But if you couldn't keep your marriage together, I can hardly be expected —'

'You think I didn't have children because I couldn't keep my marriage together? Don't you realise, you fool, that the reason we split up was because I *couldn't* have children!'

This revelation threw even Lilian off her stroke and, after a pause, it was Charmian who continued, though her voice was now tight with the threat of tears. 'And the fact that you never knew that, never thought to ask about it, that I never felt able to confide it in you, is a pretty fair comment on the amount of "loving" and "caring" I expected from you.'

Lilian was still silent.

'Don't you think I wanted children? Do you think the "career girl" image was a deliberate choice? Don't you think I'd like to be looked after, bovine and protected like Merrily, always with excuses, the excuses of pregnancy, or feeding them, or cooking for them, my maternal duties of "loving" and "caring" like a sick note excusing me any need for wider responsibility or charity? Don't you think . . .'

But there the emotion swamped her eloquence and, before she was caught short by tears, she moved abruptly to the door. 'I'm going.'

Graham drew aside, then followed her into the hall, where she was scrabbling her way into her coat.

'I'm sorry,' he said.

She looked at him. 'Yes, I'm sure you are.'

The tears gleaming on her eyelids did not exclude irony from her tone. Graham looked away as she grabbed her bag and slammed out of the house. He did not like the way Charmian looked at him. He always thought he detected too much understanding in her grey eyes.

Lilian was weeping when he got back into the sitting-room. This was a noisy business, not uncontrolled, but with an actress's instinct for maximum effect.

Merrily stood, irresolute but somehow satisfied, her arms posed in a mannered shrug. 'Oh dear, oh dear,' she said in a little voice, then came across, with continuing theatricality, to deposit a small kiss on Graham's lips.

In the dim orange light she looked strikingly like her mother and he had to restrain himself from flinching.

'How was your high-powered weekend?'

'Fine,' he lied.

'Well, you see the squalor to which you return.' She gestured to the candles on the mantelpiece. 'Have you got your lighter to illuminate the dismal scene?'

He handed it over. Graham no longer smoked, but he always carried the lighter. Sourly, he realised that he had started to do so to light George Brewer's succession of cigarettes. He was damned if the sycophancy would continue with Robert Benham's small cigars.

'Anyway, what is all this?' he asked testily.

'No power.'

'What do you mean?'

'Saturday morning I awoke and said "let there be light" and behold, there was no light.'

'What is it? Just a fuse or . . . ?'

This time Merrily's shrug was a three-act play. 'How should I know, darling?' Her eyes widened ingenuously. 'How should two women and two children alone in a house know what in the world had happened?'

'If it happened yesterday morning you could have got someone in.'

'But, Graham, you're being so horrid about money at the moment, I thought you might be cross. I thought it better to wait for you to come home.'

'Oh, for God's sake! I bet it's just a fuse. I'll go and have a look at it.'

He snatched a candle from the mantelpiece. The unnecessary speed with which he moved had the effect of putting the flame out. Relighting it spoiled his exit.

Anyway, Lilian wasn't going to allow anyone an exit. She had been upstaged for too long by the discussion of the power failure; even her pneumatic weeping had not caused sufficient distraction. She decided it was time to reassert her star status.

Prefacing her words with a dramatic sniff, she announced, 'I am going to cut her out of my will.'

'What?' Graham asked wearily. He knew from experience that it was quicker in the long run to react immediately to his mother-in-law's bombshells. Being ignored simply challenged her to find new levels of deviousness.

'I am going to cut Charmian out of my will. I'll go up to town and see Mr. Burchfield tomorrow. No daughter of mine can speak to me like that and get away with it. No, at the moment everything's left equally between the two girls. I'm going to change that. I'll make you two my sole beneficiaries.'

Oh God, if it weren't so pathetic, it'd be laughable, Graham thought. Such matriarchal gestures might be appropriate for someone who had some property to leave, but for an old woman who survived on subs from her son-in-law, it was grotesque. The only effect of Charmian's exclusion from the will would be to absolve her of responsibility for her mother's debts.

To his surprise, Graham found himself saying, 'Thank you.' Angry for having done so, he turned again to the door. 'I must go and sort out these lights.'

'Oh, before you go,' Merrily cooed, 'could you just get

73

Mummy a drink? She needs it, she's awfully upset.'

Wordlessly, Graham went across to the drinks cupboard. Though why the hell they couldn't get drinks for themselves . . . why there was this inverse discrimination whereby men were expected to do various fatuous menial tasks and . . .

There was no sherry in the cupboard.

'No, we finished it last night,' Merrily agreed.

'But, hell, I bought a new bottle on Thursday evening.'

'I know, but last night there we were, huddled in the dark like evacuees in the Underground during the Blitz . . .'

It wasn't worth pointing out to her that anyone who was an evacuee wouldn't have been in the Underground during the Blitz. 'If you knew there wasn't any there, why the hell did you ask me to get her a drink?'

'Oh,' Merrily replied skittishly. 'I meant get her a drink from the off-licence.'

It was after ten by the time Graham finally got to his 'study' and opened the other two unwelcome surprises. He did so by candlelight, because changing all the fuses and barking his knuckles severely had not brought back the power supply.

In view of this, the first unwelcome letter was ironic. It was a written estimate from the electrician who had been so gloomy about the house's wiring. For reasons which were certainly not explained and would probably only be comprehensible to another electrician, he had seen fit to raise the price from one thousand four hundred to a round two thousand pounds. Excluding V.A.T.

The second letter was from the bank. Its tone was even less friendly than the previous one. In spite of warnings, the Marshalls' overdraft had increased and the manager demanded a 'speedy settlement'; if this was not forthcoming, he threatened 'withdrawal of facilities'.

Graham sat for some time over cheque book and calculator, trying the sums in a variety of ways, but the overdraft he came up with was still one hundred and fifty pounds short of the figure the bank quoted. The thought that the bank's computer had made a mistake began to glow inside him. He liked the idea of computers being fallible; it seemed in some way to strike back at Robert Benham. He started to frame sarcasms for the letter he would write to the manager.

'Are you coming to bed?'

Merrily's voice fluted behind him. She leaned childishly in the doorframe, a nightdress like an oversize T-shirt sagging from the sharp edges of her body.

'I will be soon. You haven't been doing any joint account cheques I don't know about, have you?'

'No. I don't think so. Not big ones.'

'Good. The bank manager's got a —'

'Oh, except for Henry and Emma's music lessons . . .'

That turned out to be the missing figure. Seventy-five pounds for each child. Graham felt too tired even to lose his temper. He made some caustic remark and turned back to his calculator.

He assumed Merrily had gone and was surprised, two minutes later, to hear her repeat, 'I said, are you coming to bed?'

Fourteen years of marriage had not left any room for ambiguity in the invitation. He swung his chair round to contemplate his wife. But he was too angry and the memory of Tara Liston's perfect proportions was too recent for him to feel any stirring of lust.

'No, not yet,' he replied.

She came across to him and, with that mistaken sense of timing she shared with her mother, kissed his lips and fumbled down at the inert folds of his lap.

He jerked his head away. Merrily's hand came up to either side of his face, holding him in imitation of some film she had once seen.

'Who is it, Graham?'

'What?'

'Who is the woman you're seeing?'

'Merrily . . .' Weariness at her stupidity sapped him.

'No, come on. Am I expected to believe this story about spending the weekend with your new boss?' Her small voice had grown squeaky with emotion. 'Go on, are you going to tell me who it is?'

Was it from now on to be his fate, Graham wondered, to be accused of peccadillos he had not committed, while his great crime went undetected? Again he felt the exhausted urge to laugh, but he restrained himself.

'No, Merrily, I am not.'

She looked at him with what was designed to be a searching, reproachful look, and walked out of the room. He watched her go, irritated by her irrelevance.

Before she was out of sight, she was out of his mind.

Money.

That was the main problem. Somehow he had to raise his income, or cut their expenses. He felt his father's meanness rising in him, and hated it. He wanted country cottages and boats and expensive women, not that awful small-minded cheese-paring to which he too now seemed to be sentenced.

He got out a bank statement, resentfully remembering the number of occasions he had seen Eric Marshall do the same, and started to check through the regular payments.

There was only one that could be reduced and make any worthwhile saving. It was the figure of nearly a hundred pounds paid each month to an insurance company, the endowment part of their endowment mortgage. If he could convert the mortgage back to a simple one . . . The endowment was a good long-term investment, but his problems had to be resolved in the short-term. He reached for the folder which contained all the documents relating to their recent house purchase.

The endowment mortgage had been arranged through a broker and Graham had not before studied the documents in detail. Now he did, and found out on exactly what terms he and Merrily had made the purchase of their house.

And what he found out, he relished.

One phrase in particular appealed to him. It was the definition of the endowment policy by which the mortgage was guaranteed:

JOINT LIFE WITH SUM INSURED PAYABLE ON FIRST DEATH.

CHAPTER NINE

Once he had decided to kill Merrily, Graham Marshall felt a kind of peace. He had reached a logical decision and now could allow himself a lull before he implemented that decision. He felt the lightness that follows arrival at a destination.

He had no doubts about the logic of what he had decided. There were three unanswerable arguments in favour of killing his wife.

The first was the financial one. To have the mortgage paid off would revolutionise his life. The payments to the building society and insurance company were by far the largest monthly drains on his income. With them out of the way, he would start again to feel some financial latitude in his affairs.

The second argument was that being married was a bar to the kind of lifestyle he was now determined to recapture. He had sufficient self-knowledge to realise that he was not dependent on close emotional ties. He should have been aware of this earlier, before he was trammelled by the bonds of family, but now he had recognised his nature, he owed it to himself to get out of his current situation as soon as possible.

The third reason for killing Merrily was that he couldn't stand her.

And the qualms and uncertainties that would divert most potential murderers between the intention and the act did not affect Graham Marshall. Thanks to the old man on Hammersmith Bridge, he had no doubts about his capabilities. He had committed murder. He had gone the distance.

Increasingly he found his thoughts translating the murder

into sporting metaphors. This was a habit that had been with him from schooldays. Though unexceptional on the track and field, he had always seen academic competition in terms of a race. Revision had been a period of intensive training, to ensure peak fitness and performance on examination day.

The murder was now part of the same imagery, a major challenge which he had met. It was as if he had completed his first marathon. From now on he knew he could go the distance; it was just a matter of improving his performance.

Having decided Merrily's fate, he felt again as if he were entering a period of intensive training.

He also felt renewed strength in his identity when it came under threat.

Which was just as well, because his identity received a considerable blow on the Monday morning, when he was summoned to Robert Benham's office.

After Stella had showed him in, Graham began by thanking Robert for 'a really terrific weekend'.

'Oh yes. Glad you enjoyed it.' The dismissive tone made this sound like a reprimand, as if Graham were gratuitously introducing his private life into office hours. Robert moved quickly on. 'Listen, I've just had a letter about a three-day conference in Brussels. Set up by some EEC committee. I gather it's a comparative study of personnel methods in the member countries. I want you to go and wave the Crasoco flag.'

Graham was gratified. Very few foreign trips came the way of the Personnel Department. He got the occasional day or maybe an overnight at one of the regional offices, but other countries were administered either locally or from America. On the rare occasions when opportunities for travel had arisen in the past, George Brewer had appropriated them.

So it was good news. The Brussels trip sounded like a classic non-essential freebie. Maybe, Graham began to think, life under Robert Benham wouldn't be so bad.

'Oh, that sounds . . .' He was about to say 'fun', but realised that the word might lack gravity, so substituted,

'. . . interesting. When is it?'

'22nd to 24th of April,' replied Robert, looking at him with unusual intensity.

'Well, that should be . . .' Then Graham realised the reason for the look. 'But the Departmental Heads' Meeting is on the 23rd.'

'That's right.'

The Departmental Heads' Meeting was an important part of Graham's power-base within the company. Twice a year the heads of all the London departments, as well as the regional ones, met to discuss staffing problems and proposals. Chairing the meeting was one of the tasks George Brewer had willingly relinquished to his assistant, and it was a job that Graham enjoyed. It also gave him an insight into the fortunes of the various sectors of the company, privileged information that fuelled his own scheming over the next six months. Excluding him from the Departmental Heads' Meeting would remove his finger from the company's pulse.

'But, Robert, I chair that meeting.'

'*Have* chaired it in the past. I think it's a job that should be done by the Head of Personnel.'

Graham considered his position. There was no doubt that Robert had planned this annexation of responsibility. The casual line of 'just had a letter about a three-day conference' did not fool him. Robert had certainly made up his mind to send Graham to Brussels the previous week; the softening-up of the weekend had been calculated and this new assault was definitely a challenge. Graham now understood the game Robert was playing. It was the tactic of any conqueror – to relax his victims with assurances, and then to remove their liberties piecemeal, in a series of small raids, none in themselves big enough to warrant resistance. Robert was working on the assumption that the worm wouldn't turn.

But Graham was not prepared to submit that easily. 'O.K., that's a point of view, Robert. I don't agree with it, but obviously you're entitled to your opinion.' He paused. 'However, I would point out that on April 23rd George Brewer

79

will still be Head of Department. I think I should consult him before I agree to go to this conference.'

'I've squared George.'

Robert spoke with finality. Graham knew there was no point in appealing to the older man. George would only bid for sympathy, agree that no one took any notice of him any longer, and plead for company in another maudlin drinking session. Graham had been thoroughly outmanoeuvred.

It was like the weekend, designed to diminish him and make him feel subservient to Robert Benham. The only thought which protected Graham from its full effect was the knowledge that he had done something that Robert had never achieved. He had committed a murder.

And was going to commit a second.

As he left Robert's office and passed George's he gave himself another boost by inviting Stella out for a drink after work. She consented, suggesting that this time, rather than leaving together, they should meet in the wine bar. He liked her practicality, the precision with which she followed a sequence of steps she had certainly trodden before. He wondered how many of his colleagues had trodden them with her.

He liked talking to Stella. Again he found that evening it was a relief to be with a woman who made no demands on him and who talked about things that were not part of his daily life. He relaxed, and felt his relaxation was justified, a licensed day out from training so that he didn't become obsessed with thinking of the challenge ahead.

As they emerged after three glasses of wine, Stella said she'd be happy to cook him supper one night, and Graham realised with slight shock that this was a sexual invitation.

Sex had not figured much in his thoughts since he had killed the old man. His fantasies of expensive women were intellectual, not physical, desires. No doubt he had made dutiful love to Merrily a few times and he had certainly felt sexual envy for Robert and Tara at the weekend, but lust had not been a strong motive. He wondered if it ever had for him. The

'Swinging London' experiments of his twenties and his marriage to Merrily had, in retrospect, been prompted more by the demands of convention than importunate desire. And now that there was something else of significance in his life, he felt no shame in admitting that sex was not very important to him.

It was certainly not the main reason for his consorting with Stella. He did that for a change of company and, he realised, from a shrewd sense of survival. If Robert Benham was set to exclude him from the legitimate sources of information within the company, then Graham was going to have to build up his own underground network. And Stella, soon to take over as secretary to the new Departmental Head, would be an essential contact.

But, though he had no particular desire to capitalise on it, Graham recognised that her sexual interest was flattering and might, in time, prove useful.

Keeping his options open, he said that supper one night would be very nice, kissed her gently on the cheek and left.

CHAPTER TEN

It was not until the weekend that he began to think seriously about the murder. The euphoria which followed his decision about Merrily's fate had begun to dissipate from inaction. Also, Lilian was staying again 'because she's still so upset over Charmian'. His mother-in-law's presence was the reminder he needed of his intolerable situation.

And his money worries remained. A grovelling letter to the bank had bought time, but not a solution. So many of the family's expenses were essentials paid by standing order that, though he made himself unpleasant to Merrily about house-keeping and to the children about their entertainments, he knew that their actual savings could only be nominal. No, he had to stop paying the mortgage. And there was only one way to do that.

Murder, however, is easier in the abstract than it is in reality. Though the lack of repercussion from the old man's death gave him an occasional glow of unassailable immunity, Graham did not delude himself that Merrily's would be as easily achieved. For a start, it had to look like an accident. And, since he knew that the first port of call for every murder-investigating detective was the partner of the victim, it had to be accomplished in a way that absolved him from all suspicion.

The more he thought about the problem, the more his respect for successful murderers increased.

He quickly rejected the devices recollected from his occasional reading of detective fiction. Stabbing with icicles, bludgeoning with deep-frozen chops, injecting air bubbles into the bloodstream and employing Pigmies with blowpipes all seemed likely to raise more problems than they would solve.

Poison, though . . . Poison did have possibilities. Not for nothing was it one of the favourites of the domestic murderer. Everyone ate and drank and, without resorting to the fictional hope of a poison unknown to medical science, there were an adequate number of lethal compounds around most houses.

Some research was needed. Graham went to the local library.

The girl behind the counter did give him a slightly odd look when he asked what they had on poisons, but directed him, without much confidence, to the SCIENCE section. Failing that HEALTH or HANDICRAFTS. Or she had a feeling there was something on famous murderers in BIOGRAPHY. Or, of course, there was the *Encyclopaedia Britannica* in REFERENCE.

Graham hummed cheerily to himself as he set out along the stacks.

SCIENCE proved unavailing. He fell eagerly on the Chemistry text books that were there, but they only glanced incidentally on poisons. Still, they did at least remind him of the little chemistry he had done at school. Maybe all those boring practicals hadn't been wasted. Maybe they'd had some use other than getting him an O-level. Might be worth checking through his old notes when he got home.

HEALTH was also, perhaps predictably, unhelpful. There were plenty of references to poisons, but all concentrated on how to cure someone who had taken them. Which was the last thing Graham wanted to know.

HANDICRAFTS, he decided, had just been an optimistic guess on the part of the librarian.

BIOGRAPHY looked too dauntingly large a section for him to go through, so he went over to REFERENCE and took down the volume of *Encyclopaedia Britannica* which covered POISONS.

He sat down at a table and, amidst pensioners going

through the newspaper racecards, mothers planning holidays with hotel guides and schoolchildren working on 'projects', he tried to find out how to murder his wife.

He stayed there for about an hour, rising periodically to fetch a new volume for a cross-reference, but at the end felt little further advanced. The editors of the *Encyclopaedia Britannica* did not appear to have had the would-be poisoner in mind when they compiled their great work.

Graham found out a good deal about the triumvirate of arsenic, cyanide and strychnine, but no clue as to how they might be unobtrusively obtained. Did rat poisons still contain arsenic? And if they did, how did one set about extracting it? Or feeding it to the victim? It didn't seem the ideal solution. And he didn't feel any more optimistic about building up a supply of cyanide from almonds or apricot kernels.

At the end of the hour the only hopeful fact he knew was that poisons were much used as weed killers and insecticides.

Graham Marshall set off for the garden centre.

There, too, there was a Saturday morning crowd, of husbands with worried expressions and steel tape-measures estimating paving stones, of pensioners carefully stocking window-boxes, and wives loading Volvos with dahlia tubers and garden furniture. Graham again felt light-hearted, even light-headed, as he walked between greenhouses and Gro-bags to the covered part of the garden centre. He felt a gleeful immunity from suspicion, just another commuter bent on titivating his rectangle of urban soil. His intentions were deliciously private.

As he went through the glass doors, a word came to him. A word he should have thought of earlier, a word whose dangers had recently received considerable press coverage.

Paraquat.

There seemed to have been a little spate of cases of children dying from accidental consumption of paraquat. Most of these had occurred on farms where the concentrated form of the poison was to hand, but Graham felt sure that a gardening version was available.

He also felt it was the ideal treatment for Merrily.

He looked along the rows of proprietary weed killers, but none was labelled 'Paraquat'. Obviously an ingredient rather than a brand-name. He started taking down bottles and cans to check their contents.

'Can I help you, sir?'

The assistant was young, with transparent down as yet unshaven over a spotty face. The green overall he wore was too large, suggesting that he was weekend staff, perhaps even still at school.

'Yes. I'm looking for something with paraquat in it.'

'Oh, yes, sir. Why? What exactly did you want to kill?'

Graham looked up sharply, but of course there was no suspicion in the boy's eyes. It was a logical question to ask of someone selecting weed killers.

'Well, er, weeds,' he replied feebly.

'Yes. Any particular sort, sir?'

Graham searched quickly through his memory and managed to come up with 'Ground elder.'

'Oh, well, sir, I think you'll find this very good.' The boy displayed a small bottle between finger and thumb.

'Does that contain paraquat?'

'No, sir. Glyphosate, sir.' If he was still a schoolboy, the young man certainly seemed to know his business.

'Oh, thank you.'

'That is the best, sir.' The boy hovered. 'The check-out's over there, sir.'

'Yes. Yes. I'll . . . thank you. A few other things and . . .'

At last the boy wandered off and Graham resumed his study of the shelves. He felt disappointed. He had taken a fancy to the word 'paraquat'; 'glyphosate' had not got quite the same ring. Anyway, his eroded recollections of chemistry could not provide a precise definition of 'glyphosate' or its likely effects on Merrily.

Then his eye lighted on something else. It was the word he was looking for. 'Contains paraquat', it said on the packet. He picked a middle-sized box and read the cautions on the side.

Yes, that sounded suitably dangerous. He was about to go, then changed his mind and took a large box instead.

Four pounds twenty. A bargain, if it did what he wanted it to do.

Jauntily, he walked up to the check-out.

'Not much good for ground elder, sir.'

The omniscient youth had appeared round the corner of a garden gnome display.

'You want something more selective,' he continued. 'What you got there'll kill everything.'

'Oh, don't worry,' said Graham on a bubble of laughter. 'That'll do.'

If his resolve had been slackening (which it wasn't), Saturday lunch would have tightened it up again. The children were at their most repugnant, cross at being refused money to go to the cinema that afternoon. Lilian had moulded her face into an expression of brave anguish, and kept asserting how sharper than the serpent's tooth it was to have an ungrateful child. And Merrily, still basking in the fact that she was not the child in question, was at her most infuriating. She had taken to playing a brave little woman role. Yes, they were hard up, but she wasn't going to be daunted by that. She'd fight back. Maybe she could make a large batch of chutneys and sell them. Perhaps a little stall outside the front gate . . . ?

Graham might have minded less if he had thought his wife really meant it, if these suggestions were genuine attempts to improve the family finances. But he knew they were made only for effect, obscure flanking movements in a campaign directed at him. He noticed she never mentioned actually getting a job. On the one occasion when he had suggested it, Merrily had gone all frail and exploited, saying yes, of course, if he really wanted it, he could 'send her out to work'. She was sure she could somehow manage to fulfil what she still regarded as her primary duty of 'giving him a good life'. And she was sure that Henry and Emma would get used to being 'latch-key kids'. And, as to the shame, the public admission that they needed

86

the money, well that wouldn't worry her, she had asserted with a bulldog jut of her little chin, so long as it didn't worry him . . . As she got older, Merrily used her mother's methods of exaggeration more and more.

The Saturday lunch ended with Graham losing his temper. This prompted bad language from Henry, tears from Emma, and from Lilian and Merrily the identical expression of a camel patiently inviting the final straw. Merrily said they could take a hint and they would all go out for a walk in Richmond Park, 'because at least then he couldn't object that they were spending any money'.

Graham foolishly mentioned that the petrol in the car which would drive them the two miles to the park was not exactly free, and got a predictably dramatic reaction from Merrily. She produced her housekeeping purse and emptied its contents on to the kitchen table, begging Graham to help himself to however much it cost. She would hate him to feel that his wife was trying to cheat him.

When the house was finally empty of these elaborate ironies and recriminations, Graham poured himself a large Scotch and sat down. The awfulness of the lunch gave him a sense of righteousness. Everything awful that Merrily did now gave him strength, justification, a confirmation that his decision to murder her was the right one.

The shed was rarely used. Since they moved, the Marshalls had had too much to do in the house to pay much attention to the garden. The tools lay stacked against the wall as the removal men had left them. The hover-mower, the only piece of equipment which had been used the previous summer, lay across the floor, impacted grass beneath it giving off a damp vegetable smell.

Graham cleared the clutter of shears and bamboo canes from the table-top under the dusty window, and put down his equipment. A dark green bottle half full of sherry. A wine glass. And the large box of weed killer.

He broke off a foot-length of bamboo and was ready to

begin his experiment. He hadn't done anything comparable since school and then it had been in rather different laboratory conditions. But this would be good enough to tell him what he wanted to know.

He poured an inch and a half of sherry into the wine glass. The brand he bought for Lilian was darker than the Tio Pepe she preferred, yellowish in colour.

He took the box of weed killer and shook out its contents. The poison was contained in little sachets, eight in all. With a Stanley knife he nicked the corner off one and looked inside.

His first shock was that the stuff was blue. Little blue granules rather like those tiny cake decorations known as 'hundreds and thousands'.

Oh dear. Maybe they would change colour as they dissolved. He poured a few granules into the wine glass and stirred vigorously.

At first they seemed unwilling to liquefy at all, but then they did. The colour, however, remained. The sherry turned bright, bright blue.

He wondered, not very seriously, about weaning Merrily off sherry and on to Blue Curaçoa, but, even if that could be achieved, he couldn't see her being fooled. The liquid had a nasty livid sheen on the top, and an opaque sediment was forming at the bottom.

He sniffed it. The smell hadn't changed. That was one thing in its favour.

Hmm. Nobody was going to drink from a glass like that by mistake. Maybe from a bottle, though . . . ? It was worth trying.

He emptied the remains of the sachet into the sherry bottle and shook it vigorously. For a moment he set aside the problem of getting Merrily to drink straight from the bottle. Just see if it works first.

He looked through the dark green glass. The adulteration of the contents was not apparent at first glance. The colour didn't look odd. But when it was held up to the light the thick sediment showed, and when he looked close, undissolved granules clustered against the sides like some obscene Chinese meal.

It was pretty obvious it wasn't going to work, but something kept him going. Maybe it took time to dissolve. Maybe more would have the required effect.

He ripped open another sachet and, forming a funnel from a piece of cardboard torn off the box, poured the contents in. Another shake and the bottle's contents looked even more bizarre.

Suddenly the incongruity of his actions struck and he found himself laughing. The whole situation was farcical and filled him with a strange elation. He slit open the remaining six sachets and poured their stock of granules into the bottle. Then he shook it, like a rattle, singing, through his giggles, the South American tune 'La Bamba'. What he was doing seemed the funniest thing that had ever happened to him. The seriousness of his intention and the crass incompetence of what he was doing triggered his wild hilarity.

At last he sobered up and looked at the bottle.

No. No one would ever be taken in by that blue mass of half-dissolved granules. The person who drank through that lot would have to be very, very determined to die.

He heard a noise from the house and looked up to see Merrily waving from the kitchen window. Damn. Hadn't noticed the time. Well, he couldn't wash up his experiment now. Do it some other time when he was alone in the house.

He shoved the bottle, the glass and the remnants of the weed killer packing on a shelf behind a large rectangular can of creosote.

Need for a rethink. Silly to imagine it would have been as easy as that. He went indoors, mildly irritated but not depressed by his failure.

He carried the Stanley knife to explain his presence in the shed. 'Wondered where it had got to, darling,' he said kissing Merrily perfunctorily on the forehead.

'I'm surprised you can find anything in that shed,' she accused. 'It's a terrible mess. Really needs tidying.'

'Yes. Yes. Yes.'

'You must get round to it some time.'

'Sure.'

'Though I suppose I'll have to end up doing it myself. Like most things,' she concluded with a long-suffering sigh.

The remark was meant to make Graham feel guilty. But he was damned if he was going to let it. Guilt, he had decided, even for trivial matters, was not an emotion in which he intended to indulge in the future.

He was coming down from having shouted the children into bed when he met Lilian in the hall. She moved her arm behind her back, but too slowly. He saw the bottle of sherry in her hand.

'Where did you get that from?' he snapped.

She gave him the defiant look of the boy in *When Did You Last See Your Father?*, an expression that didn't suit her.

'In the shed.'

'Why on earth did you go in there?'

'The bottle was around at lunchtime. I saw it. I knew you had hidden it somewhere, Graham.'

'Why should I do that?'

She straightened up into a posture of martyrdom.

'I know you don't like me, Graham.' She left a pause for the flood of contradictions, which didn't come.

'But I do think hiding the sherry's pretty petty.'

'But I wasn't hiding it. I was just using the bottle. It's not sherry in there.'

'It smells like sherry.'

Oh God. Had she snatched a quick tipple out in the shed? What effect would it have? He had wanted to test the dosage somehow, but this was not the way he would have chosen.

'Well, it isn't sherry!' He snatched the bottle from her quite roughly. 'I was just using it for something in the garden. If you want a drink, there's some wine in the fridge.'

A deep breath telegraphed the start of Lilian's weeping. 'I think you're very cruel to me, Graham. You know I'm desperately upset about how Charmian behaved. And now you . . . I expected a bit of support from you . . . I wouldn't have changed my will if I'd known –'

'Oh, for God's sake!' Graham stumped off towards the garden. Going through the utility room, he saw the sticky labels Merrily used to identify food in the freezer. He tore one off and wrote on it with felt pen: 'POISON. NOT TO BE TAKEN.'

He stuck it over the bottle's original label. Out in the shed he hid the bottle deep in the corner behind a pile of seed trays. Too risky to put it in the dustbin. He'd dispose of it another time.

He looked out of the dusty window to the lights of the house next door. How warming, welcoming other people's lights looked. Perhaps, he thought wryly, that was how the lights of his house looked to outsiders, the glow of a happy family within. Huh.

It was going wrong. Lilian's finding the sherry shouldn't have happened. He had taken a stupid, unnecessary risk.

In fact, his whole approach had been wrong. Slipshod. Inefficient.

He had killed the old man effortlessly and that was now a source of fierce pride. But killing Merrily would take more cunning. In the euphoria of having made the decision he had been careless, underestimated the difficulties that faced him.

Just because of his failure to get George's job, he must not let his standards slip. He had always prided himself on efficiency, and now he had to demonstrate that he was more efficient than Robert Benham. Since he was prevented from deploying his skills at the office, then he would apply them to his wife's murder.

No more carelessness.

Detailed, systematic planning.

He was determined that the murder was going to work.

CHAPTER ELEVEN

It was Merrily herself who showed him how to do it.

On the Sunday evening, after Lilian had finally gone off to what she insisted on calling her 'lonely little room', Graham was watching something less than riveting on the television, when he thought of a new potential economy and went up to his 'study' to work it out on the calculator.

He had assumed Merrily to be pottering around in the kitchen, so was surprised to see her kneeling on the floor in front of his desk, sifting through the contents of the drawers. She turned round guiltily at his approach.

'Lost something?' he asked.

'No.'

'Then what are you looking for ?'

'I'm looking for some evidence of what you've done.'

That gave him a momentary *frisson*, but then he realised that she was once again referring to his imagined infidelity. God, her stupidity infuriated him.

'What sort of evidence had you in mind?' he asked lightly.

'It might be anything. You never know what's going on behind a *man's* bland exterior. Vivvi found a whole *library* of pornographic magazines at the back of Will's sock drawer.'

He understood. Merrily had been talking to her friend. Vivvi was, if possible, more affected than Merrily herself and the current form her affectation took was feminism. In her case all this involved was wearing designer dungarees, talking about menstruation a lot and refusing to cook meals when she felt like being taken out by her long-suffering husband.

'I'm sorry to disappoint you. You won't find any porno-graphy here. I suppose I could get some if you fancy it,' he added ironically.

'It wasn't pornography I was looking for in your case.'

'What then?'

'Letters.'

'What sort of letters?'

She stood up and faced him. Defiance did not add to her charms. 'Vivvi's mother,' she began, 'works at Sotheby's. She's a porcelain specialist.'

'Ah.' Graham was utterly bemused by this. Merrily, he thought, as she went on, has gone off her rocker. Maybe I could get her certified and solve the problem that way.

'On her way to Oxford Circus last Monday evening she walked past a wine bar. She saw you coming out with a woman.'

So that was it.

'Whom you kissed,' Merrily continued inexorably.

Graham's first instinct was to explain. It was only Stella from the office, after all. There was no sexual interest on his side. Merrily's spy had got the wrong end of the stick.

But another instinct stopped him. There was something of value in Merrily's suspicion. He could not yet identify what it was, but he knew he must foster her distrust.

'She was talking rubbish,' he blustered, too vehemently. 'It must have been someone else she saw.'

'You were late that evening. I remember. And you'd had a drink.'

'Yes. O.K., I had. But just with someone from the office.' He carefully made the truth sound like a lie.

'I don't believe you, Graham.'

'Well, you bloody well should. You're not going to find any love letters in here.'

'No?'

'No. There aren't any.'

'Then you won't mind my looking.'

She spoke with triumph, but in fact was playing straight

into his hands.

'Yes, I bloody do mind you looking! It's an invasion of privacy. This is *my* room. These are my papers. Get out!' And he hustled her to the door.

She turned on the landing and looked at him piercingly. Lilian Hinchcliffe would have been proud of the way her daughter was playing the scene.

'Very well, then,' said Merrily.

She used her littlest voice, but there was no doubt that her words were a challenge. She would be back for further snooping.

With a show of anger Graham slammed the study door. But when he sat down in his swivel chair, he was smiling.

Merrily having given him a lead, Graham found that the rest of the components of his plan slotted quickly into place. He had the feeling that his luck was in, that he was working well. His training programme was right and he would peak at the proper time. It was the same good feeling that had always come to him, until the last year, in the run-up to examinations and job interviews. He felt that he was in charge of events, almost that the world span at his bidding.

Robert Benham had, unwittingly, given him another vital component. The trip to Brussels, designed to frustrate Graham's progress at work, was going to prove an important boost to his other career. It would provide what is essential to any serious murderer, an alibi.

Graham also realised, his mind working gleefully well, that the trip could be used to increase Merrily's suspicions of his fidelity.

He had mentioned Brussels to her once or twice, but now if she brought up the subject he veered guiltily off it, apparently unwilling to give details of the nature of the conference. He also made tactical purchases of new pyjamas and a different aftershave which he hid with minimum efficiency at the back of his shirt drawer.

Stella had to play her part, too, though she was unaware of

it. Meeting her alone in the corridor one day, Graham said yes, he'd love her to cook supper for him one night. She responded eagerly, suggesting the next evening. No, he didn't think he could make that . . . or he might be able to . . . He'd have to consult the diary at home. Could she ring him that evening to check? Merrily would be out till ten.

Merrily, who had made no arrangement to go out, took the call, as intended. Graham watched covertly as she reacted. Stella, taken off her guard, must have said something before she rang off, because it registered on Merrily's face before she turned accusingly to Graham.

'Wrong number, was it?' he asked with innocence.

'I'm not sure,' said Merrily slowly.

He continued the campaign when he saw Stella at the office the next day. Yes, he'd gathered what had happened. Merrily had come home unexpectedly early. Yes, it had given him a nasty turn, too. Meant he'd have to tread a bit warily for a few days. So supper might be a risk. But how about a drink after work?

In fact, going to Stella's flat for supper might have advanced his plan further, but Graham did not relish the inevitable sexual dimension. It was not that he felt any physical revulsion, just that sex seemed decreasingly relevant in his life. For the same reason, it was some weeks since he had made any physical approach to Merrily, a fact which, working like everything else in his favour, gave her more food for suspicion. He added to this by ringing his wife from the wine bar and saying he was having to work late. Then he went back to chatting with Stella. Again he kissed her as they parted. You never knew who might be watching. But he felt no sexual interest.

Even the pornography he bought raised no excitement. He was interested, particularly to see how candour and photographic techniques had advanced since such material had last been important to him, in his late teens, but the interest was dispassionate. His preoccupation with the murder gave him an ascetic sense of purpose, of all his concentration being focused on a higher goal.

95

The purchase of the pornography was perhaps an indulgence, gilding the lily, but he did need a lure for Merrily. She had been looking for letters, but he could not supply any, unless he resorted to forging them. She had, however, also mentioned pornography as evidence of masculine perfidy, so that would have to do.

He bought some half-dozen magazines for spankers, suckers and mammary fetishists. Deciding that to leave them in his sock drawer would be too slavishly imitative, he put them underneath some insurance brochures in the lock-up part of his desk (to which he was confident Merrily had a key).

The Brussels trip was not the only reason why he had to complete his preparations quickly. Another approaching deadline urged speed.

He did not get a chance to test the next part of his plan until the weekend before he went away. Showing a calculated softening in his attitude, Graham allowed his family the Saturday afternoon trip to the cinema which he had previously denied. He encouraged Merrily and Lilian (it was the long Easter weekend and his mother-in-law was going to be there for the duration) to accompany the children. He would stay and watch the sport on television. Merrily had looked suspicious of his altruism, which was no bad thing from Graham's point of view, but agreed to go. Lilian said it was a great treat; no one ever asked her to go anywhere.

Over lunch, casually, he mentioned that he thought it was about time they had some new curtains in the spare room. Merrily said, yes, fine, she agreed but thought that they hadn't got any money to have them made. Graham said he remembered how, when they moved into their first house in Barnes, she had made all of the curtains herself. Now they were hard up again . . .

Merrily's little face hardened. 'Very well. Of course, Graham. I'm sure I can find time, *along with everything else*, to make some curtains. Mind you, Graham, you will have to fork out for the actual material, and the lining, and Rufflette tape.

Or perhaps you'd like me to *weave* the stuff myself . . . Perhaps we could organise the children to go into Richmond Park and collect dog hairs. Then we could spin them into yarn and . . . What do you say?'

Graham didn't rise to her. Awfulness from Merrily could now only add to his serenity. 'No, I'm sure I can afford to buy the material. Is the sewing machine working?'

'I imagine so. I haven't used it since we moved, so it's still where the removal men left it.'

'Where's that?'

'In the loft.'

As he climbed the folding steps and slid aside the wooden covering to the loft entrance, an unpleasant thought struck him. Suppose the light up there had been added later, an extension in modern white plastic-coated flex taken off the antiquated wiring . . .

The fear was quickly resolved. At the top of the steps, he pulled himself up on a pipe which led from the hot-water tank, and reached for the switch. The naked bulb threw instant light over the draped and dusty shapes under the rafters. And revealed that the light switch dated from the same time as the rest of the house's electrical system.

He stood astride the opening and surveyed the scene of the crime. The pipe against which he steadied himself could have been designed to conduct electricity.

He looked closely at the switch. That too couldn't have been better. It was the old brass type with a scalloped dome. The switch had a round metal end. Red and black rubber-covered wires emerged from the rose for about four inches before they disappeared into a metal tube fixed along a horizontal rafter. Gingerly he felt the thick, stiff wire through its coating and noted with satisfaction that the rubber already showed the crosshatched lines of perishing.

He hummed contentedly to himself as he went down to the cupboard under the stairs and switched off the power. Then he pulled on a pair of rubber gloves he had found in the kitchen; they were rather tight and squeezed his hands. He picked up a large rubber-cased torch and a pair of pliers and set off back upstairs.

He didn't need the pliers. The old insulation crumbled off the wire like pastry. Soon the golden glow of the two wires showed in his torchbeam. He squeezed them gently together between finger and thumb.

Then he unscrewed the dome of the switch, fretted away at more of the insulation inside and bent one of the wires up out of its porcelain protection until it would touch against the metal cover when he replaced it.

He screwed the top back on. The brass gleamed too much where his rubber gloves had wiped off its accumulation of dust. He reached up to an overhead rafter, scraped some of the sooty sediment into his rubber-covered palm and gently blew it over the switch. The brass turned uniformly dull.

His hum became a jaunty whistle as he bounced down the stairs to the main switches. Then, with another stroke of serendipity, he remembered what Lilian had given him for Christmas. At the time his reaction had been that the gift was rather mean and totally useless, but at the time he had not visualised needing to test the mains.

The screwdriver was still in its package, so he was able to follow the instructions exactly. The point was to be placed against the suspect appliance and the other end lightly touched. If current flowed, the neon in the handle would light.

He switched the mains back on and returned to the loft. Laying his torch on a rafter so that it was trained on the switch and holding the screwdriver tentatively between finger and thumb, he brought the blade down on to the brass casing.

Nothing happened.

A surge of anger swept through him. This was not the way it should be. Everything was going right for him, he was invincible.

Then he chuckled. Of course. Elementary electrics. He took the rubber glove off his left hand and tried again.

The neon glowed.

Methodically, he went downstairs, switched off the mains, returned to the loft and defused his booby trap. Down again to restore the power, and up again to check the switch was no longer live.

Then he climbed from the ladder to the opening again to see if there was any way the pipe could be avoided. There wasn't. The light from the landing shone on it, and the height of the steps was such that one needed a handhold for the last pull. He might have been able to heave himself up on the frame of the opening, but Merrily, being some nine inches shorter, would be bound to use the pipe.

Once in the loft, it would be natural for her to keep hold of it. The rafters were not boarded so she would have to balance with care, and lean across towards the light switch. Even though she was lighter than he, her weight would press her hand against the live metal. The shock would pass from arm to arm, through her chest and heart.

Graham picked up the torch and screwdriver and went back down through the opening. He replaced the cover, folded the steps and put everything away. Then he sat down to watch the wrestling.

The final part was easy. On the evening of the 21st of April, Graham packed his bag for Brussels before supper and then went into his study, leaving the door ajar. He sat in the swivel chair, got out one of his pornographic magazines and studied its splayed orifices with detachment.

He was aware of Merrily's presence behind him before she said, 'Supper's ready.' He shoved the magazine into a drawer. Quickly. But not quickly enough.

'What's that you're reading?'

'Oh, nothing. Just some insurance thing.' He rose this time too quickly. 'Supper, good.' He hustled Merrily out of the doorway.

'What have you got in there, Graham?'

'Nothing, nothing. Come on, I'm starving.'

'Graham, there's no point in keeping secrets from me. I'll

99

find out.'

'No, you won't.' He slammed the study door. 'Now, listen! I will not have you snooping in my things.'

Merrily put on her little girl pout and a voice to match. 'Do you think little me'd do a thing like that?'

Yes. Yes, I hope so, he thought, as he said, 'No. Of course not,' and kissed her.

After supper, he acted restless and tense. He was getting good at acting. Only a few weeks earlier the tension had been real, but now he knew what he was doing, he felt increasing self-control.

Then, suddenly, he announced. 'Oh, I knew there was something. I was going to get that sewing machine down from the loft for you.'

'There's no hurry. I'm not going to have time to–'

But Graham had gone. With elaborate caution he went into his study and opened a few desk drawers. He contrived to be on the stepladder to the loft with his arms full of papers when Merrily was drawn by curiosity upstairs.

'What are you doing?'

'Oh, just having a clear-out. Taking some rubbish upstairs.'

He wondered if he was overdoing it. Under what circumstances would he take wastepaper to the loft? But Merrily's suspicion, though rampant, was aimed in a different direction.

'Really?' she asked drily.

'Yes. I thought, while I've got the stepladder up . . . Nothing you want me to put up there for you?'

She shook her head.

'I mean you never go up there, so if there was anything . . .'

'No. I never go up there.' She gave him a mocking look that was almost a challenge, and drifted downstairs.

He worked quickly on the switch. He knew he was taking a risk fitting it without turning off the mains, but he had bought wooden tongs to handle the metal parts, and felt safe. Within five minutes the job was done and he received a comforting glow from the neon of his screwdriver. He used the wooden tongs to switch off the light and went back downstairs.

Merrily looked at him contemptuously as he entered the sitting-room.

'Where's the sewing machine?' she asked.

CHAPTER TWELVE

Graham enjoyed the conference. It was like being back at school. Though the class was made up of international personnel experts, though the surroundings were the impersonal, dust-repellent luxury of a new hotel, though the equipment included videos, computers and interpreters, it was still the values of school which prevailed. What counted were the questions raised after each dissertation, the points brought up in discussion groups, and in supplying these Graham, with his quick wits and lack of real commitment to the subject, was able to excel. He also had the comforting sensation that all the delegates were being assessed, and that he was coming out better than the rest. Graham Marshall felt his old self again.

He was untroubled by what he was missing back at Crasoco. The Departmental Heads' Meeting was less interesting than the Brussels conference and, he decided, probably no more useful. Already he was forming sentences with openings like 'Of course what they're doing in Holland about this problem . . .' or 'I think the statistics from West Germany are relevant in this matter . . .' He was refurbishing his armoury of information, little details which could be used in his old game of confusing his colleagues. He might not fool Robert Benham, but he could still fool the rest of them.

And Graham was now feeling more confident about Crasoco. Yes, he'd missed George Brewer's job, but he wasn't written off yet. A hatchet man like Robert Benham was bound to make enemies, and a focus would be needed for the disaffection he created. George Brewer's policies had become unfashionable and been reversed by the appointment of his successor, and exactly the same might happen when Robert Benham went.

Because there was no doubt that Robert Benham would go. He had made it clear that Head of Personnel was just a rung on the ladder he had planned for himself. Within five years he would have moved on to another company or . . . or who could say what might have happened to him?

Graham found that being away from London gave him objectivity. Since he lost the job, he had been too bound up in thoughts of his own failure and Robert Benham's success. Now he could achieve a more balanced view of his position. All was by no means lost.

He also liked living in a hotel. He liked the anonymous cleanness of the decor, the polished tiles of the shower, the paper-wrapped individual soap, the breakfast that appeared in obedience to a form hung on the door. He liked the impersonal luxury of a world where every service was part of a financial contract, where nothing depended on the inefficient motivations of duty or goodwill, where environment was merely a support system, not an expression of personality. This was the style in which he intended to live in the future.

The thought process of removing Merrily from his life was now complete. He did not think of her at all, just of himself as a skilled athlete returning to peak efficiency. There had been a hiccup in his training, a virus perhaps, which had laid him low, but he was now on the mend and would soon be capable of even greater feats.

So totally had he expunged the memory of his wife that when the call came through, his first reaction was of irritation. Reality was limping too slowly behind his thoughts. The new structures in his mind were all designed, but he had to deal with a few niggling details before he could start building them. Merrily's death became a formality, no more than a planning permission, but one that still, exasperatingly, had to be obtained.

He had flown to Brussels on Wednesday, 22nd April, and

the conference had started that afternoon. He had an untroubled expectation that he might hear something from London the next morning, but the call did not come, so he was able to enjoy the point-scoring of the second day. He was in the hotel foyer on his way to the first Friday session when he was paged for a phone call. He took it in a booth near the Reception Desk.

His first feeling when the speaker identified himself as a policeman was one of annoyance. He had been looking forward to the day's events. The second session in particular, a seminar on redeployment of staff too inefficient to be left in their current jobs but too senior to be demoted, was exactly the sort of occasion when Graham would excel. Still, he had to get the planning permission, tedious though it was.

'I'm very sorry, sir. I'm afraid I have some bad news for you.'

'What? Something hasn't happened to one of the children?' He was gratified by the glibness with which the right words came into his mouth.

'Not the children, no sir. I'm afraid it's your wife.'

'What? Has she had a car accident?' Again, he congratulated himself.

'No, sir. Not a car accident. A domestic . . . an accident with electricity.'

'Oh, my God. Is she all right?'

'I'm sorry, sir. I'm afraid she's dead.'

Mentally he counted up to ten before saying, 'Oh no! She can't be!'

And while he counted, he felt the glow of satisfaction spread within him.

The water of the Channel gleamed enticingly as he looked down from the plane. He had enjoyed the last few hours, making his excuses to the conference organisers, booking his flight, dispassionately explaining the circumstances of his need and feeling the officials' admiration for his bravery. Having lost his wife was like holding a sick-note, an excuse only to do the things he chose.

But it was much, much more than that. It was an achievement, an ambition realised. He had decided to kill her and, almost by remote control, he had brought about her death.

His point of vantage over the Channel was suitably godlike. He was in charge, a puppet-master pulling the strings he selected at the moment he chose.

He felt a sense of power.

CHAPTER THIRTEEN

He had told the police when he was arriving and there was a uniformed constable at the Boileau Avenue house to meet him.

Graham's first question was: 'Where are the children?', which he thought sounded properly concerned. He had devoted the journey to thinking of appropriate emotions for a widower. What he was really feeling, a gleeful confidence, he knew would not fit the bill.

'They've gone to their grandmother's, sir,' the constable replied. 'She said she could cope. Obviously very upset she was, but said it was her duty to look after the poor motherless little ones.'

Graham's knowledge of his mother-in-law left him in no doubt that the policeman was quoting her verbatim. Merrily's death, he felt sure, had provided Lilian with an irresistible new range of scenes to play to the extent of her histrionic powers.

'Yes. The children. It's terrible. It's going to scar them for life.' He felt these disjointed sentences were suitable for a man in his supposed state of shock.

'They recover, sir. Remarkably resilient. Though I'm afraid your daughter . . . She actually found your wife's body.'

'Oh no.'

The constable nodded lugubriously. ''Fraid so, sir. Not till the next morning, but – You know how your wife died, sir?'

Yes, of course I do, Graham was about to reply, but then remembered that no one had told him the precise details. He must concentrate. Step warily. Not allow the bubbling confidence inside to let down his act of bewildered bereavement.

'I just know it was an electrical accident.'

The policeman outlined what was believed to have happened, and Graham found that the official conjecture was gratifyingly close to his own projection of events.

'. . . and the shock ran along her arms and stopped the heart. Then she fell down from the loft on to the landing, but the children didn't hear anything. It was next morning that your daughter found her.'

'They sleep so heavily,' said Graham in a dull voice. Then, feeling an outburst might be timely, added, 'Oh God! If only they'd woken! If she'd got to a hospital in time, she might have been saved.'

'I'm afraid it wouldn't have helped, sir. Death must have been instantaneous. She wouldn't have felt a thing.'

'I suppose that's some kind of comfort.' Graham allowed his voice to break a little. Then he swayed and reached for the wall to support himself.

The constable was instantly solicitous. 'Here, you sit down, sir. Come on, you've had a terrible shock. Look, I'll go and make you a cup of tea.'

Graham sat and waited, rationing out occasional sighs and sobs when he thought the policeman was in earshot. The tea came; standard practice in dealing with shock had been followed and it was very sweet. Not to Graham's usual taste, but he drank it gratefully.

When he reckoned sufficient time had elapsed for him to have recovered, he decided to show more curiosity. He didn't wish to appear unsurprised by what had happened. 'But how? Why was the switch live?'

'Old wiring, sir, I'm afraid. The insulation was perished. She'd probably have survived just touching the switch, but supporting herself between it and the water pipe, she didn't have a chance.'

'Oh God,' Graham intoned. Then threw in another for good

measure. 'Oh God. I knew the wiring was dangerous. We were about to have it done. I'd got the estimate in. It was going to be started next week. He couldn't do it . . . any . . . earlier . . .'

He was rather pleased with the way he let this sentence tail off. Lilian was not the only member of the family with dramatic talent.

'Our people have looked at the wiring, and made it safe temporarily,' said the constable. 'Death trap they reckon, the whole house. If it hadn't been the loft switch, it could easily have been somewhere else.'

Good, thought Graham, good. That all helps to make the killing more plausible. He felt the welling confidence, which had been so slow to arrive after the old man's murder, that he was going to get away with it. An involuntary smile began to twitch at the corner of his mouth. To maintain appearances, he bit on his knuckle and shook his head in ostensible disbelief.

It was as well he was looking away, because the constable's next speech was tinged, for the first time, with suspicion, and Graham had to plan his reaction.

'One thing that did puzzle us, sir . . .' the policeman began diffidently, 'was why your wife went up to the loft, anyway . . .'

'Why?'

'Seemed a strange thing for her to do, while you were away. According to her mother, she had never been up there before . . .'

Trust Lilian to put her oar in. 'No, no, I don't believe she had.'

'Her mother said your wife was planning some tidying, but not in the loft. Presumably she was looking for something.'

'I suppose so.'

'We had a look round up there to see what it might be she was after.'

'Oh yes.' Graham gave little. He would wait until the direction of the man's words became clear before he chose his reaction.

'What we did find . . .' the policeman paused, assessing his impact, 'was some magazines.'

'Magazines?'

'Pornography.'

'Oh. But surely it's not illegal to –'

'No, no. Fairly soft stuff, these were. No grounds for prosecution or . . . No, the interesting thing about them was that they'd been put up there quite recently. Get a lot of dust in a loft, you know. There was hardly any on them.'

Graham met the constable's eye, which was curious and unyielding. Embarrassed honesty, Graham knew, was what was called for, and that was what he supplied.

'All right. I put them up there.'

'Thought that must have been the case, sir.' The policeman nodded complacently.

'Yes, I . . . I mean, lots of men buy material like that. It's no reflection on how well or badly your marriage is going . . .'

'No, no, of course not, sir.'

'So, anyway, I would sometimes look at that sort of stuff and . . . Anyway, one day I found my son in my study. He was looking for something in my drawers . . . something quite innocuous, a stamp or an envelope or . . . and it struck me that I didn't really want him finding the magazines, so I moved them up to the loft. Preparatory to chucking them out of the house.'

'Of course, sir. When was this?'

'Last week.'

'Hmm. About what we reckoned. So you did actually go up to the loft last week?'

'Yes.'

'What interests us about that is . . .' the man paced his sentence ponderously, 'why you didn't get a shock when you switched on the light?'

Graham had not been prepared for that. He felt himself colour and begin to sweat. 'Well, that's simple. I . . . I didn't switch it on.'

'No?'

'No. You see, we only moved into this house last year and, quite honestly, since getting the removal men to chuck various bits up into the loft, I've hardly been up there. I couldn't remember whether there was a light rigged up or not. So I used a torch. I was in a hurry, you see, because, well . . .' A little embarrassed cough. 'Merrily was out just for a few minutes and . . . she didn't know I had these magazines and I didn't really want her to . . . to . . .'

'I quite understand, sir.' The policeman's soothing voice was another part of his training in the treatment of shock.

Graham could still feel his face burning and the sweat starting on his temples. Still, a recently bereaved man has cause to look upset. He decided to capitalise on his physical symptoms and stage a little breakdown. 'Oh God, to think of those magazines – deceiving Merrily – they didn't matter – but it just seems so petty – and now she's dead and . . .' He managed to produce some quite presentable sobs.

'Have some more tea, sir.' But the constable didn't let him off the hook. 'We still haven't established why *your wife* wanted to go up to the loft, sir. She couldn't have had any suspicion that the magazines were up there, could she, sir?'

'What? No, it's – oh my God!' Graham manufactured a larger sob. 'The sewing machine.'

'What?'

'The sewing machine was up there. Oh, and she said she was going to make some curtains for the spare room. Yes, she talked about it Saturday lunchtime a couple of weeks back. Her mother was here, I remember.' (If Lilian was going to tell the police her recollections, then she could also make herself useful and corroborate his.)

'Yes, that must have been it – the sewing machine was up in the loft.' Time for the big, weepy finish.

'Oh God, she was going to do the curtains for me . . . As a surprise . . . For when I came back . . . Merrily . . . And now she's gone . . .' He judged it to be the moment when tears would be more eloquent than further words.

The policeman was very sympathetic. He apologised for having to ask the questions, realised that Mr. Marshall was in a state of shock, and asked if he would feel all right to be left on his own.

The last suggestion appealed strongly to Graham. The strain of curbing his glee was beginning to tell. Only one more thing he needed to know. 'Where is Merr . . . my wife . . . her body?'

'At the police mortuary, sir.'

'Oh. I suppose I'll have to sort out funeral arrangements and . . . We both agreed we'd want to be cremated if . . .'

His voice faltered while his mind thought, Destroy the evidence, destroy the evidence.

'I'm sure that'll all be possible after the inquest, sir.'

'Inquest?'

'Of course, sir. With all violent deaths there has to be an inquest.'

Sweat prickled on Graham's forehead. He felt the emptiness of nausea. An inquest was something he hadn't reckoned with.

After the constable had gone, Graham took a large Scotch to steady him. Soon he would have to face Lilian and the children, but they could wait a little longer.

News of the inquest had shaken him, but a core of confidence remained. He could cope. He would get away with it. The inquest was a formality. There was nothing a police investigation could find to incriminate him. If there had been, his reception on his return would have been very different.

Mentally, he reviewed the crime, testing it for flaws, pulling it this way and that, probing for weaknesses.

No, there was nothing. No careless fingerprint to expose him. His planning had paid off.

Lucky, he thought wryly, that he had chosen the method he had. He thought back, with indulgent disbelief to his earlier ideas, to his fumbling attempts with the paraquat, to –

Oh, my God!

His body was seized by a tremor as violent as his first reaction to the old man's death.

The sherry bottle.

He ran on legs of jelly to the shed. If the police had been in the house, investigating, inspecting, they might also have gone to the garden, might have found the adulterated sherry, might have started to harbour unwelcome suspicions of him, might have . . .

He snatched open the shed door.

It all looked different. The clutter was gone, the lawnmower and tools stacked neatly against the wall. The seed trays, behind which the bottle had been hidden, were now piled neatly on the shelf.

The sherry bottle, with its fatal contents, had disappeared.

He reeled, clasping at the wall for support. The police must have been in, examined the whole building, taken off the sherry for analysis . . .

Graham thought he was going to be sick.

But he wasn't sick, and after a few minutes the rhythm of his breathing steadied. As he reasserted control over his body, he did the same with his mind. Keep calm, keep calm, he told himself. Think it through.

Thinking it through helped. He had leapt to conclusions. It might have been the police who had been in the shed, but there were other explanations. Indeed, if it had been the police examining the building, why should they have bothered to tidy it? The shelves had been dusted down and the floor swept. That was surely beyond the scope of their investigation.

Wasn't it more likely, Graham thought with a little glint of hope, that Merrily had had one of her rare bursts of domesticity and attacked the shed herself? She had commented before on how much it needed tidying, and to do a major clear-out while he was away would have been in character, a flamboyant gesture to make him feel guilty on his return. Yes, and the policeman had quoted Lilian about Merrily's 'planning some tidying'.

Fuelled by hope, he hurried to the dustbins. That's where she would have put the rubbish she'd cleared out.

But they were empty. Of course, the refuse collectors came

on a Thursday.

He was about to replace the lid on the second bin when he saw something. Just a scrap of damp cardboard which had stuck to the inside and escaped the refuse truck.

It was a piece of the weed-killer box. The piece he had torn to funnel the granules into the sherry bottle.

He slumped against the wall with relief. It was all right. Merrily had tidied the shed. She had consigned the damning sherry to the dustbin and it was now lost and anonymous in some council amenity tip. Graham was safe. His late wife had obligingly destroyed the evidence against him.

He returned to the house for another large Scotch. That panic had passed, but other problems remained.

Whenever he was in danger of complacency, there was always the inquest to worry about.

It was a bad ten days.

Deaths generate work for the survivors. And the death of the active mother of two children generates more work than most. Though he had often castigated her minor inefficiencies, and though he had early recognised her native laziness, Graham was still surprised at how much Merrily had done, or perhaps by how much needed to be done by other people now that she was dead.

Unfortunately, the person who saw it as her God-given rôle to do most of these things was Lilian. Though Graham was glad of the help, he wished that it had come from another quarter.

Immediately after Merrily's death, her mother had taken Henry and Emma to the custody of her flat, but as soon as Graham returned, they all came back to the Boileau Avenue house. Immediately Lilian took domestic control, and her approach had an unnerving air of permanence. Within three days she spoke of the spare room as 'my room' and by the end of the week was saying it would be more practical to sell her flat, 'since I'm going to be needed here'.

This was not at all how Graham had visualised his future. If

113

all his wife's murder had achieved was to replace her with her mother, it had been a wasted exercise. Lilian around the house was even more annoying than Merrily. She hadn't even her daughter's minimal efficiency. Though she made much of dressing the part, with housecoats and turbanned scarves, her aptitude for housework was nil. Years of being cosseted by domestic staff and helpful lovers had left her without the basic skill of assessing a job and deciding how long it would take.

The kitchen floor would be left half-washed, two garments put in for a whole cycle of the washing machine, the Hoover would be abandoned half-way up the stairs, as Lilian launched herself into another scene.

Needless to say, her daughter's death gave her full scope for drama. Her shock and misery were no doubt real, but through them Graham could detect a core of satisfaction, even of triumph.

Lilian knew that Merrily's death had pushed her centre-stage and strengthened her power-base in the family. Her old complaint that no one needed her any more (though Graham had his doubts that anyone ever had needed her much), could no longer be justified.

But consciousness of her advantage did not stop the tears and the wailings and the scenes. She had lost her favourite daughter, she was alone in the world. Graham, now firm in his habit of objectivity, watched through these outpourings, feeling nothing but contempt. The situation could not continue for ever, but he would have to bide his time before he sought its solution.

His own behaviour he monitored with care. For him to appear unfeeling might raise suspicion, so he needed the occasional breakdown to maintain his image as the shocked and grieving widower.

In presenting this front he was helped by his panic over the inquest. The outsider only sees the physical manifestations of mental turmoil, not its cause. Hot flushes, sweating, restlessness, uneven speech patterns, sudden fluctuations of mood are all signs of a troubled mind, but the same symptoms could be triggered equally by the death of a much-loved spouse or the fear of being exposed as a murderer. Even through his anxiety, Graham could feel a perverse satisfaction that the cause of his discomposure could be so readily misinterpreted.

The inquest did worry him, there was no doubt of that. Though so much in the planning of the murder had worked in his favour, there were still too many variables about which he knew too little. How skilled was the police's forensic investigation likely to be? Had he left some blatant clue to his sabotage? Was foul play suspected?

Occasionally confidence again flooded his being, but such moments of peace were rare. He worried that his preparations had not been sufficiently meticulous. If he ever committed another murder (and something told him that if he got away with this one, it was not impossible that he might) he would take a lot more care.

But never for a moment did he regret having killed Merrily. His anxiety was only about his chances of getting away with it. Her absence brought new inconveniences, but those could be resolved. He felt again that mixture of apprehension and excitement that had always preceded examinations at school. The inquest was his latest and most demanding test.

If he passed that one, nothing could stop him.

The inquest was not an isolated event; there were more police enquiries before the bereaved Marshall family and Lilian Hinchcliffe appeared in the Hammersmith Coroner's Court. Graham underwent further meticulous questioning, which paradoxically he enjoyed. He had the feeling of being in a game, a quiz-programme perhaps, but one for which he had made adequate preparations and one which he stood at least a fifty/fifty chance of winning.

His daughter also, as discoverer of the body, suffered further questioning. The shock had told badly on her and in her emotion she became more of an adult. Not, though, the sort of adult who appealed to her father. She took on more and more of her mother's mannerisms, which were of course Lilian Hinchcliffe's mannerisms. As her grandmother's influence

115

grew, Emma became more like her. It was as if, with her daughter removed, Lilian immediately worked to replace her with another clone. Emma was fully recruited into the exclusive conspiracy of womanhood. The two now wept and emoted in unison.

Henry was apparently taking his mother's death less hard. With the brutality of adolescence, he was even heard to make jokes about it. A psychologist might well have recognised this behaviour as a defence and discovered the suffering core of a bewildered child, but Graham was no psychologist and did not feel the interest to investigate.

With the frail link of Merrily removed, his children seemed more than ever strangers. Four of them sat side by side in the Coroner's Court, but to Graham the others were irrelevant. He was the champion, in peak condition, though he still faced the most daunting challenge of his career.

The proceedings were short. The Coroner called a variety of witnesses. A doctor gave the evidence of the post-mortem on Merrily's little body. A statement by Emma was read out. Lilian described her arrival at the house on Emma's summons and the policeman, whom she in turn had called, stated what he had found. The electrician who had surveyed the house for rewiring confirmed his views of its lethal state. The Coroner regretted this terrible tragedy to a young family, spoke of the need for constant awareness of the dangers of superannuated electrical systems, and a verdict of accidental death was recorded.

Graham Marshall had cleared another huge hurdle.

The cremation had been set up in advance; only the Coroner's verdict was required before the arrangements could proceed.

It was fixed for the following day. Lilian scoured the house for black and kitted out herself and the children like something from a Dickens serial on BBC-2. Graham wore a light suit and a black knitted tie. He tried to keep the bounce out of his step as he walked from the hearse to the crematorium chapel.

It was as he would have wished it. Clean, anonymous,

functional. It reminded him of the hotel in Brussels where he had been only ten days before.

The officiating clergyman also achieved anonymity. His short address made no secret of the fact that he had never met Merrily. Her virtues were generalised, her identity withdrawn into platitude.

The turnout was small. Beyond the family, the odious Vivvi and a couple of other representatives of Merrily's gynaecological Mafia had come, but none of their husbands had deemed the occasion worth a day's leave.

At the back of the chapel Charmian sniffed quietly, alone. She had tried to greet Lilian, but her mother had cut her dead, shepherding the children away from their aunt as if from a flasher in the park.

Lilian and Emma also snuffled throughout the service. Henry remained balefully impassive. Graham managed a few coughs and throat-clearings that could have been interpreted as emotion and which contained the exhilaration inside him.

At the appointed moment the anonymous curtains slowly closed on the futile expense of the pale pine coffin. When they slowly reopened, the ponderous conjuring trick was done. The coffin had vanished, consigned to the fierce blue gas jets within.

And Merrily was gone. A powdering of ash to be scattered. More plantfood for the roses in the Garden of Remembrance.

The feeling of power surged through Graham like lust.

The few friends shook hands with the family outside, murmuring stock condolences. No arrangements had been made for a drink afterwards and none seemed required. Vivvi and her coven drifted away.

Charmian was the last out of the chapel. She had spent a moment repairing her make-up. The tears were gone, but she was still in the grip of deep emotion.

Lilian bridled instantly at the sight of her prodigal daughter. 'Come on, Emma. Henry. We must be moving.' She started towards the car. Then turned back to her son-in-law.

117

'Graham.'

'I'll be along in a moment.'

Lilian's parting sniff contained more affront than suffering.

Charmian looked at her brother-in-law. The grey eyes were full of pain, but had not lost their knowing quality. He felt a strange bond with her, an urge to confide, to tell her what he had done, in some obscure expectation of praise.

But he said nothing, just her name. 'Charmian.'

The grey eyes still held his stare. They disconcerted him. They seemed to see too much. He looked down at the ground, conscious of a scuff-mark on one of her black patent shoes.

'Graham, I want to talk to you. It's very important.'

'Yes?'

'Yes,' said Charmian. 'It's about Merrily's death.'

CHAPTER FOURTEEN

'My feelings about Merrily are complex. Always have been. Now she's dead they are even more confused.'

Graham's eyes wandered round Charmian's living-room as she spoke. It was the evening of the cremation. He had left Lilian to settle the children and gone out without specifying his destination. Deviousness, covering his tracks, was becoming a habit.

His flickering glances took in the dark brown paint, the loaded pine bookshelves, the terra cotta plant pots suspended in harnesses of knotted string, the giant floor cushions, the hand-woven rugs on the wall. It was all yesterday's trends, dating from the time when Charmian was at her most successful, when pop journalists were being snapped up as feature writers, when she had had a regular column in one of the Sundays. She had been married then, too. The house had been a mutual project, the work of a pair of London trendsetters. But now the marriage and the column were long gone. Charmian survived as a freelance journalist, spreading her net ever wider to increasingly obscure publications as the impetus of her reputation slowed. If she had not received the house as part of the divorce settlement, her life would be precarious; as it was, she was safe but not affluent. Her surroundings reflected this. The paintwork was a little battered, there was too much dust, the windowpanes wore a filter of grime.

Through the front windows Graham could see the spiked railings that protected the steps down to the basement. He had a quick image of a body impaled on them, one viscously gleaming point emerging from the stretched bulk of clothes. Anyone who jumped from the upstairs window would land like that. So would anyone who was pushed.

Pleasing fantasies of murder methods were now part of the regular stock of his thoughts. His imaginative life, he felt, had been considerably enriched since he became a murderer. Railings, yes, good. With comparable satisfaction he noted the tangle of wires and adaptors that fed the randomly assembled stereo components. He didn't want to repeat himself, but the set-up offered plenty of opportunities for electrical accidents.

It was all hypothetical, of course. Casual conjecture. He was merely making a professional assessment of the situation and its possibilities. At the moment he had no reason to kill Charmian. It rather depended on what she felt such urgency to discuss with him.

He concentrated his mind on her analysis of the relationship she had had with her sister.

'It's an awful thing to admit, particularly of someone so recently dead, but I never liked her.'

Graham offered no reaction, and Charmian continued, 'Obviously childhood recollections are all mixed up and it's hard to disentangle my feelings for Merrily from those I have for my mother. I think I turned against Lilian when our father walked out, when I was about twelve. We never got on after that. I just became increasingly aware of her selfishness and affectation. And Merrily seemed to get daily more like her. I'm sorry, but I thought my late sister was a profoundly silly woman.'

Graham was surprised to discover how closely her view coincided with his, but recollection of his bereaved status prevented him from endorsing it. He bided his time. He still wasn't sure where Charmian's discourse was leading and, until he was, felt mildly apprehensive.

'The fact is,' Charmian continued, 'I often wanted Merrily dead.' Graham did not comment. 'It's only now she *is* dead that I can recognise the violence of my feelings. I thought I

120

just disliked her; in fact I hated her. And if I knew who caused her death I'd like to shake him by the hand and thank him.'

Graham tensed, but with her next words the danger passed. 'Oh, that's metaphorical, but it is what I feel. I know I'm taking a risk talking to you like this, Graham. You were married to Merrily, you must be in a terrible state, and perhaps you don't want to hear her abused. But I need to say these things to you.'

'Why?' He bleached the monosyllable of intonation.

'Because I have to know whose side you're on.'

'I don't understand.'

'Listen, my mother fucked my life up completely. I think if my marriage had worked, if I could have had children of my own, I might have been able to break free of her influence. As it is, I'm stuck, a menopausal divorcee, full of hatred.

'She also destroyed Merrily. Not in the same way, because I resisted and Merrily never resisted, but quite as completely. She destroyed Merrily by absorption, by making her into a facsimile of Lilian Hinchcliffe. And I'm glad Merrily died before she could repeat the process on her own children.'

She paused, momentarily exhausted by the outburst, and looked at Graham for reaction. He did not know what response to give. He was surprised; he had feared suspicions about the circumstances of Merrily's death, but never anticipated this statement of sisterly revulsion. Also he found himself in more or less complete agreement with Charmian, though he was wary of confessing it.

He looked blank and confused, which he was, and once again a favourable construction was put on his lack of emotion.

'I'm sorry, Graham, I'm being stupid and insensitive. Showing a sense of timing almost as crass as my mother's. Oh God, I keep recognising bits of her in me! I've tried to suppress them, blot them out, but they're still there. I sometimes wish they could be cut out by surgery, that I could just go into hospital for a few weeks and come out a normal person.'

He waited for the end of this spasm of self-hatred before he spoke. 'I still don't understand why you're saying all this. You said you wanted to know whose side I'm on. I'd like to know what the alternatives are.'

'All I'm asking is: do you like Lilian?'

It did not require a lot of thought to answer that one.

'Right. Good. Which means you're on my side.'

'I still don't understand, Charmian.'

'There are no half-measures with Lilian, no truces, no alliances. Either you're for her or against her.'

'Well, we've established where I stand.'

'Yes. So my next question is: Do you want her looking after your children, repeating what she did to Merrily and me in another generation? She's already started on Emma, I could see that at the cremation, already she's training her into a "little woman", teaching her the rules of alternating blackmail and collapse, the system of militant pathos by which she's always run her own life. God knows what effect she'll have on Henry, but I can't think that it'll be for the good.'

'No.'

'So do you really want her to look after them?'

'No, of course not. It isn't settled yet, what'll happen to them. Obviously, it's going to be difficult for me, being at work most of the time, you know . . .'

'Yes. Listen, Graham, I have a proposition to put to you. Let me look after the children. Let them come here to live with me.'

'Charmian –'

She raised a hand. 'No, hear me out.' Which was just as well. It wouldn't do for him to accept the offer with too much alacrity. He should hear out her justifications, make some pretence of assessing the proposition. It didn't look good for a new widower to abandon his children with too much enthusiasm.

'Graham, I know some of my motives may be suspect. I know I was jealous of Merrily having children and no doubt I want to take hers over because I will never have any of my

122

own. Also my career's not going well, and maybe I fancy the option of doing less and staying at home to look after children. And I don't know how good I'll be at it. The only things I do know for certain are that I love the children and that, whatever I do, being brought up by me will do them less harm than being brought up by Lilian Hinchcliffe.'

Graham's mind was working fast. This was better than he had dared hope. If Charmian took the children off his hands, then he could sell the Boileau Avenue house and buy the service flat he so yearned for. With Merrily's death, the mortgage would be paid off, so whatever he got for the house would be pure profit. Of course, if Charmian was going to give up work, he would have to support her, have to pay her maintenance for the kids . . .

Her voice broke into his calculations. 'I'm sorry, Graham. I'm going too fast. I shouldn't have rushed in. You need time to think about it. Or perhaps you think what I'm suggesting would break up your family completely . . .'

He gave a little, confused shake of his head.

'Perhaps you think I should be offering to come to the house, as a kind of housekeeper. But I can't see that working, Graham.'

'No.' His voice still sounded puzzled.

'I can't really see us as a foursome,' she continued with her customary bluntness. 'I'm just talking about the children.'

'Yes. I understand that.' But he didn't sound as if he understood.

'Sorry. I shouldn't have barged in like this. Maybe you don't want Henry and Emma to leave the house. Maybe you'd rather get in some sort of professional housekeeper . . .'

Oh no, that sounds expensive, thought Graham. His mind was absolutely made up, but the scene, he knew, required some token prevarication.

'I'm sorry, it's a bit sudden . . .'

He looked at Charmian. The grey eyes were tense, dependent on his response.

What she had offered made excellent sense from every point

123

of view. She had a core of common sense which the rest of the family lacked, and her current feud with her mother was bound to minimise Lilian's influence.

Once again he felt the strange need to confide in her, to confess his murder – no, he wasn't doing himself justice – his *two* murders. He felt a need for outside commendation. Again he missed his parents. He knew it was idiotic, but he wanted to phone them, to hear their impressed and reverent silence as he described his latest success. In his parents' absence, Charmian seemed the most likely person to give him the reaction he needed.

He felt very drawn to her. Sex played no part in the attraction. Sex was now a vague recollection from his past, like a journey walked daily to school, presumably important at the time, but instantly forgotten once discontinued.

Charmian's grey eyes looked sympathetic. She had said she always hated Merrily. She had said she would like to shake her sister's killer by the hand. Graham wanted to see the eyes light up with surprise and admiration when he told her of his achievement.

'Charmian, there's something you don't know . . .'

'Yes. What?'

He suddenly realised what he was about to do, and stepped back from the brink. 'I'm sorry. I didn't . . . I'm confused . . .'

Again she misread the cause of his incoherence.

'I know it's a shock. Take time. Let the idea sink in. Think about it. Or ask me any details you want to know.'

'Yes. Yes.' And with the broken delivery masking the baldness of the question, he asked, 'What about money?'

'Money?'

'Yes. I mean, if you were to look after them, you couldn't do it for nothing.'

'Ah, I see what you mean. Yes, I had thought about that.'

She had. Sensible woman. She had thought it out in some detail and she presented her suggestions with clarity. The appeal of the idea to Graham increased. It would move the obligation to his children to that area of contractual agreement he so favoured.

But the greatest appeal of Charmian's proposal lay in how little she was asking. With no mortgage repayments and the children mopped up by such a modest monthly outlay, he was going to be quids in. True, there were school fees, but they couldn't possibly get to their current schools from Islington, and he recalled with relish that Charmian was a great advocate of State education. Still, time enough to sort that out.

He felt light-headed. He couldn't believe with how little effort everything was working for him. That the force of Charmian's hatred of her mother should be channelled so conveniently was pure serendipity. What she had offered him completed his desires. He had removed his wife from his life. Charmian was proposing to do the same service for his son and daughter. And, incidentally, for his mother-in-law.

All was quiet when he returned to the Boileau Avenue house. He had taken a taxi all the way, feeling he deserved a little pampering and celebration. He had contained the urge to leap about and shout for joy until he got home.

Inside he found the post, which had been neglected in the upheaval of the cremation. Amongst other less important items was a letter from the broker through whom he had arranged the mortgage.

From a flurry of condolence, one hard fact emerged. The letter confirmed that, following the tragic death of his wife, the outstanding mortgage on the Boileau Avenue house would be paid off by the insurance policy.

It had all worked. Graham poured himself half a tumbler of Scotch and, drinking it, began to laugh, softly at first. But as the tensions of the past weeks, of the old man's murder, of Merrily's murder, of the inquest, the cremation, drained out of him, the laughter increased in volume.

He was aware after a time of the door being opened and of Lilian's bemused face framed in the space. Hers was soon joined by the shocked faces of Henry and Emma.

And the sight made Graham Marshall laugh all the more.

CHAPTER FIFTEEN

An unpleasant shock awaited Graham the next morning. He had not been in to work since Merrily's death, claiming a week of compassionate leave.

When he walked into his office he found that his desk had been moved from its central position to one side and directly opposite it was an identical desk, at which sat a young man in an open-necked shirt and brown leather blouson. The young man smoked a small cigar. Graham recognised him as Terry Sworder, one of the brighter Personnel Officers who had been recruited from Operations Research Department.

'What the hell are you doing here?'

The young man looked up at the question. 'Oh, hi. Very sorry to hear about your wife.'

The sentiment was delivered without interest, purely as a matter of convention. Ironically, though Graham was not aware of the irony, he felt affronted that the young man was not showing more respect for the dead.

'Thank you. But that doesn't answer my question. What the hell are you doing here?'

'Oh, Bob asked me to sit in while you're away,' Terry Sworder replied languidly.

'Bringing your desk with you is a rather elaborate way of "sitting in". If your presence was really necessary, I wouldn't have minded you sitting at mine.'

The young man shrugged. 'Bob said I might as well make myself at home since we're going to be working together.'

'Who's going to be working together?'

'You and me, pal.'

'On what?'

'Bob reckons it's daft not having someone who can use the computer in this office, so I'm going to be here to help you with that.'

'Oh, are you?'

Terry Sworder seemed not to notice the sarcastic emphasis. 'Yes. We're going to put in a terminal over there.' He gestured vaguely to the corner of the room.

'And you're really asking me to believe that you're going to stay in here?'

'Oh yes.'

'We'll see about that.'

Graham stalked out of the door and set out along the corridor towards Robert Benham's office.

The Head of Personnel Designate's secretary directed him to the office of the retiring Head of Personnel. 'Bob's with George, I think.'

Graham didn't like the way Robert Benham had suddenly become 'Bob' to everyone. It betokened a certain mateyness of management style that didn't appeal to him. He didn't want the Personnel Department filled with scruffy young men in denims calling everyone by Christian names. Christian names should be reserved for colleagues at the same level, and their use extended beyond that by invitation only.

He met George Brewer in the corridor outside his office. The old man was moving about nervously, as if anxious to get to the Gents, but his movement had no direction.

'Graham, hello. Very sorry to hear about Merrily. I know how I felt when my own wife . . . when . . . I . . . I don't know what to say.'

Again Graham felt that this response was only just adequate. He said yes, it had been a terrible shock, and the reality of what had happened would only sink in gradually, and he would have to learn to live with it, and he thought hard work was going to be his best therapy for the time being.

'But what are you doing out here, George?'

The old man looked shifty. 'Oh, I . . . It's Bob.'

God, the mateyness had even infected George.

'What about him?'

'Well, he's, er, he's in the office with the Head of Office Services, and I thought it might be easier for him if I just slipped out.'

'Slipped out? Waited in the corridor for him to finish?'

'Well, er . . . not exac . . . yes.'

'God, you are still Head of Department, George.'

The old man's eyes appealed pathetically to him. Their corners, he noted, were gummed with yellow. 'Don't want to make waves,' he murmured.

Graham snorted and pushed into the Head of Department's outer office. Stella looked up at him over her typewriter.

Her expression was strange, tense and excited as if she was expecting something. With a feeling that was not unpleasant he realised that this was in response to his new status. The intent of their encounters at the wine bar had been ambiguous when he was married, but now he was a widower the potential of the relationship had changed. He recognised Stella's awareness of this change and felt mildly flattered. The way his life was currently going, anything might prove of advantage to him.

'Graham, I was very sorry to hear about your wife.'

The response was becoming automatic. He nodded grimly. 'Yes, it was a terrible shock. Be years before I really take it in. Still, life must go on.'

He injected just enough twinkle into the last sentence to keep Stella's hope alive, and continued, 'Is Bob in there?'

'Yes. He's with –'

Graham didn't wait for the explanation, but walked into the office.

Robert Benham was leaning over George's desk. The Head of Office Services, a thickset man in his early fifties, was showing colour samples. 'I want something bright,' Robert was saying, 'get away from the terrible institutional drabness

128

of – ah, Graham. I was very sorry to hear about your wife.'

Graham didn't bother with any response this time, just demanded, 'What the hell is Terry Sworder doing in my office?'

'Didn't he explain?'

'He gave some explanation, but I couldn't believe he'd got it right.'

'Why not?'

'Robert, I have been in that office for four years. Lionel Agate was in it for five years before that. It is the Assistant Head of Personnel's Office.'

'Things can change, Graham.'

'It's something that goes with the job.'

'It's staying with the job. It's just that you'll be sharing it.'

'But that's ridiculous! Think what it'll do to my status in the company if I'm shoved into the corner of my office like some junior filing clerk.'

'Graham,' said Robert Benham coolly, 'I don't give a shit about your "status in the company". I don't give a shit about anyone's "status in the company". All I'm after is an efficient operation.'

'Oh yes? If you don't give a shit about status, why are you having your office redecorated? Go on, that's what he's doing, isn't he?'

The Head of Office Services, appealed to directly, took the opportunity to say what he'd been wanting to for some time. 'Perhaps I'll just slip out and wait while you finish this discussion. Then we –'

'You stay,' snapped Robert Benham. 'This interruption won't last long.'

'No?' Graham was shouting now. 'Go on, if you don't care about status, why don't we move half the typing pool into *this* office? I'm sure it wouldn't inconvenience you much.'

'Graham, I know you're upset about your wife –'

'Don't try that one! Oh yes, pretend I'm only behaving like this because I'm under emotional stress. Listen! I have a perfectly legitimate complaint, and I demand that you send

129

Terry Sworder back to the Computer Room or wherever he crawled out of!'

'No.' Robert Benham shook his head briskly.

'Come on, you haven't answered my question. Would you object to having some "assistant" shoved into your office? Go on, of course you would.'

'The two cases are not comparable. First, I am Head of Department'

'Not yet you aren't!'

'In all but name.' The words were delivered with great forbearance. 'Secondly,' he continued, 'if I thought I needed an assistant in here for the efficient discharge of my duties, I would install one.'

'Meaning I don't discharge my duties efficiently?'

'Meaning that it is insane to have someone in that job who's not computer literate.'

'What?' This frontal attack winded Graham. Mustering what reserves of sarcasm he had left, he asked, 'If that's how you feel, why don't you just get me out of the job? Kick me out?'

'I have investigated the possibility,' Robert replied coolly, 'and unfortunately it can't be done. You're too senior in the company to be removed for any reason other than gross misconduct.'

'Terrific,' said Graham. 'I'm honoured that you've taken the trouble to find that out. And bear in mind, you're less senior in the company, and getting you removed may prove a lot easier!'

Graham Marshall looked down at the swirling waters of the Thames from Hammersmith Bridge. The place now held no fears for him; rather it was a source of strength, a shrine almost, the scene of his conversion, of his rebirth.

The sun that glinted on the water was warm with the promise of summer. It made him think of holidays. Yes, he would have a nice holiday this year. Somewhere hot, somewhere rather luxurious. He would put behind him the rowdy family heartiness of Cyprus, the awful memories of self-catering in Wales, and go ... where? The West Indies, maybe ... Yes, that had the right sort of feel. And he'd certainly be able to afford it now. Luxury for one was comparatively inexpensive.

He thought about his scene with Robert Benham. The skirmishing was over; both sides had nailed their colours to the mast. For Robert to have admitted that he had investigated removing his rival left no further ambiguity in the relationship. It was now open war.

Graham had spent lunchtime in the company bar with other members of the Department, and then set off home, an action that could be interpreted as a symptom of bereavement, or an expression of pique against Robert Benham.

The bar-room conversation had given Graham considerable encouragement. His were not the only hackles which had been raised by Robert Benham's ungentle style. Already, before he had taken over the job, a power-base of opposition had built up against him. Marshalling that opposition was the kind of task for which Graham's skills were uniquely formed. He began to relish the guerrilla warfare ahead.

Robert Benham would fight hard, but Graham knew that Robert Benham would not win. He might have a formidable armoury of skills and talent, but he did not possess Graham's ultimate weapon. It was a weapon that might not be brought into play, but it was there, and in extremity Graham Marshall would not hesitate to use it.

On his way home Graham walked past an estate agent. He went in, announced that he wished to put his house on the market and arranged a time for a valuer to call and assess the profit of his crime.

CHAPTER SIXTEEN

'I think we really ought to sell it. I'm sure we could use the money.'

'What?' Graham looked up. He had only half heard his mother-in-law's words, engrossed in the book he had just got from the library. It was a book about famous murder cases, and he was reading it with amused relish. It boosted his confidence. They had all been such incompetents, such amateurs, all weakened by lapses into inefficiency or pity. His feeling of untouchable exclusivity increased.

Lilian repeated her words, exactly, an habitual form of reproach she had used on her daughters when they weren't listening to her. She prefaced the statement, as ever, with 'I said'.

'I *said*, I think we really ought to sell it. I'm sure we could use the money.'

'What do you mean?'

'Go to an estate agent. Put it on the market.'

'Ah.' Graham smiled. 'I've already done it.'

He anticipated an explosion, and rather enjoyed the anticipation. The scene had to come, and it was as well to get the future sorted out sooner rather than later.

But he was disappointed. Lilian did not seem put down by his revelation; if anything it cheered her up. 'Good,' she said. 'We want to get things sorted out as soon as possible.'

This sentiment so exactly mirrored his own that he stared at her with some bewilderment. It did not seem likely that Lilian Hinchcliffe should succumb to a sudden flush of reasonableness at her advanced age.

She looked quite girlish as she continued. 'Might get as much as thirty thousand for it now.'

'Thirty thousand? You're out of date, Lilian. If I only got thirty thousand, I would have been done. Do you know how much I paid for this house?'

'This house?' In the echo her girlishness was gone. Every year of her age, and a few more, showed in her face.

'Yes. This house.'

'But, Graham, you can't sell this house. I was talking about my flat.'

'Ah.' He laughed good-naturedly at her error.

'You can't sell this house. It's ideal for us and the children.'

'I disagree.'

'Is it the money? I thought the mortgage was paid off by Merrily's death. But if it is money, when we've sold my flat I'd be happy to lend you—'

'It isn't the money. I just want to sell the house.'

'Oh yes, that's a natural reaction. Straight after Merrily's death, with the cremation only yesterday, of course the house is full of memories . . . But you mustn't do anything hasty. Henry and Emma need stability at the moment. Don't you see that, Graham?'

He shook his head with some impatience. He had always found it exasperating how much slower most people's minds worked than his own. And now that he had planned his future with such sense and precision, it was annoying to encounter someone unable to appreciate his logic.

'Lilian, I will tell you what is going to happen,' he began patiently. 'Merrily's death has merely crystallised something I have been thinking for a long time. I do not enjoy family life. I would like to live on my own. And I am now free to follow my inclination. Because she is dead.' And then he added, for form's sake, 'Sad and regrettable though that undoubtedly is.'

Lilian Hinchcliffe's mouth gaped open. 'You're in shock. You ought to go and see a doctor. Graham, you're not talking sense.'

'On the contrary. I am talking better sense probably than I have ever talked to you. There is no need for me to go and see a doctor. I am not in shock. I am simply telling you that I wish in future to live on my own and am therefore going to sell this house. It seems a perfectly logical decision to me.'

'But no, no it's not logical. You are forgetting that there's not just you. There's Henry and Emma, and me. You do not exist on your own.'

Ah, but I do, thought Graham smugly. Very much on my own. Two murders have set me apart from everyone else in the world. And the thought gave him a burning, exhilarating sense of identity.

But he still had the boring process of spelling it all out to go through. 'Listen, Lilian, the only thing you and I ever had in common was Merrily. We never liked each other. No, don't argue, don't pretend, we never did. Merrily was our sole, circumstantial link. With her gone, there is no reason why we should ever see each other again.'

'But, Graham, she's only just dead and . . . I've just lost my daughter, I . . .'

'Better to get it sorted out now,' he said soothingly, 'than for either of us to continue under any illusions.' In the circumstances, he really thought he was being very understanding, breaking it to her with great sensitivity.

She gaped more. Tears appeared in her eyes, their appearance delayed by genuine shock rather longer than in most of her scenes.

'But, but Graham, putting me on one side for a moment . . .'

Which is exactly what I'm doing, he thought.

'What about the children? You are Henry and Emma's father. You can't just abandon them.'

'I am confident that Henry and Emma will be well looked after. Better looked after than by me. By someone who really cares for them.'

'Oh, I see.' Sarcasm now overcame the self-pity in her voice. 'You're just relying on me to come up trumps. You throw them over and you know their grandmother will cope. Well, of course

134

I will. But I can't cope without somewhere to live.'

'You have somewhere to live. Your flat.'

'There's not room for Henry and Emma in my flat.'

'I am not suggesting that there is. You live in your flat. They don't.'

'But where do they live? You said they were going to be looked after by someone who really cares for them.'

'Henry and Emma are going to live with Charmian.'

The words were softly delivered, but their effect could not have been more devastating. Her jaw did what only the cliché describes, and dropped. She mouthed, as if the whole world contained insufficient oxygen for her needs. Graham wondered idly if she was about to have a heart attack. In many ways it might simplify his life if she did.

But eventually her voice returned. 'Graham, you're mad,' it whispered. 'Quite, quite mad. Certifiably mad.'

'No,' he replied gently.

'Yes, you talk as if you've planned this for years.'

'Not exactly planned it – certainly thought about it.' Which was an accurate assessment, he reckoned. There had been a bit of planning, yes, but there had also been strokes of pure luck, like Charmian's offer, symptoms of the fact that everything was going his way.

'Oh yes, planned it.' Lilian's voice was recovering strength; her theatrical training never deserted her for long. 'You were just waiting for Merrily's death. In fact . . .' her eyes widened as the thought struck home, '. . . perhaps you even planned Merrily's death.'

A week before this would have really rocked him; now he felt confident to field any accusation. 'What, you mean murdered her?'

Lilian nodded, wordlessly.

Graham smiled. 'I think for me to have murdered her, Lilian, I would have had to be here at the time of her death. Don't you? Also the police did make rather exhaustive investigations. Didn't they? Had there been the slightest suspicion of anything other than an accident, I think it might have come up at the inquest. Don't you?'

There was a long silence. Lilian regarded him with acute distaste. Then she changed direction, and changed style. The first impact of the shock had limited her histrionics, but now it was fading, and her customary manner reasserted itself.

'I can't believe how cruel you're being,' she sobbed. 'I've never been so hurt, never. Just after Merrily's death, to hear what you've said . . . I've suffered a lot in my life, but never like this. Even lovers have never hurt me like . . . Even when William Essex broke off our *affaire*, I didn't feel like this.'

'Well, you must have seen that coming.'

'What?'

He knew he was being vindictive, but he felt she deserved it. The accusation about Merrily had been nasty; a revengeful home truth was therefore justified.

'You must have known why William Essex broke off your so-called *affaire*.'

'Why?'

'If indeed it ever started.'

'What do you mean?'

'I mean that William Essex was gay. Was always gay.'

'No!'

'God, it wasn't just people in the business who knew. It was virtually admitted in *The Times* obituary. He was one of the country's most famous old theatrical queens.'

'He may have turned strange as he got older, but when we were lovers –'

'If there ever was a moment when he made advances to you, it must have been just a test, a challenge to himself, to see if he could make it with a woman.'

'No. We were in love.' She broke down in tears.

He knew it was cruel, but he was sick to death of her. All her posturing and embroidered reminiscences seemed irrelevant. Irrelevant and annoying. Now the confrontation had come, he was prepared to use any trick to hurry her out of his life.

The sobbing subsided, and when she spoke again, the subject had changed. She sniffed. 'I must repair my face before I get the

136

children from school.'

He said nothing as she moved across the room. At the door she turned back to him. 'Why?' she asked softly. 'Why Charmian?'

'Because,' he replied in a logical tone, 'I think she'll bring them up better than you will.'

'I see.' The voice was very small, just like the little voice Merrily had always used in reproach.

It was that which prompted his next callousness. 'Besides, you talked of their stability. Charmian's forty-five. Just from the practical point of view, she's going to be round a lot longer than you are.'

'Yes,' Lilian riposted defiantly. 'You don't know how right you are.'

Graham had difficulty in getting to sleep that night. It was not his conscience that was troubling him. Any conscience he had ever had had been removed from him over the past weeks as effectively as if by a surgeon's knife.

Nor had there been any further outburst from Lilian. She had behaved quietly, fetched the children from school, given them tea, played board-games with them and put them to bed. Both had gone without fuss. They were still taking the mild relaxants the doctor had prescribed to help them over the shock of their mother's death.

Lilian had then cooked supper for herself and Graham. The meal had been consumed in silence, the television tactfully on to provide an alibi for the lack of conversation. After washing up, Lilian had retired for an early night.

Her behaviour had been exemplary. And if her expression had been too martyred or she had drawn too much attention to how good she was being, such gestures were so much part of her normal repertoire that Graham had long since learned to ignore them.

No, it was something that she had said in the afternoon's confrontation that had disturbed him. Not the moment when she had accused him of Merrily's murder; in retrospect he had rather enjoyed that. Her coming so close to the truth gave him the *frisson* of playing chicken; it partially satisfied that craving in him for confession, for sharing the knowledge of his crimes with someone. And the wildness of her accusation, and the skill with which he answered it, gave him a feeling of inner strength.

What had upset him was the moment when she had described him as 'mad'.

The word hurt and unsettled him. The slur of mental illness had never before been cast on him. He remembered acquaint-ances at university and at work who had 'cracked', proved unequal to the system and gone under. He had always felt mild contempt for them and a righteous sense of his own immunity from their disease. His behaviour had always been logical and positive; it was not in his nature to brood or feel self-doubt.

At least it had not been in his nature until recently. The compound batterings of losing the job and committing the first murder had rocked his equilibrium for a time, he was prepared to admit that; but he now felt back on an even keel, perhaps more logical and positive in his approach than at any previous time in his life.

What worried him was the knowledge that a frequent symptom of mental illness (madness, call it by another name, he knew what he meant) was delusion, a conviction held as strongly as in sanity, but a conviction based on a scale of values that are false.

He questioned himself about this. Certainly he had changed. Two months previously he would not have contemplated murder, yet now he had committed it twice without remorse, and drew strength from what he had done. Was that madness?

He knew there was a school of thought that classified all taking of human life as aberrant behaviour. But that was surely just a moral viewpoint, circumscribed by the great taboo which surrounds the crime. He, Graham Marshall, by his initially inadvertent breach of that taboo, had transcended such inhibited thinking. He knew he could commit murder and gain satisfaction from doing it, so his recent actions were no less logical and positive than his behaviour had been for the rest of his life.

Besides, he thought, giving himself the final warmth of comfort, if what he had done was madness, surely it couldn't make him feel *so good*.

No, if he couldn't sleep, it was simply excitement. And strain. The athletic metaphor returned to his mind. He had given of himself in the big event, he had won, and he must expect some reaction. He needed to wind down, take it easy, as he selected his next challenge.

In the short term what he needed was a large Scotch.

On the landing he heard moaning from inside the bathroom and threw the door open.

The noise was coming from Lilian, who lay in the bath.

Graham's first shock was the sight of her naked body, and its similarity, in shrivelled parody, to Merrily's. To the body that was now compounded to a little scattering of dust.

Then he saw the redness in the water.

He raised first one limp hand, then the other. On each wrist a narrow slit trickled blood.

But the cuts barely scraped the skin. Her arteries were in no danger.

God, if that was her idea of a cry for help, it was hardly worth answering.

'I'll ring the doctor,' he announced, fully aware that she was conscious. At the door he turned back suddenly, and was rewarded by the sight of her open eyes. Their expression was of sheepishness at having been caught out.

Downstairs by the phone was a note in Lilian's handwriting. He didn't bother to read it.

Bloody amateurs, he thought as he dialled the doctor's number, I'm surrounded by bloody amateurs.

CHAPTER SEVENTEEN

Graham looked across his desk at Terry Sworder with distaste. The young man had chosen to come into the office in an open-necked tennis shirt under a hooded cotton zip-jacket like a tracksuit top. A soggy little cigar dropped from his lip. Graham pitied the lack of style. In the days when he himself had sought to shock management by dressing boldly, it had been done with a sense of elegance; he had never been merely scruffy. Graham had passed comment on the inappropriateness of the costume when Terry arrived, but been told that 'Bob's taken me off normal Personnel stuff at the moment. Wants me to check some of the projections we've run through the computer for this survey.'

'What survey?' Graham had asked.

'Basic staffing survey. Model for Human Resources Requirements in the late 'Eighties. Bit hush-hush at the moment. Management don't know it's on,' Terry had replied gnomically.

Graham had not enquired further, recognising one of his own tactics, the deployment of a verbal smoke-screen to obscure issues. But he knew that the survey would be looking for ways of cutting staff in the Department.

Presumably it was the survey that was keeping Terry Sworder preoccupied, unaware of his superior's scrutiny. Sheets of concertina'd computer papers spread across his desk. These he pored over, stopping occasionally to use his calculator or jot down a note.

Graham pointed his foot towards his opponent, back with

140

his favourite fantasy of the loaded shoe. A slight pressure of the toe and, in Graham's imagination, Sworder flicked back with the impact of a bullet in his neck. Red from the exit-wound splattered the wall-planner behind and the young man's body twitched backwards twice before slumping still over his papers. Blood spread slowly across the tightly massed figures.

But the fantasy failed to bite. Like pornography to an adolescent who has lost his virginity, it was no longer adequate. Reality had diminished its effect.

Graham's thoughts wandered off briefly in a more pleasing direction before he reined them in. No, he had no reason to murder Terry Sworder. That would be stupid, tackling the symptom rather than the disease.

Robert Benham was his enemy, Terry Sworder a mere irritant. The young man was only being used by his master to get at Graham, to undermine his confidence and status in the company.

Graham smiled as a new thought formed warmingly in his mind. Using Terry Sworder was a game at which two could play.

Crasoco's staff management system, like that of many other large corporations, relied on annual interviews. Each member of staff, above a certain level, had a confrontation once a year with his immediate boss, who would read a report on the individual's work. This was a device to give the illusion of open management, an opportunity for commendation or criticism from the senior party, and the airing of any grievance by the junior. The report would then be placed (confidentially, the story went) in the individual's personal file. In this way honesty and democracy were in theory upheld.

In practice, the system was toothless. Though appeal procedures existed, few staff members would risk making waves by too overt complaints or criticisms, which were bound to reflect on the senior who was interviewing them. And, for their part, the bosses, except in cases of total incompetence or insubordination, tended to moderate any criticisms they might have of their staff. At a time when the management was known to be on the look-out for staff reductions, Departmental Heads had no wish to help them in their search. Any suggestion that someone was not pulling his weight might easily be interpreted as proof that a department could run as efficiently with one less member. And, empire-builders to a man, the Departmental Heads did not like the idea.

The result was that almost every annual report filed was bland and uncontroversial.

But it needn't be. That was the thought which comforted Graham Marshall. Over the last couple of years, as George Brewer's assistant, he had been writing most of the departmental reports. It was one of those routine jobs which George had been happily shedding and, though his signature appeared on the relevant pink form, the words above it were Graham's. Indeed, on occasion the signature had been Graham's too – or rather Graham's version of George's. He had found the ability to forge his boss's writing useful more than once, and even kept a Parker fountain pen and bottle of blue ink in his desk drawer for the purpose. The skill was not one he had used for criminal applications, merely for convenience and – particularly as George grew more dilatory with age – for speed.

Graham had also, as his annexations of responsibility increased, begun to conduct more and more of the interviews. For George it was a routine chore, one that he had happily relinquished to the man who, after all, he had regarded as his heir apparent. The Head dealt with the more senior members of the Department, but the lower echelons had their annual interviews conducted by his assistant.

By Graham's reckoning, Terry Sworder was just about junior enough to fall into the second category.

It had to be done quickly, before George retired.

Whistling softly between his teeth, Graham left his office for the room where the personal files were stored. Robert Benham, rumour had it, planned to put even these records on computer, but the change-over had not yet taken place and Graham had no difficulty in finding the box-file which contained the history of Terry Sworder's life with the company.

He had been there for seven years. Each previous annual report had been enthusiastic, a little more enthusiastic than the required establishment-preserving minimum. Graham recognised his own sentences on the previous year's form. He even thought – though he couldn't be certain – that the George Brewer signature at the bottom was one of his.

The date confirmed what he had hoped. Terry Sworder's next annual interview was almost due. And on the report for this one, Graham thought with a smile, there would be a few lines that would stop – or at least delay – the further progress of Robert Benham's protégé up the company ladder.

'Oh, Terry,' he said casually as he went back into their office. 'Think we ought to fix a time for your annual interview.'

He went home early, so that there would be someone there when the children arrived from school. Now that he knew he would not long be troubled with them, he found himself able to be a model father. They had been told that morning that their grandmother had been taken ill in the night. The exact nature of her complaint had not been defined, but they were told it was not serious and they were not to worry.

'How's Granny?' was Emma's first question.

The model father was able to supply an up-to-date bulletin. A doctor from the hospital had rung him at the office just after lunch. 'Of course there are no worries medically,' he had said. 'The cuts were little more than scratches, as you could see. Obviously it's her psychological state we're more worried about. Even a suicide attempt as botched as this one is a sign of pretty severe mental disturbance. Of course it's reaction to the shock of her daughter's death – and I gather some boyfriend died recently too, but there may be more to it than that. One of our psychiatrists is going to talk to her. The worry is obviously that she might try again. We'll keep her in

143

another twenty-four hours for observation, but I'm afraid we're going to need the bed tomorrow. We'll liaise with her G.P. for some sort of follow-up, of course, but . . . I'm very sorry, Mr. Marshall. I'm sure, after what you've been through over the last few weeks, this is all you need.'

Graham had liked that bit of solicitude at the end. There had been a few such unexpected benefits from Merrily's death. After the children had gone back to school, there had been a good few condoling calls from mothers of their friends, offering practical help in looking after the children and invitations to meals 'if he was at a loose end and could face going out'. Suffering nobility was a new pose for him and one he rather enjoyed.

Like that of the model father. 'Granny's better,' he replied to Emma's enquiry.

'Can we go and see her?'

This was not an idea he relished. 'No, darling. She just needs to rest. She'll be coming out of hospital tomorrow.'

'Back here?' asked Emma. 'She will be coming back here, won't she? I mean now that Mummy's dead . . .'

Graham watched unmoved as his daughter dissolved into tears. Judging her by himself, he regarded such behaviour as being merely for show. Judging her by her grandmother, he wondered what she wanted.

'I hope she's not coming back here,' grunted Henry. 'I'm sick to death of the old bat.'

Instinctively, Graham was about to remonstrate. Now you mustn't talk like that, Henry. But he didn't say it. Why should he? Why should he pretend any more? The children would soon be separated from their grandmother, the arrangements had been made, and it was about time they were informed. Henry's antipathy to Lilian (a facet of his adolescent antipathy to everything) was a bonus, something which could be used to make the news of their future more palatable.

Henry, Graham thought, might not object anyway. Charmian had more appeal for his son than Merrily ever had. Her fading connection with the pop world and her constant use of four letter words were both recommendation in Henry's eyes. Given the fact that she was an adult, a member of a species he despised, she was less unattractive to him than most of them.

Graham didn't feel so confident of Emma's reaction.

She was like her grandmother by nature and Lilian's cloning process had intensified the likeness. Also, knowing his mother-in-law's divisive instinct, he had no doubt that Emma had been turned against her aunt. As Charmian herself had observed, there were no half-measures with Lilian, no truces, no alliances; in her world it was all either for or against. Since Lilian was so firmly opposed to her surviving daughter, there was no doubt that she had enlisted the support of her creature, Emma, in the conflict.

Still, the arrangement he had agreed with Charmian was too convenient for Graham to want to change it. Telling the children their fate was an unpleasant duty, but necessary, just one of those tedious details which he must deal with on the route to his ideal lifestyle.

'Henry, Emma,' he announced, 'there's something you should know.'

He got no further. The doorbell rang.

The timing was perfect. It was Charmian.

He had rung her in the morning and told her of her mother's graceless gesture. She had come to the Boileau Avenue house from the hospital, where her mother had refused to see her. Any hopes of a rapprochement between the two had been dashed.

Both Graham and Charmian took strength from this. He was reassured, fearing that a reconciliation between the two women might lead Charmian to withdraw her offer, fuelled as it had been by hatred of her mother. And Charmian's guilt was assuaged; she had made the gesture, she had tried, she had offered the olive branch and it had been thrown back in her face.

Charmian's behaviour on arrival could not have been better. She dried Emma's tears, treating her with a brusqueness that contrasted with Lilian's customary maudlin reaction

145

to any scene of distress. Emma, Graham could see, was partly offended by this matter-of-fact approach, but also partly drawn. What Charmian offered her was the chance of being treated as an adult, whereas Lilian, despite her identification with her creatures, always cast them in a subservient role.

His aunt's approach with Henry was also just right. When Graham offered her a drink, Charmian suggested that the boy should have a small one too. It was the first time he had (at least officially) tasted alcohol, and, though he didn't care for the taste much, he, like Emma, was reminded that Charmian regarded him as an equal.

The evening, which could have been sticky, turned out rather jolly. And when, at bedtime, Charmian revealed the plan that both children should go and live with her, even Emma greeted the suggestion with enthusiasm.

'Thank you for that,' said Graham, as they sat over what Charmian had described as 'one for the road'.

'For telling them?'

'Yes.'

'I gathered you hadn't got round to it.'

'I was about to tell them when you arrived. I think it came a lot better from you.'

'Yes, I think it did.'

Once again, Graham felt relaxed by her presence. Again the silly urge to tell her about the murder was in him, but he knew he must not give way to it. Its pressure was almost titillating.

'When they do live with me,' Charmian continued, 'I don't suppose you will come and see them very often.'

'What makes you think that?'

'I don't think you care very much for them, Graham.'

He smiled. Her frankness, and the accuracy of her assessment, were disarming.

'You have it in one, Charmian.'

She didn't smile.

He pressed on. 'I don't deny it. Too many people, to my mind, pretend to emotions that convention demands of them. I have done that for too long. Now I'm going to stop. From now on I will accept what I really think, act on it.'

'Yes.' Charmian paused. 'So this has all worked out very well for you. Merrily dying, me offering to have the children . . .'

He nodded. 'It has worked out very well for me. I'm grateful to you. And I'm glad that you couldn't face the idea of their being brought up by Lilian.'

'You're right. I couldn't. I had to save them from that.'

'Yes,' Graham agreed smugly.

'But that wasn't the only reason I wanted to have them.'

'Ah.'

'No. I thought they were in danger from my mother, but, my God, I think they'd be in even more danger if they were being brought up by you.'

'What?'

The grey eyes glowed with anger. 'I don't know what's wrong with you, Graham, but it's always frightened me. There's something missing in your emotional circuitry. Your detachment is too total. You have no compassion. You are a monster. You frighten me.'

Graham Marshall felt as if he had been slapped in the face.

Leaving a large company is a slow process for senior personnel. The number of farewell celebrations increases with the number of years of service and the level attained in the hierarchy. George Brewer, who had joined Crasoco at twenty-two straight out of Cambridge and ended his career as Head of Personnel, qualified for the maximum number of send-offs possible.

The first was scheduled for a full month before his official retirement date, and took advantage of a board meeting on that day to assemble some of the company's top brass for a lunchtime drinks party in one of the twelfth-floor hospitality rooms. The atmosphere was relaxed. The board members had little idea who George was and could therefore be impersonally charming. His immediate superiors and colleagues knew there was a long sequence of such occasions ahead and felt no pressure to pass on messages of great pertinence to the retiring Head. And George himself, with a couple of drinks inside him, shed his self-pity and recaptured some of his former urbanity.

Robert Benham and Graham were both invited and they met as the uniformed waitress proffered a drinks tray. Graham took a gin and tonic, Robert an orange juice.

The waitress disappeared and left them facing each other. 'Terry Sworder,' said Robert, stripping the cellophane off a small cigar.

'Yes. What about him?'

'Gather you've set up an annual interview for him tomorrow.' Robert lit the cigar. Graham had to restrain himself from reaching for his lighter.

'Yes. It is due.'

'It's not your place to set it up.'

'On the contrary, Robert. It most certainly is my place. George asked me some years back to make all such arrangements.'

'And to actually take the interviews?'

Graham, as he knew his father would have done, noted the split infinitive and felt a sense of superiority. Robert Benham, whatever his skills, was really just a common little man.

'In a lot of cases, yes, my actually taking the interview would help George, reduce his workload a bit.'

This was rewarded by a snort of contempt which showed Robert to have little opinion of his boss's workload.

'And you were planning to do Terry Sworder's interview, were you?'

'Yes, I was. George has got a lot on his plate at the moment.'

'Bugger all, except a great series of do's like this.'

'That may appear to be the case, but I think it will be more convenient for him if—'

'The interview's been postponed for six weeks. When it happens, I'll take it.'

Graham smiled submissively. 'I don't think George will be very happy to find—'

148

'I've told George. He agrees.'

There was insolence in Robert Benham's stare. The hostility between them was no longer disguised. Then, as if he had read Graham's intentions towards Sworder, the younger man asked, 'By the way, when's your annual interview coming up?'

For the second time in twenty-four hours, Graham felt as if he had been slapped.

Later, as he half-listened to a board member's condolences for Merrily's death, his attention was monopolised by his rival's voice. He knew he was becoming obsessive about Robert Benham, but he couldn't help listening as the younger man discovered that David Birdham, the Managing Director, shared his enthusiasm for sailing.

'Oh yes, David, I've just got a little twenty-foot job. Four berths, but sails all right. Well, I get down there as often as I can. Got her moored at Bosham, yes. Not this weekend, no. My girlfriend's over from the States and we've promised ourselves a couple of days' pampering at the Randolph in Oxford. But the next weekend, certainly, I'll have the boat out on the Sunday. After that I've a feeling I'm going to be rather busy. Once George has finally gone, there'll be plenty to do. Whole Department needs a big shake-up. Actually, David, wanted to talk to you at some point about the Department's name . . . "Personnel" has a very dated feel. Really think we should be talking about "Human Resources" these days.'

David Birdham conceded that there might be something in this, and his junior went on, 'It'd just give the thing a new feel. Show that I'm not just into cosmetic tinkering, show I mean business. You see, I'm convinced that a lot of major changes are going to be needed in this Department.'

Graham realised that he was looking full at the speaker and that Robert, with an expression of irony, was holding his eye. Graham also realised that the last sentence had been delivered specifically for his benefit.

He was going to have to do something about Robert Benham.

CHAPTER EIGHTEEN

Detective-Inspector Laker looked again at the letter. It was typewritten and had arrived through the post that morning, addressed simply (and incorrectly) to 'Murder Department'.

A crank letter would normally have been dealt with further down the hierarchy. It was only because of the very specific nature of the accusation that it had been referred to him.

The message was short.

> THERE ARE CONSTANT COMPLAINTS ABOUT THE NUMBER OF UNSOLVED MURDERS, AND THAT DOESN'T DO MUCH FOR THE POLICE IMAGE. IF YOU WANT TO IMPROVE THE STATISTICS, YOU COULD DO WORSE THAN ASK GRAHAM MARSHALL OF 173, BOILEAU AVENUE ABOUT THE DEATH OF HIS WIFE, MERRILY.

Needless to say, there was no signature.

Detective-Inspector Laker looked at the paper hard. He didn't handle it. In the unlikely event of investigation being required, the less new prints the better.

From the criminal point of view, he didn't take it very seriously. The shock of death, he knew, produced bizarre reactions in people; its random nature, its lack of apparent purpose, had power to change characters overnight. The sheer disbelief of bereavement, the desperate desire to explain the inexplicable, could lead to wild accusations, usually against doctors and hospitals, but often against individuals too.

No, it was not the nature of the letter that disturbed him; it was just one phrase in it. 'The death of his wife.'

It was eight months since Helen had died. He thought he was getting better; at times he could even think ahead, make plans beyond the imperatives of work; he would never get over it, but at times he could envisage living in a kind of equilibrium with the knowledge of her absence.

And then something like this would happen. He never knew what it would be that triggered the return of his raw, uncontainable grief. It could be the sight of a woman in the street, a sentence half-heard in a television play, a smell of cooking, or something as fatuously irrelevant as those five typewritten words. And when it came, the pain still had power to destroy him, sap his strength and poison his thoughts, leaving him empty, exhausted and afraid.

Yes, obviously the letter needed some sort of token investigation. But it could wait a few days.

CHAPTER NINETEEN

Graham liked being alone in the Boileau Avenue house.

Charmian had taken the children to Islington for the weekend. This was not their final move, merely one of the steps in their process of acclimatisation. She had presented it to them as fun and, though Graham's opinion of Charmian had been soured by her statement of distrust in him, he could still appreciate her skill in managing his offspring. This weekend, she announced, Henry and Emma could come and select their rooms in her house. If they liked, they could go out and buy some paint to start decorating the rooms. At least they could reconnoitre the area, try the local hamburger joints, maybe even see what was on at the local cinemas.

Graham felt confident that they were in good hands. Absurdly, that little righteous sensation of being a model father returned to him. There he was, selflessly doing what was best for his children.

Lilian was also conveniently looked after. Though Graham's sole interest in her was that they should never meet again, he was aware that appearances must be kept up. To banish her too suddenly from his life might draw attention to his behaviour, and he knew that all his future plans depended on maintaining a low profile.

He had therefore talked very solicitously to the hospital doctor about his mother-in-law's condition. She was obviously in a state of shock, he agreed, after her daughter's death, but he did not feel this could have been helped by the additional stress of looking after her two grandchildren. He was also certain that staying in the house where her daughter had died must have been a contributory factor in her suffering, and felt it would be better if she returned to her own flat. It was not, of course, that he was unwilling to look after her, but he felt his own emotional stability to be so precarious that he feared he might do more harm than good. Since his own unhappiness sprang from the same cause as his mother-in-law's, namely Merrily's death, he feared that the two of them together might only exacerbate each other's distress.

He found, as he made his recitation, a full repertoire of pauses, sighs and sobs came unbidden to his aid, and the performance was taken at face value. The doctor agreed with what he said, regretted Mrs. Hinchcliffe's uncompromising hostility towards her surviving daughter, and arranged for her to return to her own flat, where a voluntary helper would stay with her over the weekend.

Graham was thus freed to enjoy his solitude.

That solitude was not uninterrupted. There were still phone calls of sympathy from former friends, and the estate agent sent round four couples at intervals to inspect the property. All of these were properly respectful of his recently bereaved status. They regretted, from his point of view, the need to sell the house, but could see exactly why he was doing it. Three of the couples showed a gratifying amount of interest and one implied that some form of offer might not be long in coming.

This pleased Graham, because, although he felt at ease alone in the house that day, his happiness arose from the solitude rather than the surroundings. The house was too large and raised too many responsibilities. Since Merrily's death it had quickly got untidy and Lilian's barnstorming forays with Hoover and duster had made little impression. Then Graham found that he was having to devote time to washing shirts and socks. He also looked with distaste at, but ultimately ignored, the rising tide of dirty clothes in the children's bedrooms. Perhaps Charmian should move up her proposed schedule. He couldn't cope for long with the constant kitting-out and other services that Henry and Emma required.

He also resented the clutter of the house, the volume of furniture and bits that Merrily had accumulated. Though he had been present, and even consulted, at many of the purchases, he thought of it all as exclusively hers. Now she was gone, and the house soon to go, he would sell the lot, piano, pine dressers, hatstands, rocking chairs, knick-knacks – all could go to the first bidder.

Yes, the sooner he was installed in his nice little service flat, the better.

A pleasing thought struck him. The normal inhibition of house purchase, unwillingness to be saddled, however briefly, with two mortgages, did not apply to him. Merrily's death, something he now saw as an artefact, with its own perfection of design, had freed him from such restrictions. There was nothing to stop him from looking for, or indeed buying and moving into, a flat straight away.

But not yet. He would keep this weekend to himself, cosset himself a little, recoup, build up his strength for the next test.

And read. He had bought another book about murderers, this time one by a Home Office pathologist. The subject was beginning to fascinate him, but the fascination was not that of prurience. His interest was detached, professional, almost academic. He shook his head over the follies of past murderers, their carelessness, their lack of proper planning. He felt towards them much as he had towards his colleagues at Crasoco, that they were maybe good, but that in a straight race he had the skills to beat them.

His feelings towards the murderers, however, were subtly different. With them he felt an identity, a mild regret for their failures, a unity in the freemasonry of murder.

He experienced mild anxiety about his growing interest in the subject. Any behaviour tainted with obsession was alien to him. The first murder had been an accident, and Merrily's a logical solution to a problem. He must never begin to think of murder as more than a means to an end.

And what was the end he had in view? He decided he

should devote a little time to the analysis of his motives.

His main reason for killing his wife had been financial. Her death offered him a way out of a situation that threatened to reproduce his parents' parsimonious existence. It also brought other benefits, freed him from unwelcome responsibilities, and offered him the chance of living the sort of life he wanted.

And what did he want? An hotel-like environment, and no emotional ties. Freedom to be himself, do what he chose. To have a nice flat, a nice car, enough money, go out where and when he wanted. And with whom. He was not yet sure to what extent sex would play a part in his new life, but it was an option not to be forgotten.

By one murder, he had achieved most of those objectives. With Merrily and the children out of his life, there was nothing to stop him from building up his dream.

Why then did he not feel complete satisfaction? What was the little unease in his mind?

Deep down he knew, but he teased himself by withholding the answer for a little while.

It was work. His image of his free self had projected a Graham Marshall who was Head of Personnel at Crasoco, not a passed-over and resented assistant to another appointee.

Robert Benham was the problem.

And while there might be political ways within the Crasoco system of dealing with that problem, there was another, much quicker, method. Robert might talk airily of Human Resources, but he was not aware of the inhuman resources of his rival.

It was not just a morbid fascination with murder that brought Graham to his conclusion. To kill Robert Benham was the logical thing to do.

Accepting this fact, one which had recently popped in and out of his mind with some frequency, gave it official status. Now he had declared his intention to himself, he could begin to plan.

The murder of Robert Benham would not be as easily

accomplished as that of Merrily Marshall. Though he felt pride in the achievement of his wife's death, Graham could see the advantages which he had when planning it. A knowledge of her habits and a knowledge of her environment had both helped. Lack of any motive apparent to the outside world had also been on his side. Living in the same house, he had had time and opportunity to set up the means of her removal. And his absence in Brussels had ensured its remote operation. Setting it in perspective, after the first euphoria of achievement, he could see that it was a good murder, but not a great murder.

To dispose of Robert Benham he would need something rather better. And in the case of Benham, he might be seen to have a discernible motive, so greater caution would be required.

Like Merrily's, he decided, the young man's death must appear to be accidental. Though he thought he had the skills to divert suspicion from himself in a murder investigation, life would be considerably simplified if no such investigation were ever started.

Benham had three main areas of operation where he might meet with an accident – at the office, at his Dolphin Square flat, or at his country cottage. Other settings were appealing, but impractical. For Robert to be run down on his way to work, or for him to fall down a flight of steps on one of his visits to Miami, were attractive, but hard to arrange. Or hard to arrange without Graham's involvement being too obvious. If he just happened to be in Miami at the same time as Benham, the finger of suspicion would not take too long to home in on him. No, as with Merrily, the operation had to be remote. When Benham died his murderer must not be in the vicinity; Graham must be somewhere else with an unbreakable alibi.

These were just general principles. Graham felt no great urgency to form a complete plan at once. The fact that he was making a start, that he had made the decision, gave him sufficient pleasure for the time being. He opened a rather good bottle of wine and settled down to watch Saturday evening television.

He awoke on the Sunday morning, luxuriating in the space of the double bed. He contemplated masturbating. There was nothing to stop him; it might be quite fun. But an exploratory hand stirred no response. And his mind remained empty of carnal images. Perhaps he really had managed to eliminate desire, along with so many other inconvenient distractions, when he killed Merrily.

He went downstairs to make a cup of instant coffee and collect the papers, then returned to bed. He felt deliciously unhurried. Time to savour all the irrelevancies that journalists dig up for Sundays; time, if he got bored with that, to relish a few more of the pathologist's tales of murder; time, if he felt like it, to think and plan.

The papers occupied him for forty minutes, the book a mere ten. Then, giving in good-humouredly to his mind like an indulgent father, he returned to the teaser of Robert Benham's murder.

First, the setting for the fatal accident . . .

He thought about the office. Like all buildings, the Crasoco tower offered opportunities for fatal accidents. As he knew from experience, anywhere on mains electricity could prove lethal. There were also boilers to explode, heavy furniture to crush people, lift shafts and staircases to be fallen down. Come to that, there were windows to fall out of. Only a year before a twenty-two-year-old secretary had drawn attention to the unhappiness of her affair with her boss by projecting herself from the tenth floor. As a method of killing it had been undoubtedly efficacious.

But nobody was going to believe in Robert Benham as a suicide victim. The idea was totally incongruous. And the idea of anyone falling accidentally from those windows was even less convincing. Because of the building's air conditioning, actually getting one open was quite an achievement.

Besides, even granted the gift of Robert Benham standing at

157

an open window, Graham would have to be on hand – and therefore visible – to push him.

The same objection arose with all office accidents. The Crasoco tower was a busy place; few things occurred unseen. And even if Graham could engineer an accident without witnesses, or, better, contrive one that happened by remote control, it was all too close. In the office setting, if there were the slightest suspicion, professional rivalries would instantly be investigated. The atmosphere between the two had been observed, and Graham's statements to the lunchtime anti-Benham faction would be remembered. He would be set up as a prime suspect.

No, the office was out.

He had never been to the Dolphin Square flat, but knowledge of the block and the dangers of any break-in being witnessed, ruled it out straight away.

He turned his attention to the cottage. This offered considerable advantages over the Crasoco tower and the flat. First it was remote. If, as Benham had implied, he was frequently there on his own, the danger of witnesses was less. Or if a remotely triggered method could be devised, Graham was unlikely to be observed while setting it up. The cottage was also old and, though it had been extensively modernised, its age made an accident more feasible.

Then there were all those beams. And the thatch. In a place like that fire would spread instantly. And the cottage's small windows might make escape difficult. Anyone asleep upstairs when a fire started would be lucky to survive.

As a method of killing it would undoubtedly work, but setting up a suitable conflagration posed problems. Arson was not one of Graham Marshall's special subjects, but his reading of newspapers suggested that it was a crime fairly easily detected. So shoving petrol-soaked rags through the letter box, or throwing a can of the stuff in at one of the windows, or even – in a frivolous image his mind presented – shooting flaming arrows Indian-style at the thatch, though probably efficacious methods, were unlikely to escape the notice of the authorities.

And they all had the disadvantage of requiring Graham's presence at the scene of the crime at the time of the crime.

There were remote methods that might work. Maybe he could use another act of electrical sabotage. Some appliance that could overheat near a curtain, perhaps? Or near a sofa? The flames from the burning foam in modern sofas were notoriously deadly.

Hmm, not quite. The idea had not quite the form yet, not the intellectual perfection that his plan to dispose of Merrily had had. He wondered briefly whether he really had been so convinced when he devised his wife's quietus, or whether the conviction had been added in the retrospect of success. On balance, he thought it had always been there, and felt confident that, when he got the right idea for Robert Benham's extinction, he would recognise it.

He brought his mind back to the cottage. There were arguments against the staging of electrical disasters. The timing might be a problem. Suppose the faulty appliance were spotted ... Then the sabotage might be identified and investigations ensue.

The trouble with any such plan was that it would involve housebreaking. He realised again how easy he had had it with Merrily. Was that, he wondered wryly, the reason why the majority of murders are of cohabitants?

Breaking into Robert's cottage to set a booby-trap doubled the risk. There was a danger of discovery, not only when the thing went off, but while it was being installed. And there was no guarantee that ...

Suddenly he remembered the bright blue burglar alarm on the front of the cottage.

For the time being he had reached an impasse. He took the realisation philosophically. Time enough, time enough. He was on the right track. He would get there.

It was while he was shaving that he thought of the boat.

CHAPTER TWENTY

Graham saw Stella in the canteen on the Monday lunchtime. She was sitting at an empty table, eating cheese and biscuits, when he approached with his loaded tray.

'Do you mind if I . . . ?'

'No. Please.' He sat down. She scrutinised him. 'How are you feeling?'

'Oh, you know . . .'

'Any better?'

'A bit.'

'The shock must be awful.'

'Yes. In surprising ways. It sort of upsets one's whole thinking. Whatever you think about is different. The circumstances have changed.' He was mildly surprised at the fluency with which such lines came out.

'Yes. I've never lost anyone very close to me. Both my parents are still alive. It must be terrible.' She spoke this automatically, assessing, wondering what his next move was going to be.

'I mean . . . you,' he said, fully aware of the impact of his words.

'Me?'

'Well, you know you and I . . . when we went to the wine bar those times, before . . . before . . .'

She helped him out of his apparent embarrassment at mentioning Merrily's death. 'Yes, I know.'

'Well, I enjoyed it.'

'Me too.'

'And now suddenly it's all different. I mean Merrily's dead and one part of me is reacting to that, and yet at the same time another part is saying I'd like to go on seeing Stella, but there's this sort of feeling that I shouldn't.'

'Because of what people might say, people in the company?'

'I suppose that's part of it. All of it, maybe.'

'Well then, if we do meet, we should do it somewhere where nobody in the company'll see us.'

'Yes, that's right, we should. How do you feel about going out to dinner somewhere tomorrow night?'

Predictably, she felt pretty keen about it.

He had rung earlier in the day for an appointment with his doctor and went along after work. The doctor was an earnest young man Graham had met perhaps twice when collecting prescriptions or getting forms signed. Merrily had had all the other dealings with him. She and Lilian regarded a doctor as someone central to their lives, someone with whom they had a relationship; for Graham he represented merely a convenient service, on a par with an emergency plumber or a minicab firm.

'I'm so sorry about . . . what happened,' said the doctor with a gravity beyond his years. 'A tragedy. Such a lively woman, so vital.'

Graham nodded agreement.

'And then I heard about your mother-in-law. A foolish act which must have put additional stress on you at a time when you are least able to bear it.'

Graham prepared to voice his request, but the doctor had not concluded his monologue. 'The full effect of bereavement is something we medical practitioners have still got a lot to learn about. There's research being done, and the most important thing that emerges is the need for grief, a need for the bereaved person to abandon him or herself to grief. And as soon as possible. I do hope that you are grieving for Merrily.'

Graham felt an irrepressible desire to laugh, but when the sound came out, managed to convert it into a sob.

'Yes, yes,' said the doctor soothingly, 'that's good. You mustn't have any of these inhibitions about men crying. It's just as important for a man as a woman. Grief is essential.'

Since the young man seemed prepared to go on about grief indefinitely, Graham stated the reason for his presence. 'The fact is, doctor, I am having difficulty sleeping.'

'Well, that's no surprise, Mr. Marshall – or may I call you Graham? – no surprise at all. Any normal person is bound to be affected by the sort of shock you have just suffered and the effects are most likely to take a physical form. Insomnia I would expect, or a bad back, headaches or –'

'Are you saying it's just psychosomatic?' asked Graham, sensitive to any aspersions being cast on his imagined complaint.

'By no means. Anyway, what is psychosomatic, what is real? Increasingly we medical practitioners are having to learn to treat the whole patient, not to separate the body and the mind. Your mind has experienced a terrible shock, and your body is reacting by depriving you of sleep. It is only time, and the full process of grief, that can complete the healing process.'

Since the doctor was in danger of getting on to grief again, Graham cut in. 'What I'm asking, doctor, is can you prescribe something to make me sleep?'

This the doctor did willingly. Two of the pills, taken half an hour before retiring, should do the trick. If Graham still found himself waking up in the night, he could take one more. Three was the limit, though. The doctor warned him of the dangers of overdose, hesitating slightly as he did so. Presumably, with Lilian's gesture a recent memory, he was a little worried about planting such an idea in the head of a man unhinged by grief. Graham assured him that there was no danger of that sort, and set off with his prescription, trying to look subdued.

By the time he got home, he no longer felt the need for pretence, and moved jauntily to the front door. Everything was coming together very nicely, he reflected.

He was so cheerfully absorbed in his plans that he did not

notice the occupant of the parked Ford Escort opposite, nor the intensity with which the man watched his arrival. Nor did Graham see the man get out of his car and walk slowly across the road to the house.

The doorbell rang.

Graham opened the door and looked at the stranger quizzically.

'Good evening. My name is Detective-Inspector Laker. I'm sorry to trouble you, but I wonder if we could have a bit of a talk about your wife's death.'

CHAPTER TWENTY-ONE

'Can you think of any reason why someone might make this sort of accusation?' asked the Detective-Inspector.

They were sitting quite cosily in the front room. Graham had furnished each of them with a large Scotch. He had been mildly surprised when the policeman had accepted his offer of a drink; he had expected a 'no, sir, not while I'm on duty' demur. But he was glad. He recognised the seriousness of the confrontation and wanted it as informal as possible.

'No, no, I can't,' he replied to the question. 'It just seems very vicious, at a time like this, turning the knife in a wound that hasn't begun to heal.'

Once again he was surprised at the way the words came to him. He seemed to have an instinct for the expression of bereavement.

'Yes, I can see that, Mr. Marshall,' the Detective-Inspector said soothingly. 'And I'm sorry that I have to be here to add to your troubles. The accusation in the letter is a very serious one, though.'

'But totally false. God, I mean, it's not as if there hasn't been a police investigation. And an inquest.'

'Yes.'

'You know the findings of the inquest, don't you?'

'I have read the relevant documents, yes, Mr. Marshall.'

'Well then.' Graham delivered this as if it were the Q.E.D., the end of the argument; but he watched Laker's reaction closely.

The detective was silent, and Graham felt impelled to

continue. 'It's a ridiculous accusation. And very cruel. I mean, why should I have wanted to kill Merrily? Ours was a very happy marriage.'

'Was it?' The emphasis of the question was not loaded; Laker appeared to be asking merely for information.

'Yes, of course it was. Ask anyone. Ask our friends.'

'Ah, Mr. Marshall, a marriage is the most private relationship two people can have. A profoundly secret contract. What appears on the surface can be very misleading.'

'O.K., I accept that, but even say I hated Merrily, why should I go to the trouble of murdering her? You can get a divorce easily enough nowadays. I had no motive to kill her. Come on, what did I possibly stand to gain from her death?'

'Nothing, except to get your mortgage paid off. Thirty thousand pounds.'

Graham flushed. This was getting too near to the truth. He tried to think of a blustering defence, but words wouldn't come.

The detective held the pause, then said, 'I'm sorry. This must be very upsetting for you.'

Graham sank his head into his hands. He wasn't sure. Was Laker interpreting his reaction as a symptom of outraged bereavement or was the sympathy merely delaying an accusation? He decided to stay silent until the Inspector made his position clear.

'But thirty thousand pounds is surely not sufficient motive for murder,' Laker went on. 'Someone in your position would have to be mad to take the risk for that.'

Graham had to look up to check the policeman's expression. Were the words to be taken at face value or were they to relax him, to lead him into a trap?

Laker appeared to be sincere. Graham felt marginally less tense, though a little wedge of doubt had been driven into his mind. As when Lilian had voiced it, the accusation of madness was what hurt. The Inspector's indirect aspersion cast doubt on Graham's motivation, on the system of logic which had dictated his recent actions. He didn't like it.

'Anyway,' Laker continued, moving even further from the role of accuser, 'it's ridiculous to think you could have caused your wife's death, even if you had wanted to. Say you had arranged some form of elaborate electrical boobytrap, what guarantee had you that your wife would go up to the loft?'

'Exactly,' Graham concurred.

'From all accounts she'd never been up there since you'd bought the house.'

'No.'

'And you weren't to know that she'd suddenly decide to make the spare-room curtains while you were away.'

'No.'

'No. The accusation's preposterous.'

Graham didn't feel he was quite let off the hook yet. If the Inspector was as unsuspicious as he appeared, why was he there?

'But somebody has made it,' Laker continued in a measured tone. 'That's what I don't like.'

'I'm not too keen on it myself.' Graham felt he could risk this amount of wry humour.

'No. Have you had any other hate-mail?'

'No.'

'Accusing telephone calls?'

'No.'

'Right, so we come to the crux of the matter. Have you any idea who might have sent this letter?'

'None at all.' Graham hadn't had time to think of that. Since the revelation of the letter's existence he had been too anxious about Laker's possible suspicions.

'Because I think this sort of thing's despicable!' The Inspector was suddenly incensed. 'I know how you must be feeling at the moment. I had a . . . my wife died not so long ago and I . . . I mean, if I'd known of a letter like this, I'd have . . . I don't know what I would have done to the person who sent it.'

He paused to recover himself. This was not good, not

professional. It wasn't the first time he had become too emotional since Helen's death. However much he tried to keep his private life apart from his work, he seemed now to have no control over its incursions. He knew his reasons for coming to see Graham Marshall were suspect. It was a chore he could have delegated, but the letter had unleashed such raw anger in him that he had wanted to follow it up himself. He kept projecting himself into Graham's circumstances, imagining how he would have felt in that terrible month after Helen's death if this kind of spurious allegation had been levelled at him.

'What I'm saying, Mr. Marshall,' he continued, calmer, 'is that the person who sent this letter has committed an offence. If you wished to prefer charges, you would be quite within your rights. Which is why I want to know if you have any idea who might have sent it.'

'Am I allowed to see the letter?'

Detective-Inspector Laker took a folded sheet from his inside pocket and handed it over. 'This is a photocopy. We may need to run tests on the original.'

Graham read the typewritten words.

He had not a second's doubt about their origin. The defiant flamboyance of the gesture gave it away, and the hinting style of the letter confirmed it. It had all the hallmarks of Lilian Hinchcliffe's work.

'Hmm,' he said. 'I might have an idea.'

He didn't want to commit himself yet, till he had thought through the implications of an accusation.

'Who?'

'Well, I'm . . . I'm not sure that I would want any further action. That is, of course, assuming I have your assurance that you don't take the accusation in the letter seriously.'

'You can rely on that, Mr. Marshall. But, since you obviously *do* know who sent the letter, are you sure you don't want it followed up?'

Graham was tempted. There was an attraction in the idea of getting his own back on Lilian, of having her publicly

167

reprimanded and his own absolution from guilt publicly proclaimed. But there were dangers to be weighed against that. At the moment the case was quiet, dead and buried. The inquest's findings had been satisfactory and now he had Detective-Inspector Laker's assurance that he was believed innocent. Better to leave well enough alone than risk unknown consequences by stirring it. Regretfully, he decided to deny himself the pleasure of that little extra revenge on Lilian.

'No, I think not, Inspector. As you say, the recently bereaved are in a very vulnerable state, and I think enough damage has been done.' Oh, he could sound smug when he tried.

'Well, I think that's a very altruistic position for you to take, Mr. Marshall.' Laker paused. 'From what you say, incidentally, it's not difficult for me to work out who is the author of that letter.'

Graham raised a quizzical eyebrow, but said nothing.

'I did hear of your mother-in-law's suicide attempt last week. She's obviously in a very unstable state. Death has this effect on people. They feel guilt and they want to attribute that guilt. When someone close dies, most of us blame ourselves in some way. I dare say at times, Mr. Marshall, you've blamed yourself for your wife's death.'

Graham nodded his accord, stifling the naughty bubble of a giggle in his throat.

'And in many cases the bereaved transfer the blame from themselves to someone else. As your mother-in-law has clearly done. She probably blames you first for taking her daughter away from her by marriage; and now her daughter has been taken away by death, she blames you for that too.' He paused, at first satisfied with his conclusion. Then it seemed to embarrass him. 'I'm sorry. Doing the amateur psychologist bit. Hazard of the job, I'm afraid. Anyway, you are certain you want no action?'

'Certain. Can I get you another of those?'

Armed with his second large Scotch, Detective-Inspector Laker began, 'It is terrible, the first bit . . . that slow, slow realisation that she's gone. I found at times I would forget it and then something would force me to remember again. And every time it hurts. Don't you find that?'

Graham found the right agreements coming out. Laker stayed commiserating for another hour. Since Helen had died, he had found the evenings the worst. Evenings and weekends. He now put himself forward for duties at uncongenial times, duties he would formerly have tried to duck. Anything to fill the time.

After a while he felt he had to go. He shook his host's hand on the doorstep, urging Graham to 'give him a buzz when he was in need of moral support'. And, feeling slightly sheepish at having given away so much of himself, Detective-Inspector Laker went across to his Ford Escort.

Inside, Graham poured himself another huge Scotch.

He couldn't believe it, the way everything turned to his advantage. He had feared that Laker had come as an avenging angel, and had found instead just an ally in the league of widowers.

Graham relaxed and let the laughter come. He lay on the sofa and laughed till he was weak.

He was in the kitchen experimenting with a box of Swan Vestas matches when he heard the front door opened with a key.

He walked into the hall and met Lilian.

'I left some of my belongings,' she said haughtily. 'I've still got Merrily's keys. I didn't think you were in.'

This was patently untrue. If she had wanted to come when the house was empty, she had had ample opportunity during his working hours.

'Where are the children, Graham?'

'They're staying with Charmian a couple more days.'

'But what about school?'

'I rang their teachers and said they needed a break after what had happened. The teachers agreed.'

'They mustn't miss too much school. It's unsettling for

169

them not knowing what's going to happen.'

'Everything will be sorted out.' He didn't tell her that Charmian had that day been to see the headmaster of the local comprehensive in Islington to arrange Henry and Emma's immediate enrolment.

'Yes. Soon, I hope. The sooner they're away from you the happier I'll be, Graham.' She added the last sentence with sudden viciousness.

Almost exactly what Charmian had said. What did they think he was – some kind of monster? He contemplated a riposte about the anonymous letter, but refrained. He'd store that, just as he'd stored the line about William Essex's sexual proclivities. Always a good idea to have a weapon in reserve when dealing with Lilian.

Though in fact he wouldn't be dealing with her for much longer. After she walked out of the house that evening, there was no reason why they should ever meet again. With that knowledge, she became for him just a minor irritant, not even worth baiting. (Must remember to get Merrily's keys from her before she goes, he thought.)

He drew aside. 'You came to collect some things.'

She made a great noise gathering her possessions together, but Graham paid no attention. She was an irrelevance; she could not touch him. He lounged in the sitting-room with yet another Scotch, and switched on the television.

It was not Lilian's style to leave without a parting shot. She stood in the doorway, clutching an old suitcase, and mouthed something inaudible.

'Sorry, can't hear you with the television,' he announced.

She walked into the room and switched it off.

'*I said* you won't get away with it, Graham.'

'With what?'

'With just shedding all your responsibilities like this. It's not as easy as that.'

'It seems to be,' he replied coolly.

'No. You frighten me, the way you've behaved over Merrily's death.'

He shrugged.

'And the way you've treated me, Graham.'

He looked at his watch.

'But don't you worry, you'll have your comeuppance. I'll get my revenge. One way or another, I'll destroy you.'

Deciding that she wasn't going to improve on this as an exit line, Lilian Hinchcliffe stormed out of the house.

Oh damn, she had still got the keys. Never mind, he could write to her and ask for them.

Graham switched the television back on.

He was undisturbed by Lilian's threat.

But then he thought she was referring to the anonymous letter.

CHAPTER TWENTY-TWO

There was a gratifying call at the office the next morning from the estate agent. Two of the couples who had seen the house had made definite offers. Both had offered under the asking price because – and the young man had to overcome considerable embarrassment to get the reason out – there was obviously work needed on the electrical wiring. One of the offers was a thousand pounds short, the other five hundred. Graham instructed the agent to accept the higher offer. The couple, it seemed, were currently living in rented accommodation and, since they had nowhere to sell, the young man looked forward to a speedy exchange of contracts.

Graham then consulted the Yellow Pages and rang round half a dozen Central London estate agents, asking them to send him details of two-bedroom service flats in their areas. He named as his maximum price the amount he had just accepted on the Boileau Avenue house. Without a mortgage to worry about, there was no need for him to try and save money.

Terry Sworder was out of the office communicating with one of his computers while this telephoning went on, and Graham took advantage of the young man's absence (though why he should care what Terry Sworder thought, he didn't quite know) to go out shopping.

Some of his purchases were self-indulgent, and others professional. (He found increasingly that plans for the murder were taking over the compartment of his mind which he had previously reserved for thoughts of work.)

He bought some sheets of sandpaper of different grades, a

pair of rubber gloves and a Portsmouth Tide Table.

Then he went to Tottenham Court Road and bought a telephone answering machine. From there he got a Tube to Green Park, walked to Farlow's in Pall Mall and had himself fitted with a pair of fishing waders.

He stopped at a travel agent and picked up some brochures for holidays on the Greek Islands and in the West Indies. At an off-licence he bought a bottle of Pernod, a bottle of Bailey's Irish Cream and a bottle of Advocaat. In all these transactions he paid cash.

Finally, he caught the Tube to Victoria and deposited all his purchases in a left-luggage locker.

By then it was after twelve, so he got a cab back to the office. Robert Benham's regular Tuesday squash court was always booked for twelve-thirty.

There were two glass-backed courts in the basement of the Crasoco tower. Graham walked casually past to check that Benham was playing. Yes, there he was, crouched and absorbed, his legs and arms surprisingly hairy. He played squash as he did everything else, with efficiency, aggression and total concentration.

Graham sauntered along to the changing-room. Play had just started on both courts, so there was no one there. Four sets of clothes hung from pegs.

He recognised Robert Benham's leather-patched jacket and jeans immediately, and reached into the trouser pocket.

Good. As most people would, Benham had taken his wallet on to the court, but had not taken his bunch of keys. Graham flicked through them, found the one he wanted, wrote down its serial number and returned the bunch to the jeans.

Then he sauntered up to the canteen for lunch.

There was a little locksmith he'd noticed down off Carnaby Street and he went in there after lunch.

The man behind the counter was old, with bushy eyebrows.

'Do you stock keys for Robson's padlocks?' asked Graham.

'Yes.'

'We've got one on our garage door,' Graham lied glibly. 'The wife's only gone and lost the key. Dropped it down a drain, of all things. I ask you. I don't want to have to saw it through. It's a perfectly good padlock.'

'Yes, I stock them. What's the serial number?'

Graham gave it and the man produced a key.

Easy.

But as he walked out of the shop, Graham felt chastened. He mustn't talk like that, must curb his high spirits. There was no need to make his lies so elaborate. That bit about his wife was unnecessary and, in the circumstances, stupid.

In an echo of some school sports master, he said to himself, 'Careful, Marshall, careful.'

He met Stella that evening at a restaurant near Holland Park, which was neutral ground for them, and also well off the Crasoco employees' circuit.

As they ordered coffee, the waiter asked, 'Can I get you a liqueur, madam?'

'Oh yes,' said Stella. 'I think I'll have . . . um . . . Bailey's Irish Cream, please.'

Good girl, thought Graham, good girl.

CHAPTER TWENTY-THREE

For the next couple of days Graham Marshall kept a low profile. At work he was quiet, confident that this behaviour would be interpreted as a sign of bereavement. He avoided conflict with Robert Benham and, on the couple of occasions it threatened, bowed subserviently to the other's will.

At home he conducted a few minor experiments, but most of the time just watched television, eating take-away meals. Now he had a definite offer on the house, he felt no urgency to keep it tidy.

He realised he had made one mistake, when Charmian rang him on Thursday evening. From her tone, she clearly thought he should have rung earlier in the week to enquire after Henry and Emma. Graham gave her some line about being in a bad state and not wanting his grief to rub off on the children, though he knew Charmian's piercing understanding of him would not accept that. He spoke to Henry and Emma, who sounded like children of a distant acquaintance he had not seen since they were babies. Their manner was polite, distant, but relatively cheerful. Then he spoke to Charmian again and arranged that she should come on the Saturday morning to collect the bulk of their remaining possessions.

He knew why he had made this mistake, and promised himself to be more careful in future. The trouble was that the children no longer played any part in his thoughts. He had written them out of his life as completely as he had Merrily in the weeks before her death. But reality again lagged behind the speed of his imagination. Henry and Emma still existed, and he must go through the motions of still being their father. The separation should not be a sharp break, but a gentle tapering-off of contact. It was a bore, but it was something that he must do. His behaviour must appear what is conventionally known as 'normal'. Any apparent callousness should be avoided. This was not to save the children suffering, but simply to allay suspicion. The world had certain expectations of him, and so long as he followed the observances of 'normality', the world would leave him to his own devices.

Thinking this, he decided he should also demonstrate an appearance of solicitude to his mother-in-law. He didn't fancy ringing her, partly because their conversation was likely to be vituperative, but, more importantly, because no one would know about the gesture. A call to the doctor would be a less acrimonious exchange, and would also register on a kind of objective Brownie points tally.

Lilian was now under the family G.P., rather than the hospital doctor, and Graham got through just as the young man was closing his evening's surgery. Oh yes, of course, Mrs. Hinchcliffe. The doctor's tired mind homed in on her case amongst all the other hundreds he had dealt with that day. Yes he could understand Mr. Marshall's anxiety. Well, as far as he knew, she was making a good recovery. He would check with the social worker, yes. And how about Mr. Marshall himself? Was he feeling any better? Sleeping all right? Was he managing to grieve?

In a properly subdued voice, Graham assured the doctor that his skills at grief were improving.

On the Friday, mid-morning, he went to see George Brewer. Stella looked up as he entered the outer office and, seeing who it was, rose hesitantly, perhaps in expectation of a kiss.

Graham put his fingers to his lips in a gesture of complicity. Yes, of course, I still feel the same, but keep it quiet at the office, eh?

Stella smiled and nodded.

'Still all right for tomorrow, though?'

She nodded again.

'Is the old man in?'

The shift of conversation to office matters freed her from dumb show. 'Yes.'

'Anyone with him?'

'No. Rarely is these days. Surrounded by back-slapping management at all these cocktail parties, and left strictly on his own in the Department.'

Graham smiled, went to his boss's door, knocked once and entered.

George Brewer looked up guiltily. He had been playing with the suspended Newton's Balls on his desk. This 'executive toy' had been presented to him by his colleagues on his appointment as Head of Personnel. A jocular card had accompanied it, with the message, 'This'll give you something to do when you've got nothing to do.' Now those words were all too relevant.

'Oh, Graham.' George's hands flew to pick a circular out of his in-tray. His expression was that of a schoolboy caught masturbating. The slight sheen of sweat that now seemed a permanent feature shone on his forehead. His jacket was slung over the back of his chair and the armpits of his shirt, too, were darkened with sweat. The room held a stale whiff of anxiety.

Graham noticed the discarded jacket with satisfaction.

'Morning, George. How are you?'

'Oh, you know . . .'

'Got another of your executive piss-ups today?'

'No . . . no . . . nothing today.' The words seemed to have a wider application than a mere answer to Graham's question. Then, eagerly, the old man added, 'Don't know whether you fancy a drink at lunchtime . . . ?'

'Sorry. Got to go out and do some shopping.'

'Ah.' George Brewer crumpled again.

'Actually, there's something I want to check with you . . .'

George looked surprised. It was rarely that anyone wanted

177

to check anything with him these days.

'Yes, Robert asked me to do a report on the union negotiations. You know, this tedious business about Travelling Allowances for Office Services staff off Central Premises.'

'Oh yes.' The old man still looked bewildered.

'I've been sitting in on the meetings and Robert just wanted me to do an update. You know, current state of play . . .'

'Uhuh.'

'Well, it's finished, but I thought you should cast your eye over it before I pass it on to Robert.'

'Oh. Oh.' The second 'Oh' was extremely gratified. It was a long time since George had been consulted on something like this. Over recent years Graham had done more and more of the routine work on his own and, since the announcement of Robert Benham's appointment, all important documentation bypassed George's office completely.

In fact, Graham's report was not important. It was the kind of thing that, in more confident days, George would have dismissed with any airy 'God, I don't need to look at *that*.'

But in his current reduced state, he seized eagerly on any opportunity to maintain the illusion that he was still needed.

He leant over the document. Graham picked up a pencil and moved round behind his boss's chair, close enough to feel the sting of cigarette smoke in his eyes. Graham pointed with the pencil at a particular paragraph. 'It's this bit, really. We haven't actually had the agreement ratified, but I think we're safe to take it as read, don't you?'

'Well, I . . . let's just have a look at it.' Given the responsibility, George was going to make sure he read every word. He leaned closer over the document.

Graham slipped his hand into the inside pocket of the jacket hanging over the chair. He withdrew George Brewer's wallet and transferred it into his own jacket pocket.

It was a risk, but he reckoned the risk was small. Besides, he was beginning to enjoy the tease of danger. Moments like his confrontation with Detective-Inspector Laker had been frightening, but the relief afterwards was wonderful. Danger gave him a feeling of extra professionalism. If he could keep his cool under that kind of provocation, he was obviously getting good. He was completely in control, just sailing rather close to the wind.

As this image came to his mind, he thought of Robert Benham and smiled.

He needn't have taken George Brewer's wallet. He wasn't worried about the theft ever being attributed to him, but it did raise the minimal danger of a connection being made between Benham's death and Crasoco. In some ways, Graham knew he might have done better to steal an anonymous wallet.

But that carried as many dangers, if not more.

First, there was the problem of the theft. He had no skill as a pickpocket and to get caught in the act would be shameful. Again, he couldn't guarantee the contents of an anonymous wallet. Nor could he easily return it after use, so the theft was almost bound to be reported.

Most important of all, he couldn't forge an unknown signature without hours of practice. Whereas George Brewer's he could do in his sleep.

Graham Marshall took the Tube to Marble Arch, which he reckoned was far enough away for anonymity. It was a short walk to the car-hire garage.

'Yes?' asked the uniformed girl behind the counter, with the meaningless smile of efficiency.

'Good afternoon. I'd like to rent a car for the weekend.'

'Of course, sir. What, that would be three days?'

'Yes. I'd like to drive it away now, if possible, and return it on Monday.'

'Fine. What sort of car did you have in mind?'

'Something fairly small. Ford Escort, that sort of size. Depends how much it costs.'

The girl reeled off a list of models and prices. Graham selected a Vauxhall Chevette. The girl started to fill in a form.

'Could I have your name, sir?'

'George Brewer.'

'I'll need your driving licence.'

'Yes, of course.' He took out George's wallet and put the old man's driving licence on the counter.

'No endorsements, sir?'

An ugly moment. He had no idea of George Brewer's record as a driver, but gave a confident 'No', which fortunately was not contradicted by the document.

'This address on the licence is still valid, sir?'

'Yes.'

'How will you be paying, sir? Cheque or credit card?'

He had thought this one through. Stealing George's cheque book or using one of his credit cards was not on, as the details of the transaction would be documented and even George, in his current fuddled state, would smell a rat.

'No, I'll pay cash.'

'Well, sir, we ask a fifty pound deposit, and then settle the difference when you return the car.'

Fine. He reached again for George's wallet and had another ugly moment. He had drawn out sufficient cash for the deposit that morning, but had omitted to transfer the notes from his own wallet.

Nothing for it. The girl appeared to be engrossed in the form. Graham pulled out his wallet, extracted the fivers, and returned it to his pocket.

When he looked back, the girl was staring at him. Damn. He was drawing attention to himself, the last thing he wanted to do.

'Sorry,' he apologised with a weak laugh. 'I'm just disorganised.'

The girl's expression relaxed, as he counted out the notes on to the counter. 'Oh, Mr. Brewer, when you pay in cash, we do require some other proof of identity apart from the driving licence.'

'Yes, of course.' He opened George Brewer's wallet and reached into the credit card compartment. He slid something out and looked down at it.

It was a photograph of the late Mrs. Brewer. He felt himself colour as he shoved it back. 'Damned things. So sticky.'

He managed to slide out an American Express card. 'This O.K.?'

'That'll do nicely,' she replied with a smile, in parody of the advertising campaign. She wrote down the number of the card.

Ten minutes later, Graham Marshall was driving a pale blue Vauxhall Chevette round Hyde Park Corner. He went down Park Lane and left the car in the underground car park. Then he caught the Tube back from Marble Arch to Oxford Circus.

Stella had just returned to her office from lunch and was brushing her hair when Graham came in, holding a piece of paper.

'Hi,' he said. 'I've just done a slight amendment on that report. Like to show it to George. Is he in?'

'Still in the bar, I think. He's in a bit of a state.'

'Why's that?'

'Lost his wallet.'

'Oh no!'

'He's just getting so confused at the moment. I asked if he could have left it at home, but he said no, because he must have used his season on the train this morning.'

'Hmm. Slipped out of his pocket under the desk perhaps?'

'I've had a good look around, can't see it.'

'He really is falling apart.'

'Yes, God knows what'll happen to him when he actually does retire. He'll just collapse.'

'Afraid you may be right. One of the sort who'll be dead within a year.'

'Hmm.' She indicated the paper. 'Shall I take that?'

'Don't bother. I'll put it on his desk for when he comes back.'

Inside the main office Graham looked around. The required image of executive efficiency didn't leave many nooks or crannies in the furnishings where objects could lie unseen. He contemplated the waste-paper basket, but it was empty and the idea that the wallet had dropped in by chance stretched the imagination too far. He could put it in a drawer, but that also raised questions.

Mustn't stay in there too long. To walk out to Stella holding the wallet, and saying he'd found it, linked him too closely to its disappearance.

Oh well, in George's current state he was more likely to blame himself than imagine outside action. Graham shoved the wallet down between the cushion and the side of his boss's chair.

Stella smiled as he came out.

'See you tomorrow,' said Graham, and winked.

CHAPTER TWENTY-FOUR

The meal had gone well. He hadn't overstretched his culinary abilities. Two large pieces of best fillet steak he could cope with. Grilled mushrooms he could cope with. Salads and cheesecake he had obtained from the local delicatessen.

The wine was a good bottle of Mouton Rothschild. Stella hadn't commented on the fact that Graham drank only about a glass of it. Either she hadn't noticed or she had put it down to a becoming awareness of responsibility in a man approaching a seduction. And she didn't know that he had touched no alcohol in the pub where they had gone before the meal. She had seen him return from the bar twice with what looked like two large gin and tonics, not knowing that his drinks were untainted by gin. It wasn't just that Graham wanted to keep his wits exceptionally sharp; he also had no wish to run the smallest risk of being breathalysed on this night of all nights.

Again, Stella had passed no comment on their going to the pub and on Graham's chattiness to the bar staff and casual acquaintances there, although such behaviour did not conform with the desire for secrecy in their relationship which he had stressed earlier in the week. Probably, the anomaly did not worry her. She expected him still to be in an unpredictable emotional state, and was simply relieved to see him in apparent good humour.

He had talked during the meal of Merrily. He had made it clear to Stella that the marriage had long since died, and explained to her what confusion the reality of his wife's death had unleashed in him. He felt shock and regret, of course, and yet these feelings could not swamp his knowledge that the marriage had not worked. Among all the other emotions, he felt a glimmer of hope, the possibility that, by a random act of fate, he had been given the chance to start his life again. The drift of this conversation, together with an adequate ration of soulful looks and hand-touchings, left no doubt about the way the evening was headed.

Graham knew he was taking a risk. To cultivate Stella so soon after Merrily's death could be interpreted, retrospectively, as a motive for his wife's murder. But the word 'murder' had never arisen, except in Lilian's hysterical letter, and after his visit from Detective-Inspector Laker Graham felt complete confidence that the case was closed. Besides, once again he found he was getting a charge from the element of danger in what he was doing.

As Stella trapped the last crumb of cheesecake with her fork and popped it into her mouth, Graham rose from the table, saying. 'Let's go into the sitting-room. I'll sort out some coffee.'

Stella stretched herself out on the sofa in an inviting way as Graham went across to the drinks cupboard. 'Look, I got something specially for you. I know you like it.'

He held up a brand-new bottle of Bailey's Irish Cream.

'Oh, you are an angel, Graham.'

He got out a glass and fumbled with the metal seal at the top of the bottle. 'Damn. I don't know who designs these things. They're always impossible to open. I'll get a knife in the kitchen. Black or white coffee?'

In the kitchen the coffee-machine dripped intermittently, at the end of its cycle. On the wall hung a collage picture of a girl, made from coloured seeds. It was something Emma had brought from school. For Graham it was an odd reminder that there had once been children in the house. That morning Henry and Emma had come with Charmian and collected their belongings. It seemed like years ago.

He looked at his watch. Twenty-past ten. Pretty well on

184

schedule. So long as everything else worked.

He still felt confident. He hummed tunelessly as he picked up the envelope from the work surface. He opened the bottle of Irish Cream without difficulty. Then he shook the powder from the envelope into the glass. Three tablets. He had been tempted to use more, but remembered the doctor's caution. Mustn't run the risk of accidents this end, he thought.

He poured the thick creamy liqueur into the glass and stirred the contents with a spoon. He'd experimented earlier in the week, and had not been able to detect any peculiarity in the taste of the solution.

He threw away the envelope and put two coffee cups on a tray. He took a whisky glass, poured in about half an inch of cold tea he had kept for the purpose, then added a little whisky on top to give the right smell.

He placed the whisky and the Bailey's Irish Cream bottles on the tray and returned to the sitting-room.

He waited till Stella was half-way through her liqueur before he kissed her. It was a strange sensation. The lips that his probed were different, more fleshy, moister than Merrily's, but that was not the source of the strangeness. It was the fact of kissing that seemed odd, like the fact of having had children, a distant memory from another life. His tongue did a little dutiful exploration, and his hand, guided by expectation rather than instinct, rose to circle a breast. His other arm moved behind Stella, securing her neck in the crook of its elbow.

From this position Graham could see his watch. Twenty to eleven. The timing was becoming more critical.

For everything to work, he needed to be away by midnight or very soon after.

Stella's hands were massaging his shoulders, then moved up to his neck and steadied his head for her tongue to demonstrate its own expertise. He had never felt much doubt about her response, and the event proved that confidence to be justified.

Graham felt nothing. His mind hovered above his body,

mildly contemptuous of its antics. His penis hung flaccid and uninterested.

Stella drew back her face from his and looked at him. Her eyes were not dewy with romance, but shrewd. There was no deterrence in them, just the complaisance of a woman who knew the score and had given her consent.

It was Graham's cue to say something, but he felt uncertain of the appropriate phrasing.

Stella yawned. Good, good, he thought.

That gave him the impetus to speak. He selected a voice of humility, tentative, thick with adolescent misgiving.

'Shall we finish our drinks and go upstairs?'

Stella gave a quick little nod, and drained her glass. She smacked her lips. 'Tastes a bit funny.'

He brought his right hand swiftly down from her breast to her thigh, which diverted her thoughts sufficiently.

Then he took her hands and they rose. She pressed her body against him. He edged away to hide his lack of physical response. 'Upstairs,' he murmured throatily.

On the landing, he indicated the bathroom. 'Do you want to have a pee?'

'No, not at the moment.'

'Who knows when you'll next get the chance?' he said. It sounded provocative, promising unrelenting sexual activity, which was how it was meant to sound. The real motivation of the remark was more pragmatic. He didn't want the pressure of a full bladder to wake Stella up in the night.

She smiled. 'O.K. You know best.'

As she disappeared into the bathroom she stifled another very satisfactory yawn.

Graham put on one bedside light, which gave a suitably muted glow. He looked at the clock radio on the shelf his side. 11:02. All right so far. The next hour was the tricky one.

He kicked off his shoes and lay down on top of the double duvet. He felt he should have been thinking about Merrily, but his wife's image was now too thin and insubstantial to stay in his mind.

Stella came into the room. The front of her dress was unbuttoned to the waist in a way that Graham recognised should be enticing. She stretched her arms back, jutting her breasts forward, and yawned hugely.

'Oh, I feel so sleepy.'

'Yawns are just a nervous reaction. Anticipation,' said Graham, holding out his arms towards her.

She grinned and slouched towards the bed. 'Well, I wonder what you're after . . .' She affected a mock-innocent little girl's voice.

Graham felt a violent spasm of hatred. It was Merrily's way, the sort of line Merrily would have used. Suddenly he felt for this new woman all he had come to feel for his wife in the last years of her life. As Stella slumped on to the bed, he found himself on top of her, his hands reaching to encircle her neck.

'Hey. Steady. Steady!'

With an effort of will he made his body relax.

The light of panic faded from Stella's eyes. 'What are you doing, Graham?'

He smiled boyishly, suppressing the shock inside him. The force of that sudden hatred had frightened him. At that moment he had wanted to kill Stella, and he had no illusion about how easily he could have given in to the impulse.

'Sorry,' he murmured, affecting a schoolboy voice. 'Just the force of mad passion.'

Then, again before his lack of erection gave the lie to his words, he rolled off and lay beside her.

This impotence was worrying. Not from the psychological point of view – he didn't feel personally diminished by it. Sex was no longer important to him, and this knowledge gave him a sensation of refinement, of ascetic superiority over the rest of mankind. But his impotence was actually threatening his plans, and that was serious.

What he had had in mind for the evening had been to get to this point and then make love to Stella. The confusion of intercourse and its consequent sleepiness might make her less aware of her sudden drop into sleep. But if he couldn't do

187

it . . .

Still, mustn't write off the possibility yet. Maybe, with a little more stimulation, something could be achieved. He leant over towards Stella and started to undo the remaining buttons of her dress. As he did so, he evolved his contingency plan if sex proved impossible.

'Like Christmas,' he murmured. 'Unwrapping the goodies.'

She smiled and reached up to the top button of his shirt. Swallowing a yawn, she asked, again in the baby voice, 'And what has Santa brought for me?'

Not what you asked for, thought Graham, controlling the anger her affectation sparked in him.

Two people undressing each other as they lie side by side is not the most efficient way of removing clothes. It takes a long time. Which was exactly what Graham had planned. Minute by minute, Stella was yawning more, and her eyelids flickered with increasing frequency.

But eventually the two of them were just down to briefs and Stella's searching fingers made further concealment impossible. Graham rolled away and sat on the edge of the bed with his back to her, as though to hide his shame. Time for Plan B.

'I'm sorry,' he announced brokenly. 'It's too soon.'

'Too soon?'

'Too soon after Merrily. It's not that I don't want you. God knows,' he lied, 'it's not that I don't want you. It's just . . .'

'Don't worry about it.' He felt Stella's hand on his shoulder, pulling him round. Again he experienced a flash of fury, which he managed to extinguish. He turned towards her, framing his face into an expression of shame.

She was all motherly now, her arms threatening to smother him. 'It's all right. It's only to be expected. Let's just have a cuddle. That'll make you feel better. It's just warmth you need, warmth and . . . comfort.'

The last word was interrupted by a jaw-stretching yawn. Graham complied and lay in her arms. Continuing Plan B, he maundered on for a while about how ashamed he felt, how awful, how debased, how abject.

'Yes,' Stella murmured at intervals. 'Yes . . . it's only to be expected. Yes . . . yes . . . of course . . . you mustn't worry about it . . . yes . . .'

The intervals between the words grew longer, and then there were no more words. The rhythm of her breathing grew thick and heavy. Her mouth dropped open and a soft vibrating resonance began to sound with each breath.

Graham squinted round at the clock radio. 11:43. Good.

He waited unflinching for a few more minutes. As he did so, he looked at Stella's face thrust close to his. He saw each pore and imperfection, as under a microscope. He saw the dark hairs that sprouted at the corner of her mouth and from her nostrils. Onion smell from the salads breathed across his face. Stella's body twitched a few times as sleep took command.

And Graham knew that if anything went wrong, he would have no hesitation in killing her. More than that, he would take pleasure in doing it.

Another look at the clock. 11:54. Time.

He gently disengaged Stella's arms from his body. She shuddered and rolled over to lie on her back. The vibration with each breath now took on the rasp of a snore. He tugged the duvet from under her, producing no reaction, and covered her with it.

He dressed quickly in the old jeans, shirt, pullover and sports shoes he had left in readiness behind the chair.

Stella did not stir.

He went across to the clock radio and, with one finger on 'Time', pressed the 'Hour' button through twenty-two numbers. When the display read '9.59 p.m.', he released the buttons.

He moved across to the side of the bed and switched off the light. The click did not change the heavy rhythm of Stella's sleep.

He slipped out of the front door and walked the quarter mile to where he had parked the Vauxhall Chevette.

By nine minutes past twelve, he was on his way, driving out of London in a south-westerly direction.

189

CHAPTER TWENTY-FIVE

He took the A3 to Milford, and thence the A286 through Haslemere and Midhurst to Chichester. There was very little traffic about at that time of night, but even on the good bits of dual carriageway he did not exceed sixty. It was not a night to do anything that would attract attention.

He made good time, and a little before half-past one turned off the A27, following the sign to Bosham and Bosham Hoe. He turned again for the quay and parked up a side street. The back walls of gardens gave him some protection from curious insomniacs, and he avoided the exposure and double yellow lines of the main thoroughfare. Again, he did not wish to have the success of his great transgression jeopardised by some minor infringement.

Before he got out of the car, he checked the breast pockets of his shirt. New padlock key, a tube of glue, some small strips of sandpaper, a selection of knives, gimlets and screwdrivers. And a box of Swan Vestas matches.

He pulled the waders and torch over from the back seat and got out of the car. He closed the door and locked it.

Immediately his nose caught the seaweedy smell of exposed mud. Please God, to his surprise he found himself praying, please God may I have read the Tide Table right.

If he had, the timing for his adventure was ideal. High water at Portsmouth that evening had been at 18.27. It was neap tide; a spring would have been better, he reflected, but you can't have everything. According to his reckoning, adding the specified time difference for Bosham (five minutes for a neap tide), low water would be about quarter to two in the morning.

He took off his right shoe and started to pull on one of the waders. He leant against the car to do so. No lights shone in the side street. There was very little moon, the sky cloudy. All he could hear was the susurration of the invisible sea, and a distant incessant rattling, which at first he could not identify but then recognised as the banging of metal halyards against the masts of boats.

As he pushed his foot into the wader, the studs of its sole rasped on the tarmac surface of the road. No, not here. Someone might hear the clatter of his footsteps. Carefully he withdrew his foot and replaced the shoe. Eliminate unnecessary risks, that was what he must do. Just keep calm, and eliminate unnecessary risks.

He rounded the corner into the main street, and he could see the creek ahead. The seaweedy smell was stronger, the chattering of the halyards louder. A few lights shone on the opposite side, others on boats winked as they moved in the swell. A notice warned him that the road was liable to tidal flooding.

He moved left across the shingle, trying to remember where *Tara's Dream* was moored. On the previous occasion, of course, he and Robert had been in the dinghy and rowed round from the quay. But he remembered how he had looked back wistfully at the shore and tried to reverse that bearing. He kept looking back to the picture window he had seen then and trying to reproduce his point of view.

His shoes sounded softly on the shingle. Again he was glad he had not yet donned the waders. Eliminate risk. He was glad he hadn't used the torch yet either. His eyes were accustoming well to the gloom.

He looked back to the frontage of houses. A light shone from one upstairs window, but that had been on when he arrived. No cause for anxiety. His eyes knew rather than saw where the picture window was. The angle of his advance seemed correct.

Ahead of him the outline of a boat took shape. Beached by

191

the ebbing tide, she listed slightly, held upright by props. She had the hunched shoulders look of a sailing boat with a cabin. The shape was deliciously familiar.

He felt a surge of confidence. Everything was going to work. And the boat was right out of the water. He wouldn't even need the waders.

He drew closer, but the meagre moonlight was inadequate. He risked the flash of the torch against the nameplate on the prow.

Kittiwake III.

He reeled in sudden panic, whirling round. The darkness offered no other comforting outlines.

His heart thumped and he felt dizzy. For a moment he contemplated turning back. There was no need for it to be done that night. He'd have plenty of other opportunities to get at Robert Benham. Or perhaps, the idea came to him suddenly, there was no need to do it at all.

This thought tasted at once seductive and traitorous. For a moment it invaded his whole mind. Forget the last couple of months, the old man's death, Merrily's death, thank his good fortune that both crimes had gone undetected, and leave it at that. Don't push your luck, Graham.

For a few seconds he was almost convinced, but then he felt a growing emptiness inside him. He had lost the job he wanted, he was without wife and children. On that evening's showing with Stella, he was now impotent. If he removed the excitement of murder from his life, what would be left? Killing could still make him feel power, still provide him with an ecstatic sense of his own identity.

No, to give up now would be cowardice. Worse than that it would be laziness, lack of tenacity, capitulating the first moment the going got difficult. Come on, you must do it, he reprimanded himself piously. Remember how neatly you disposed of Merrily. You're good. Come on, Graham, you're good.

His breathing calmed to a steady rhythm. He suppressed a panicky query as to how steadily Stella was breathing at that moment. If he started to think of the risks he was taking, he might as well give up straight away.

He moved slowly round the hull of *Kittiwake III*. His right foot landed in the pool of water that had formed around her keel. The ground was getting squelchy underfoot. He leant his back against the weedy hull and pulled on the waders, buckling the straps to his belt. His shoes he left neatly beside the boat like slippers under a bed.

Then he dared to look ahead. Of course there were more boats there. He shouldn't have panicked. Of course he'd find *Tara's Dream*.

He looked back, sensing the outline of the houses and the position of the picture window. He still seemed to be on course. Two other boats lay one each side of him, but their outlines were wrong; one was a motor launch, the other a huge dinghy. But there was something else ahead.

This boat was shifting and swaying as it felt the tug of the tide. The keel was still grounded at the front, but the boat's stern twitched.

Graham flashed his torch, again to be disappointed. *Spray Queen*.

But there was another shape just beyond that moved more regularly, responding to the ripples of the sea and the drag of its mooring chain. Graham's eyes strained to prise apart the darkness, but he couldn't be sure.

He moved forward slowly. Each raised footstep made a sucking sound as it left the mud. He stepped into the water till it tickled at the wader's ankles.

Then he flashed the torch.

Tara's Dream. He had found her.

The boat was definitely afloat, only some two metres away from him. Graham looked at his watch. 1.54. He wished he had understood the Tide Table better and knew whether the water was still receding or had started to rise.

But he couldn't worry about that. Having got so close, he would complete the job. In ten minutes he reckoned he could be on his way back. He stepped forward.

He was surprised by the power of the current that dragged at his legs, but he managed to keep his balance. He was also surprised by how quickly the ground shelved. And by how much further away the boat was than it had at first appeared.

He concentrated hard on the placement of his feet. He tried shuffling, but the mud was too sticky, so he had to risk the lift of each foot and subsequent moment of imbalance. His pullover felt suffocatingly hot; sweat dribbled down his sides to the top of his trousers.

At last he had one hand on the side of the boat and felt the stippled effect of its non-slip surface under his fingers. It was then he remembered that he had not brought his rubber gloves.

But nothing was going to stop him now. He threw the torch into the boat, hearing it clatter on the wooden boards within, then moved round to the stern, where the vessel was lowest in the water. The top of the transom was at chest height, the water level round his knees, though it splashed higher.

The first attempt to heave himself up failed. His body slipped back, raising a spout of spray between the hull and his chest. He felt the shock of the water's coldness and tasted salt on his tongue. Damp trickled over the top of his waders.

The second attempt succeeded. He jerked the weight of his body over the transom and, in an ungainly scramble of flailing legs, slid down into the well of the boat.

Swivelling his body round, he lay on his back, with his feet still over the side. He was about to bring them in, when he was halted by a caution. Muddy footsteps all over the clean fibreglass and bottom-boards were not the kind of signature he wanted to leave on the job. He unbuckled the straps from his belt and slid his legs out with some difficulty. He left the waders flat with their feet dangling over the transom.

When he stood up, the boat's movement brought immediate queasiness. In his state of hypertension, nausea seemed dangerously close. That really would do it, to leave a neat little pool of vomit as a calling-card. He forced control on himself and reached under the damp pullover to the key in the breast pocket of his shirt.

God, if it didn't fit, after all this . . . He tottered forward to the cabin hatch and felt for the padlock with his right hand. His left hand trembled so much that he couldn't guide the key into its socket. He dropped it and had to scrabble through the bottom-boards by torchlight. He was careful to switch off the torch before the beam rose above the side of the boat. Eliminate risk.

Imposing calmness, he approached the padlock again. The key slid into its aperture and clicked home. He turned it. Another click, and the padlock sprang open.

Graham felt a deep peace. It would be all right. It was all going to work, after all.

He pushed back the sliding hatch at the top, gently, then lifted out the vertical wooden section. With a surge of comfort, he realised that his memory of how the opening worked had been accurate.

Now he felt relaxed. Steady against the rocking boat, he turned back for the torch and then stepped down into the cabin.

The tiny windows were curtained, so he felt safe to use the torch. Keeping its beam low, he made a quick survey of the cramped space. Forward, the recess with its four bunks was illuminated. He drew across the thick curtain which separated this from the tiny galley area. The torch beam passed across the folding table, nylon sail bags and the two hot-plates fixed over the curtained space where the Calor Gas cylinder was stored.

He directed the torch to the hatch above his head. It was as he had remembered. The fibreglass top slid back and forth on wooden rails.

It was perfect.

He slid the hatch backwards and forwards experimentally. Then, with all the time in the world, he selected one of his strips of sandpaper and glued it along the underside edge of the hatch, just above the rail. He closed the hatch and marked a point on the rail a couple of inches in front of the sandpaper,

195

Pushing the hatch forward again, he got out his gimlet and, from above, drilled a neat hole in the rail where he had marked it. He slid the hatch back to check the alignment. It was right.

He reached into his shirt pocket and brought out the box of Swan Vestas matches.

As he felt it a new, cold horror struck him. The cardboard was damp and soft to the touch. He snatched it open and struck a match against the side of the box. Nothing. Maybe it was just the abrasive surface that was wet. He tried a match against one of his own dry pieces of sandpaper. Nothing. He tried another, and another, and another.

'Fuck it! Fuck it!' he screamed in childlike frustration. He dropped the matches, and sank to the floor of the galley, weeping.

It was a look at his watch that finally brought him to his senses. 2.17. He must either sort something out or get away quickly. If Robert Benham arrived next morning for a day's sailing and found his office rival in *Tara's Dream*, it would not look good.

Robert Benham. Robert Benham was of course hyper-efficient. He was the sort of man who would ensure that his boat contained all requisite stores.

Graham straightened out of his crumpled heap of self-pity and moved across to the gas rings.

Good old Robert. There, tucked behind the blue metal frame lay not one, but two boxes of Swan Vestas matches. One match on its own wobbled sideways in the hole he had drilled. Two stayed, but didn't feel very secure. Three, however, jammed in, tight and unshifting.

He moved the hatch back gingerly, but the matches stood too proud. He took them out and cut them down to the right length. The matchheads almost touched the underside of the hatch. They would definitely touch the sandpaper as it was pushed over them.

He couldn't resist one practice go. He moved the hatch to its closed position, very slowly, so that the sandpaper just

196

caressed the red matchheads.

Then, with only average force, he opened the hatch. There was a little rasp and a flame flared.

It worked.

He closed the hatch hastily and the action put out the flame. When inspected, the fibreglass showed a slight discoloration behind the sandpaper, but the flash had been too brief to deform its shape.

Graham took out the three spent matches and, almost as if he were blessing them, cut three new ones to length and set them in place.

Shining the torch on the floor, he meticulously picked up all his spilled, damp matches and put them in his pocket.

Then, covering his hand with a tea-towel that lay neatly beside the stove, he turned the switches of both hot-plates on, low. Reaching through the curtain beneath, he found the domed stopcock of the Calor Gas cylinder. One way it would not turn.

The other way it gave. He unscrewed it as far as it would go.

CHAPTER TWENTY-SIX

The night was darker when he emerged from the galley. He guided the vertical board into its slot, moving the top hatch forward a few centimetres to do so. This was done with infinite care; he had no wish to fire his detonator too early. Then he replaced the padlock and pushed it together to lock. A quick wipe round the hatches and padlock with a handkerchief was the only fingerprint precaution he took.

Still keeping the muddy feet out of the boat, he contrived to pull the waders back on and fix the tops to his belt. Ducking under the ropes which lashed tiller and boom in place, he eased his body round until he perched on the transom.

The darkness was too thick now for him to see the water's edge, but the one upstairs light still on in Bosham Quay showed the direction he had to take.

With one hand on the stern of the boat and the other holding the torch, he launched himself into the hissing blackness.

The shock was how far he fell. Water closed, growling, over his head. The tide had risen faster than he had expected. His feet, muffled in the waders, touched nothing solid. He kicked upwards towards the surface.

Then he felt a new wetness as the space around his legs filled. Kicking became harder as the weight of water dragged him down. He gasped, salt water rasped through his nose, mouth and trachea. All was darkness, noise and pain.

His hands fumbled in panic for the buckles of the waders, but their new leather was stiff and reluctant. Then, thank

God, he thought of his belt. Though he could feel it constricting around him, he managed to undo the buckle and tug it free. With a lung-bursting effort, he kicked and kicked, until at last the waders' weight slipped away from him. He kicked again and at last his head broke the surface. He gasped for air and the waves slapped in another mouthful of salt water.

His chest was tight and the cold bit into his bones. He knew he couldn't survive long in these conditions.

Tara's Dream was no longer visible. Graham was so low in the water that he could see nothing but the sky. But even without bearings, he could feel that the water was propelling him along at some speed.

Despair threatened, but he fought it. He hadn't come this far to be snuffed out so easily. He commanded an extra kick from his trembling legs and managed to raise himself a little out of the water. Fortunately, he was facing the right direction. For a second he saw above the waves the gleam of light from Bosham Quay. He kicked towards it.

His clothes clung and dragged at him, but he did not pause to remove them. He could not spare the energy to manoeuvre himself out of the pullover, and, though the jeans would slip off easily enough, he remembered the car keys in the pocket. To be stranded, drenched through, beside a locked hire-car in Bosham, was not going to help the secrecy of his mission.

Progress was agony, but he was going with the tide and eventually one foot scraped on mud. Graham tried to stand and received another scouring mouthful of water. He forced his limbs onward and at last both feet were grounded. His arms still made swimming movements and though the water was shallow enough for him to stand, he had no strength, and shambled ashore on all fours.

He lay, beached and panting, thinking he would never move again. But he felt the lapping of water round his legs and knew that the tide was rising fast. He eased himself to his feet and tottered towards the quayside light. His teeth chattered and his whole body was shaken by spasms of shivering. His

199

shoes had been taken by the rising tide and shingle scratched at his feet.

He willed himself not to look at his watch until he was by the car. His shaking body was moving as fast as it could; and extra panic was as likely to slow him down as spur him to greater effort.

The tarmac pressed sharp stones into his soles as he inched forward. The pavement was less painful, but his first two steps had left large give-away footprints, so he stuck to the road. He was relying on the tide to erase his traces over the mud.

At last he leant against the Vauxhall Chevette and dared to turn his arm and raise the bedraggled sleeve that covered his watch. In his exhaustion he would not have been surprised to discover a whole day had elapsed since last he stood there.

2.53. The journey from the boat had taken little more than half an hour. It seemed incredible. He felt an urge to laugh, from sheer weakness and relief.

But he curbed it. He was not far behind his schedule. Having survived this far, he mustn't fail now.

As quietly as he could, he unlocked the car and extinguished the interior light which came on when the door opened. He was still trembling, but that was just a physical reaction to exposure; emotionally he was beginning to regain control.

He reached into the back of the car for a black plastic bag he had in readiness and then, standing in the street, took off all his clothes and placed them in it.

The risk of being nicked for indecent exposure was perhaps an unnecessary one, but Graham hadn't reckoned on being soaked to the skin. And he decided that he was less likely to be discovered by some affronted resident of Bosham at two a.m. than to receive unwelcome enquiries from the car-hire firm about salt and mud stains on their upholstery.

He reached again into the back of the car for the shirt, jacket, trousers and underpants he had ready and, in spite of his trembling, was quickly dressed. He brushed the worst of the sand and mud off his wounded feet before donning socks and shoes. His body felt salty damp under his clothes, but

200

there hadn't been time to dry himself properly.

Turning the neck of the black plastic bag, he slung it into the well behind the front seats. He would have put it in the boot, but didn't want to risk the noise of slamming the lid.

He sat in the car, breathed deeply and tried to control the chattering of his teeth. A light came on in a curtained upstairs window of a house opposite. Probably just some elderly incontinent making his way to the bathroom, but Graham didn't want to wait to find out.

With a little choke, the car started first time. He turned the heater on full and drove slowly out of Bosham.

As he did so, it started to rain. Heavy, steady rain. Rain to wash away footprints and mud from the fibreglass and boards of *Tara's Dream*.

Graham grinned. The random gods of chance were on his side.

It was 3.13.

There was a builder's skip outside a demolition site on the outskirts of Haslemere. Graham's bag of sea-wet clothes was shoved into it under a pile of broken lathes and torn wallpaper.

When he reached Barnes, he parked the Chevette exactly where he had driven it off from some four and a half hours earlier.

He put his key in the door of the Boileau Avenue house at 4.54. As he did so, he caught a strong whiff of seaweed. At the same moment another panic gripped him. Suppose Stella had woken up.

The light from the landing was sufficient for him to see her through the half-open door. In fact, the breathing reassured him before he looked. The snores had given way to deep sighs. She had shifted her position and now lay sideways, the slipped duvet revealing breasts squashed together by her arms.

3:01 was displayed by the clock radio.

The immersion heater had not been switched off since

Merrily's death. Since she had spent more time in the house than Graham, she had always controlled the central heating and immersion. And since the latter had been switched on at the time of her death, Graham found a plentiful supply of hot water for his bath.

He had to wash everything including his hair.

Already Stella was no doubt finding his behaviour in bed odd; if he came to her smelling of seaweed she was going to find it odder still.

The hot water restored him. He still ached, but he felt very satisfied, warm and drowsy. Mustn't go to sleep yet, though. A large Scotch after the bath and then to bed. Must remember to wash his shirt and underpants. And his socks. Yes, and take the jacket and trousers to the cleaners, get rid of the smell.

'What on earth are you doing?'

Stella stood in the doorway. Her body sagged and bulged. He realised that in his preoccupation he had not previously taken in her nakedness, the tight little breasts, not stretched like Merrily's by children, the bulge of the hips, the surprising tuft of blackness between her legs. He felt distaste for what he saw.

But her eyes mattered more, and they were still rolling with satisfactory drowsiness.

'What are you doing?' she repeated.

Time for a bit more of the abject act. 'I just thought it might relax me.'

'What?'

'I've been lying there awake for hours, after . . . you know, after I couldn't . . . we didn't . . .'

'I told you not to worry.' It was automatic reassurance; she was still very sleepy.

'It's different for a man. It makes you feel . . . I don't . . . I don't know how long I'd been lying there.'

'It's about quarter past three now,' she slurred.

Wonderful. How kind. She was doing his job for him. He'd had visions of having to wake her and draw her attention to the time.

'Well, I was just feeling so awful, so strung up, I thought maybe if I had a bath, calmed down, it might be better.'

'Let's have another try when you come back to bed. Eh?' Her wink was meant to be provocative, but it gave Graham a stab of anger, again for her likeness to Merrily.

'Just have a pee and see you in a minute,' she mumbled, and disappeared.

He didn't hurry out of the bath and when he got to the bedroom she was, as he had hoped, once again deeply asleep.

Just as well. Behind the curtains the sky was beginning to lighten.

Graham's hand was now steady. With the buttons of the clock radio he corrected the time to 5:52.

Then he lay back and thought of his victim. High tide at Bosham that morning was round quarter to seven. Knowing his rival's enthusiasm for sailing, he reckoned it wouldn't be long after that that Robert Benham boarded *Tara's Dream*.

With that comforting reflection, Graham Marshall drifted easily into sleep.

They woke about half past eight. Graham felt as if he had been dragged from the bottom of a deep well, encased in an old-fashioned diving suit, or as if he was into his third month of Gestapo interrogation. Every tiny muscle of his body ached.

Stella, too, claimed to be exhausted, which surprised her.

'It's that Bailey's Irish Cream,' Graham joked, taking pleasure in the irony of the remark.

'But I don't feel hungover. Just incredibly sleepy.'

'You must be relaxed.'

This she took as a cue. 'And how about you? Are you more relaxed now?'

Her right hand came across to his stomach and started to make ever widening circular movements. It stirred nothing. Then she took his penis and tried to coax life into it, first with one hand, then with two. When this proved ineffectual, she threw back the duvet and brought her lips into play. Graham looked dispassionately down at her head, noting that a few of the hairs were grey at the roots, and wondered which of his colleagues had taught her this particular trick.

But the kiss of life was as fruitless as her other ministrations. She might as well have been playing with an empty balloon.

Time for more histrionics, Graham thought wearily.

'I'm sorry. I had hoped . . . it just seems that so soon after a wife's death – even a wife you didn't care for . . .'

Et cetera. Et cetera. Et cetera.

He felt quietly confident about what was happening in Bosham, though he was of course desperately anxious to know the outcome of his plan. But he could ruin everything by unseemly curiosity. He had to wait until something was publicly announced. Possibly wait till the next day at work. Possibly even, if the booby trap had failed, he would wait for ever. If the matches didn't light, or if the lethal combination of gas and air didn't ignite, or if the gas had all seeped away, he might never hear anything. Robert Benham might not even be aware of the sabotage.

An empty gas cylinder would perhaps puzzle him briefly, but the triggering device might never be noticed. Since the top hatch was usually only closed when *Tara's Dream* was empty, and in the forward position the sandpaper was invisible, it could easily pass undetected for years.

But this was defeatist thinking. Graham convinced himself it was going to work. All he could do was wait.

And cultivate his alibi. To this end he took Stella out for a walk by the pond in Barnes and repaired to the 'Sun' pub at lunchtime. Both of these excursions produced a few nods from acquaintances and, to make the alliance even more public, Graham took her for a large Sunday lunch in a local restaurant.

He found conversation difficult, but she appeared not to. They talked of colleagues at work and a variety of subjects they had discussed before. Graham was very tired, but did not worry about occasional silences. He could rely on the aptitude of his emotions for masquerade. Silence and a soulful look would be interpreted as anxiety, born of bereavement and impotence, and rewarded by a gentle squeeze of the hand.

After lunch, when they had enjoyed a lot of wine, they returned to the house and lazed on the sitting-room floor with the Sunday papers. By four o'clock they were both asleep.

Graham woke with a start and looked at his watch. 5.52. Twelve hours exactly since he had completed his plan. He rose slowly, stretching his aching limbs. Stella lay splayed against the sofa, breathing evenly. He went into the kitchen to make some tea. While he was waiting for the kettle to boil, he switched on the radio.

It was at the end of the six o'clock news. With the approach of summer, Sunday evening news often listed the leisure disasters of the weekend. Two children drowned in Cornwall. A hang-glider crashed in Sussex.

And a man killed when his boat caught fire at Bosham near Chichester.

Graham Marshall felt dizzy with excitement. His body started to tremble again, but this time with life and power.

He went into the sitting-room and threw himself on top of Stella. His hand tearing away obstructions beneath her skirt, he thrust himself into her. And continued to thrust, with considerable savagery, until their shuddering mutual climax.

CHAPTER TWENTY-SEVEN

There was no other topic of conversation in the Personnel Department the next morning. Robert Benham's death was all over the newspapers. This was not because of his own fame; he may have been a big fish at Crasoco, but for the outside world he signified little. It was his connection with Tara Liston that made him newsworthy, and most of the more popular papers had photographs of her drawn face as she had arrived at Heathrow the previous evening.

The papers, in the knowledge that an inquest was still to come, were appropriately cagey about the causes of death, though one was indiscreet enough to mention a faulty gas appliance. None of them made any suggestion of foul play being suspected, and the word 'accident' appeared with gratifying regularity.

Graham swelled with pride as he sat over morning coffee in the canteen and listened to the conjecture around him. All the anxieties of the past forty-eight hours had vanished, all the moments when his plan had nearly failed. In retrospect its form was perfect, better even than his disposal of Merrily. He had returned the hire-car on the way into work that morning, dropped his clothes at the cleaners, and felt the satisfaction of a job well completed. The only slight regret came, once again, from the impossibility of sharing his elation, of being commended for his skill. But that was a cross he would have to bear.

A self-appointed expert, who claimed knowledge of comparable accidents, was giving the rest of the canteen the benefit of his conjecture. 'Oh, it happens quite often, you know. Get a leak in one of the gas pipes or forget to turn the cylinder off and the stuff just dribbles out, very slowly. Well, in an enclosed space, mixed with air, it's, well, it's like a bomb. Get a naked flame near that lot and – woomph!'

'But why do you reckon Mr. Benham got a naked flame near it?' asked one of the dumber secretaries.

'Could be anything – starting the outboard, lighting a cigarette, trying to light the stove to make a cup of tea . . .'

'But surely,' insisted the secretary, 'he wouldn't have done that. I mean, he would have smelt the gas, wouldn't he?'

This gave the expert pause. Graham listened with particular interest to how he would explain it away. 'Well, O.K.,' the man conceded, 'not lighting the stove. Some other way I suppose it happened.'

'Anyway, the police'll be able to find out when they examine the boat,' said the secretary, who, Graham began to think, was not as dumb as she appeared.

But her words restored the expert's confidence. 'Don't you believe it, darling. Won't be hardly anything left for the police to examine. Tell you, those fibreglass boats – go up like Roman candles. Gas explosion like that and she'd burn down to the waterline in a couple of minutes. Then probably the weight of the keel'd take her down to the bottom. Don't think there'll be a lot left of that boat now.' Then he added ghoulishly, 'Don't think there'll be a lot left of Bob Benham either, come to that.'

'What, you mean they'll never find the remains?'

'Oh yes, they'll have found whatever's left. Boat was on its mooring, I gather, so even if it went to the bottom, they'd be able to pick it up at low tide. I just don't think what they find's going to give them much clue as to how it happened.'

This was delivered very wisely and confidently. A few heads nodded in subdued agreement. A few were shaken ruefully at the sadness of life. Graham Marshall glowed.

Later in the morning he received a summons to the office of

the Managing Director, David Birdham.

'You've heard about Robert?' Birdham said, gesturing to a chair.

Graham nodded. 'A terrible shock.'

'Hmm. Yes, he could have gone a long way.' With that formal dismissal of the dead man, he moved on. 'Puts us in a spot in the short term. I know George is nominally still Head of Personnel, but quite honestly, he seems to be losing his marbles.'

Graham would not have dared to venture that opinion himself, but now his senior had said it, felt safe in nodding agreement.

'Fact is, Personnel's an important department and doesn't run itself. I've seen what's going on and it's clear that Robert was in charge from the moment the appointment was announced. And from what I saw I liked the way he was taking things.'

'Yes.' Graham spoke without intonation, not daring to hope.

'Well, now we've lost him, and life has to go on. At the moment I wouldn't trust George to run a white elephant stall at a village fête. Anyway, he's got more or less wall-to-wall cocktail parties for the next fortnight, so he's going to be even less use than usual. What'll happen to him when he finally leaves, God knows. Drink himself to death, I would think. Still, that's not our problem.'

Graham was tempted to say 'No', but thought it might sound too callous.

David Birdham tapped his desk. 'What I want you to do, Graham, is run the department during this little interregnum. O.K.? Nothing official. No title, no extra money, I'm afraid. I just want you to keep it going until the board makes another proper appointment.'

Evidently Graham had not managed to keep the disappointment out of his face, because the Managing Director continued, 'I know it's a lot to ask and I'm aware that this is a difficult time for you after your . . . recent problems. It may

208

also seem that there's not much in it for you, but rest assured it's the sort of thing that won't go unnoticed. I mean, you may know that when the job last came up, more than one of the board preferred you to Benham, but they were overruled. You would certainly be thought a strong candidate next time round.'

Graham nodded. It was all he had wanted to hear. He could do a lot, even in a fortnight, to strengthen his hold on the Department.

'So will you help us out?' asked David Birdham.

'Of course.'

'You'll just retain your Assistant title, but be a . . . rather more forceful assistant.'

Just as I was before Robert Benham's elevation, thought Graham.

'Very grateful to you, Graham, very grateful. Sort of thing that doesn't get forgotten in a company like this. By the way, though, I'm sure I don't need to say that you may need a touch of the kid gloves with old George. Tact, you know.'

'I can handle George,' said Graham with a smile.

Stella gave him a puzzled look when he came into her office. Perhaps he had been a little brusque in getting her out of the house the evening before. Or perhaps she was still shocked by the violence of his assault. Still, she had been begging for it all weekend.

He winked, but her reaction remained ambivalent.

'Thank you very much for the weekend,' he whispered. 'You really . . . I can't tell you how much you helped me.'

She didn't appreciate the irony of his words, and softened. After the hurried parting, all she needed that morning was the reassurance that he was still interested. She looked hopeful, anticipating perhaps some new assignation, so he moved on quickly. 'Can't talk now. George in?'

She nodded and, without knocking, Graham pushed into the inner office. Once again the old man looked as if he'd been caught playing with himself.

'Oh, er, Graham, hello. Terrible, this, about Bob, isn't it?'

'Frightful.'

'Must be absolutely awful for you in particular.'

Graham looked up in surprise as George expanded his remark. 'I mean, to have lost Merrily and then, so soon after, to lose such a close colleague . . . I mean, you and Bob were chums, weren't you?'

Good God, if George thought that, he really was losing his marbles. Many remarks sprang to Graham's lips, but he contented himself with, 'It's very sad.'

'Yes, lucky you weren't sailing with him this weekend.'

'Sure.'

'Though apparently Terry's all right.'

'What? Terry? Terry who?' The old boy's mind has really gone.

'Terry Sworder. Didn't you know? Terry Sworder was staying with Bob this weekend. He went sailing with him.'

Graham gaped.

'Apparently he was in the—what? Dinghy, fender . . . whatever they call it, when the fire started. He was blown free by the blast. Bob wasn't so lucky.'

Graham's throat was dry. He seemed once again to taste salt in his mouth.

'Wh . . . where's Terry now? Is he in today?'

'No.'

'What, in hospital?'

'No, he wasn't hurt much. Just shock, I think. No, I had a call from him.'

'Oh yes?'

'He's with the police.'

'Why?'

'Well, he's a witness, Graham. Obviously. He saw exactly what happened.'

CHAPTER TWENTY-EIGHT

He was back to being an amateur. Constantly fear took hold of Graham and shook him. Sweat oozed coldly from his body. He started at every knock on his office door, every ring from the phone, every stranger he met in the corridor. Each one could be the summons, the polite voice of officialdom asking for a few words in connection with the death of Robert Benham. And this time there would be no easy let-off, no grieving widower to be distracted by commiseration. This crime wasn't on Laker's patch, this one, he felt sure, was being investigated by a mind as cold-blooded and as logical as his own.

As he thought of this, he realised what a blazing trail he had left. He had been relying on the assumption of an accident; once the idea of crime had been planted in an investigator's mind, there were any number of pointers that would lead straight back to Graham Marshall.

Suppose his shoes had been washed up. Or the brand-new waders. It wouldn't be hard to trace those back to Farlow's in Pall Mall and, even though he had paid cash, he was sure that his ignorance of technical details, where he was going to fish and so on, had made him memorable to the rather snooty assistant.

Then there were footprints or fingerprints. It was only canteen conjecture that most of *Tara's Dream* had been immolated. Robert might have been killed just by the blast and the fire quickly extinguished. Graham thought uncomfortably of all those shining fibreglass surfaces and bitterly regretted his omission of rubber gloves.

Or the car might have been seen, its number memorised and traced back to the hire firm. Thence to George Brewer and, once he had been eliminated, suspicion could not be long in moving to his assistant.

Then there were the clothes in the skip in Haslemere . . . Everything he thought of had the same effect. It was as if, suspended over his head, was a huge black arrow with the legend 'HE DID IT'.

The rest of the Monday in the office was excruciating, but even then, through his fear, Graham could see once again how his emotions were misinterpreted. Everyone recognised his state of tension, but everyone put it down to shock at the news of Robert Benham's death. Rather than revulsion, the murderer attracted sympathy.

Things were even worse when he returned home. He was back to the state he had been in after killing the old man. There was no confident glow, no feeling of immunity, of being set above the herd. Graham Marshall felt terrified, and abjectly ashamed of his own incompetence.

He couldn't eat, but managed to drink a lot of whisky. He tried watching television, but nothing could engage his attention for more than a few minutes.

Sleep was as much out of the question as eating, and Graham spent the night in the sitting-room, where Sunday papers were still scattered over the floor. He drank steadily and the whisky aggravated the rancid taste of fear at the back of his mouth.

His thoughts spiralled ever downwards. At one point, for the first time in his life, he contemplated suicide. Death, he knew, had power, and bringing about his own might perhaps be the last expression of that power he could achieve.

But the idea did not stay with him long. He knew he lacked the kind of nerve the act required and, besides, even at this nadir of his hopes, some tiny glimmer remained. His luck had been incredible over the last few months; why shouldn't his ration last just a little longer?

The deepest of his pain came from the knowledge that he

was no longer in control of events. Nothing he could do now could either slow down or accelerate the investigation into Benham's death. He could only sit and wait. And go through the motions of as normal a life as possible.

He bathed at about six and put on clean clothes, but the change didn't refresh him. The whisky, of which he had consumed the best part of a bottle, had not made him drunk, but left him with a grinding headache.

He geared himself up to leaving at the normal time for work, and then remembered he had arranged to go in late. The Post Office engineer was coming that morning to make the connections for the Ansaphone in his study.

Now even having the device seemed pointless. He tried to recall in what mood of euphoria he had bought it and realised, with shame, that it had been simply in imitation of Robert Benham. So much of his recent motivation had been to reproduce the lifestyle of his latest victim. In Graham's current state, it all seemed rather petty.

He also shared, for the first time, some of the belittling contempt for the Personnel Department which prevailed throughout the rest of Crasoco. Even the job for which he had strived so hard, he realised, was a failure's job, chief elephant in the elephant's graveyard. He had taken all the risks for nothing.

Cramming himself into normality like a smaller man's clothes, he waited for the Post Office engineer, then watched the fitting of the new jack plug and made suitable jokes about the sort of outgoing messages he could leave. When the engineer departed, Graham congratulated himself that the man would have found nothing untoward in his client's behaviour.

But that small triumph gave only brief respite from the fear. Next Graham had to go into the office.

Terry Sworder was sitting at his desk. The right side of his face was red. His eyebrows and the fringe of his hair were frazzled to wisps of woodshaving.

Graham was momentarily immobilised by shock, then felt a perverse kind of relief. At least now he could find out how much the police knew, and begin to put some timelimit on his fate.

'Terry, are you all right?' he asked as he sat down.

'Still pretty shaken.' The young man withdrew a thin cigar from his mouth with trembling hand as if to emphasise the point. 'Physically O.K. But it's the shock, you know.'

'Of course. What actually happened?'

In the previous forty-eight hours Terry Sworder had become accustomed to this question and polished his reply into a neat little dramatic routine. But none of his audiences had listened to it with as much attention as the current one.

'It was terrible. So quick, for a start. And I was bloody lucky. What happened was . . .' He paused, warming to the performance. 'I was in the rubber dinghy and Bob had stepped on to the boat. He told me to hang on a min. till he'd opened the cabin, because it's fairly cramped in the well there, and fortunately I didn't tie the dinghy up, just hung on to the back. They reckon that's how I was saved from worse injury. Because what happened was, the minute Bob opens the hatch – woomph, the lot goes up like a bomb . . .'

Even through his anxiety Graham felt a little spurt of excitement.

'Well, the blast tosses the dinghy back just like it was a balloon and that's what saves me. It seems I keep hanging on to a bit of rope on the dinghy's side and, God, I go through the water upside down, arse over tit, don't know where I am. When I come to, I'm beside the dinghy and that's upside down and deflating fast, and I'm still hanging on to this bit of rope.'

'What about *Tara's Dream*?'

Terry Sworder would not have his narrative hurried. 'And I look across the waves and there I see this great column of flame on the water, and black smoke pouring out above it. There's other boats rushing there to help, but *Tara's Dream* burnt down to the waterline before anyone can do anything.

214

Then there's this great hiss and a load of steam and what-have-you. And down she goes.'

'The weight of the keel . . .'

'That's it. And whatever's left of Bob gone down with it.'

'Yes.' Well, at least it had worked. There was comfort in that. And not much had been left for forensic examination – also a bonus. But there remained a grave danger to Graham's safety, a danger that the accident's witness could unwittingly have unleashed in his account to the police.

Graham shook his head. 'It's terrible, really terrible.' Time for the big question. 'How do the police reckon it happened?'

'Well, it was the Calor Gas of course that went up. Must've leaked. The police don't reckon Bob would have left it on by mistake. He was too careful for that. Anyway, he hadn't been on the boat for a couple of weeks, and most of the gas would probably have leaked out and dispersed in that time if it had been left on.'

'Oh?' Graham had difficulty keeping the tension out of his voice.

'No, what they reckon happened was that the boy from the boatyard who changed the cylinder, he left it on.'

Another 'Oh', equally non-committal.

'Apparently, Bob gets down there so rarely, so pushed for time usually, that he gets the boatyard to do all that routine stuff, so's the boat's ready to sail when he wants it, see. And this poor sod who changed the cylinder must've left it turned on. Only put in last Friday, so just nice time to build up a really explosive mixture of gas and air.'

Graham could hardly believe how miraculously everything had worked to his advantage. One detail remained, though, one detail that could either destroy him or free him for life.

'But what on earth sparked it off? Surely there must have been a flame or something to . . . ?'

Terry Sworder hung his head. 'This is where I feel really shitty, Graham. You know, like guilty. Just when we were in the dinghy on the way out, I gave him one.'

'One what?'

215

'One of these.' Terry gestured with the little cigar in his hand. 'He said, no, not so early in the morning, and I said go on and he . . . well . . .'

The young man shook his head. Perhaps it was as well that he wasn't looking and didn't see the blaze of joy in his colleague's eye.

Graham could hardly contain himself. He had won; everything was on his side; now he was truly invincible.

But he controlled his exhilaration. He too shook his head and murmured, 'Terrible business.'

Then he looked firmly at the young computer expert.

'Still, life has to go on. Work in particular has to go on. You know that Human Resources survey you were doing for Robert . . .'

'Yes. The model for –'

'When were you reckoning to finish?'

'I don't know . . . Ten days . . . ? Mind you, now Bob's not around, I don't know whether –'

'I'd like it by the end of this week,' said the Assistant Head of Personnel.

CHAPTER TWENTY-NINE

It was just under a fortnight till George Brewer was finally to leave, but Graham Marshall could do a lot in a fortnight. All the old sporting imagery reasserted itself. He felt he was in peak condition, had just put in another superlative performance and was equal to any new challenge that might be thrown at him.

His first move was to be nice to Terry Sworder. Rather than treating the young man like some boffin unfit for civilised society, as he had done in the past, Graham started to take an interest, and even had the humility to let Terry show off some of his beloved computers. Graham understood little, but he was properly appreciative and afterwards took his guide to the company bar, where he was introduced to more of the staff who had risen on computer skills. He proved to them to be affable and properly impatient of the company's laggardly approach to the new technology.

At the same time Graham started to be less nice to George Brewer. He had never doubted his influence over the older man, but always previously had humoured George's rambles through his early days in the company, problems with *The Times* crossword and increasingly maudlin melancholia. Now he showed less patience, and was often short to the point of brusqueness.

He also began to disparage his retiring boss behind his back, in the canteen, or the company bar, or round the office. This he did with some subtlety. He knew a complete volte-face would be suspect and so only hinted his criticisms. He gave the impression of a man who had gone along with his superior's ideas from a misplaced sense of loyalty, but whose mask, as that superior's departure grew more imminent, was beginning to crack. Though it hurt him to disagree with George, he really didn't feel he could hold back his real views much longer.

The most public difference between the two came at another of George Brewer's farewell drinks parties. This one was set up to coincide with the visit of some of the company's top brass from the Middle East. Among these were a couple of old mates of George's and once again the conviviality of the occasion lifted him out of his habitual depression.

'God, when I think back to how we started . . .' He was addressing a massively fat red-faced man in a blazer, and Graham stood by his side. 'All very *ad hoc*, wasn't it? If any calculations needed doing, did them on the back of an envelope, or a Craven 'A' packet or whatever was to hand. None of these bloody calculators and computers and . . . dear, oh dear. Mind you, we didn't often get the answers wrong, did we?'

With a guffaw, the fat man agreed that they didn't.

'Don't see the need for it all myself,' George continued. 'Technology for its own sake, I call it. Glad I'm getting out before the bloody government makes understanding it compulsory!'

This merited another guffaw from both of them, though George's was muted by the mention of his impending departure. He picked himself out of the trough by turning to Graham for support. 'I've been lucky, though, having an assistant who thought the same as me.'

'Not about everything, George,' Graham interposed gently.

'No, no, of course not. Had our disagreements, but in outline . . . thought on the same lines. Neither of us had a lot of time for the Space Invaders, eh?'

'Well, I know you didn't, George, but I always rather thought you underestimated the contribution computer science could make to our business.'

George just stared, his mind not working fast enough to catch up with this new development.

'Sorry, George, but since you raise the subject, I'm afraid I've always found your attitude rather head-in-the-sand. I think if we'd put more reliance on computers a few years earlier, you'd be leaving a much more efficient Department.'

There was a silence. It had been said quietly, but enough people had heard. Graham gave a little diffident smile. 'Sorry,' he lied, 'but you did ask.'

George looked pained and confused. To cover his embarrassment he reached in his pockets for another of his little cigarettes. He put it in his mouth and blinked around for a light.

Graham's hand was instinctively in his pocket, but he was relieved not to find his lighter there. Must have mislaid it. Good. His toadying to George Brewer was at an end.

The other crease on the surface of his life that needed ironing out was Stella. He felt nothing for her. She had done all that he had needed at the weekend in her role as safety net, and, though it now seemed unlikely that his alibi would ever be checked, he was glad that he had taken the precaution.

Now she had outgrown her usefulness – though, from the odd whispered aside in the office, it appeared that she was unaware of that. She evidently had seen the weekend as the beginning of a relationship. It was a notion from which she had to be disabused.

He could of course just tell her to get lost, but Graham didn't want to draw attention to himself. Given her proximity to him in the department, that approach could lead to undesirable scenes along the corridors.

No, obviously he had to let her down gently. He managed another wine-bar drink after work, but regretfully cried off the next weekend on the grounds that he was sorting out the children's final transfer to Islington.

He didn't want to repeat the physical encounter of the previous weekend. Complete insensitivity to desire had returned after that savage moment of triumph, He was not sure whether any women would be involved in his new lifestyle, but he knew that if he did look for other companions, they would need to be more glamorous than Stella.

So he resorted to the established company procedure for shaking her off. On the Friday afternoon, five days after Robert's death, Graham went to see the Secretarial Organiser, Miss Pridmore, known throughout the company, with typical office wit, as 'Head of Secs'. She was a daunting lady of stout moral principles, who ruled her charges like a malign Mother Superior.

He took great pleasure in telling her at least an edited version of the truth. 'I'm sorry, Miss Pridmore. I'm sure you've heard this sort of tale before, but mine has a rather nasty twist. No doubt most executives are worried that their wives will discover about their liaisons with secretaries. In my case I'm afraid it was because of my wife's death that the liaison started. I've been in a very confused state since it happened and . . .'

He was good. He knew he was good. As he shed more and more of his real emotions, the ability to manufacture convincing imitations increased.

Miss Pridmore was of course disapproving, but also sympathetic. She could understand the anguish he must be going through. And yes, of course, it would be advisable to have the girl in question transferred to another department. No, it wouldn't be done straight away. And yes, it would be done discreetly. Of course.

And so, following the anti-feminist convention that still rules in most offices, Graham's inconvenience would be removed.

Robert Benham's funeral was scheduled for the following Monday. This delighted Graham; he knew it meant there had been no awkwardnesses at the inquest.

The ceremony was in Rugby and a contingent of half a dozen from Crasoco attended. Tara Liston was there, attracting a couple of local newspaper photographers, and Robert Benham also proved to have had a mother, father and two sisters.

Like Merrily's, the ceremony was a cremation and, as the velvet curtains did their dramatic close, Graham couldn't help wondering how much of the body was left to cremate. He felt better than at any other time in his life.

On the train back to London, most of the time was spent in the buffet. At one point, Graham found himself alone over a drink with David Birdham.

'Know I shouldn't really talk business at a time like this . . .'

'Business doesn't stop, Graham. It goes on, whatever happens.'

'Yes. Well, just to say there'll be a report on your desk tomorrow morning. A model, a sort of blueprint for the future of Personnel Department over the next decade. Some of it's quite strong. There'll be people who don't like it.'

'Who's done it?'

'Well, obviously, the computer boys have helped out on the figures, but . . . the thinking's mine.'

The Managing Director smiled. 'I will read it with interest, Graham.'

CHAPTER THIRTY

The next day Graham didn't wear a tie to the office. At lunchtime he went out and bought a dark brown leather jacket, cut on casual lines. After work he had fixed to join George Brewer for a drink, but he stood his boss up. Instead, he had an estate-agent-guided tour round a new block of service flats just off Sloane Street. A one-bedroom studio cost almost exactly what he had been offered on the Boileau Avenue house. The flats appealed to him. Without furniture, with bare polished floors and newly white walls, they appealed to him a lot. Hotel-like, uncluttered, anonymous.

When he got back that evening there was a message on the Ansaphone from Charmian. She sounded extremely angry. It was ten days since he had last seen Henry and Emma and since then he hadn't even phoned to check that they were still alive. What kind of father was he? Had he no interest at all in his children?

The final question was easily answered, but there seemed little point in ringing Charmian to tell her. Instead, he wrote to his bank manager, arranging the agreed monthly standing order into his sister-in-law's account. After that, he felt he had fulfilled his paternal duty.

It was on the Thursday that the summons to David Birdham's office came through. Terry Sworder's report lay on the Managing Director's desk.

'It's good, Graham, bloody good. Pulls no punches. Lot of redundancies, though. Many people won't like that.'

Graham shrugged. 'You can't make an omelette without cracking a few eggs.'

'Oh, sure, sure. And I could nominate a few eggs in Personnel Department who are ripe for cracking. What I'm saying is, it's one thing to produce a report like this, it's another to put it into practice. Whoever does it is going to have to work very hard and be prepared to make himself unpopular.'

'I'm sure it could be done.'

'By the right person, yes.' David Birdham toyed with a paperknife. 'Management has known for some time that this sort of shake-up was needed. We're not daft, you know, we do notice things. But, though he's been a brake on progress for years, we wanted to hang on till George went. Not just sentimental, we could easily have put him out to grass even earlier, but we didn't want any half-measures. Which was why Benham was appointed. He seemed to have the right thick-skinned qualities for the job. It needed a blunt instrument and he fitted the bill. We all felt that you . . . were too much of a traditionalist, too tarred with George's brush . . .'

Graham was silent, waiting.

'And then you send me a report like this.' David Birdham tapped the papers on his desk. 'It is exactly what is needed, and I won't say I'm not surprised that it came from you. You always seemed to follow George's line.'

'I suppose that was out of . . . what? Loyalty?' Graham poised the word diffidently.

'Loyalty can be dangerous in business. Lost you the job the last time around.'

'Yes.'

David Birdham rose from his chair and walked across to the window. He spoke with his back to his junior. 'Listen, Graham, I want you to take over from George next week. I've spoken to most of the board and most of them'll accept any recommendation of mine. May have a bit of a problem with the Staff Association over the job not being properly advertised, but we can ride that. Thing is, these are exceptional circumstances, with the Heir Apparent dying before the old

223

King goes, and in my view a quick decision is needed. Nothing like an interregnum to get a department out of hand. And since there's no doubt you were runner-up last time round, I think you should definitely have the job. What do you say, Graham?'

He had done it. The failures of the last two and a half months had been wiped away and he stood where he had hoped to stand. But his position was so much stronger; three murders had elevated him way beyond his prosaic former hopes.

'It's a big challenge, David,' he said grittily, 'but it's one that I'd welcome, and one that I feel confident I can cope with.'

'Good man.' The Managing Director turned, came towards him and shook his hand. 'I'm relying on your discretion. All got to be hush-hush at the moment. Certain amount of bumf has to be passed around before we can make any official announcements. So keep it under your hat, eh? Don't tell anyone, even at home . . .'

David Birdham realised what he had said and coloured. For the first time in Graham's memory, the man looked embarrassed. 'I'm sorry. Insensitive. I mean . . . Well, all I hope is that your taking over the job will be some – of course inadequate – compensation to you after your wife's death.'

Graham made his smile of response properly reflective, the smile of a man who has just been reminded of his greatest sadness rather than one of his greatest triumphs.

George Brewer's previous farewell celebrations had been local, carving up little sectors of different departments, but the one which started at six o'clock in the eighth-floor conference room on his final Friday of employment included everyone.

Its guest of honour seemed subdued, if not downright depressed. Whereas the previous crowds had lifted him to a feverish jollity, on this occasion the reality of his departure seemed to crush his spirit. He no longer had merry quips of golf and gardening to answer the enquiries about how he

224

would spend his retirement; he replied, 'I don't know. I just don't know how I'm going to fill the time.' He no longer even pretended to crow at the prospect of increased leisure and his index-linked pension, but listened wistfully as his colleagues inadvertently excluded him by their talk of future plans. He looked like a man on the edge of a dark precipice, afraid and ignorant of how far he had to fall.

His assistant, by contrast, was in ebulliently cheerful mood. He chatted lightly with his older colleagues and his new friends from Operational Research. He had whispered, complicit conversations with members of senior management. He flirted harmlessly with secretaries under the benign eye of Miss Pridmore. And every now and then, when someone mentioned his late wife, he looked appropriately grave.

He saw Stella from time to time. She tried to pierce his bonhomie with meaningful looks, but achieved no deeper conversational engagement than the other girls. At one point she actually took his arm and hissed, 'When are we going to see each other again, Graham?'

'Soon, soon,' he replied airily, and whisked away to share a joke with Terry Sworder.

Eventually, after a great deal of drinking, a glass was tapped for silence and David Birdham gave a brief, professional encomium on George Brewer. He started with an ancient, mildly risqué anecdote of George and a long-vanished secretary at a conference in Manchester, which achieved the required raucous laugh, then moved on to list the Head of Department's qualities of good humour, patience and common sense, and to say how much they would be missed. He made a brief reference to 'the cloud cast by recent events' and assured 'George's successor, whoever he might be' that he'd have a tough job in maintaining the high standards of his predecessor. David Birdham did not mention his personal view that George was 'losing his marbles' and had been 'a brake on progress for years'. In conclusion, he asked everyone to raise their glasses to George Brewer, as Miss Pridmore wheeled in the gift to which they had all so generously contributed – a new golf trolley.

After the applause had died down, George made a broken-backed little speech of thanks. Perhaps he was drunk, perhaps it was emotion, but he kept losing his thread. He mistimed his jokes, stuttered his gratitude, and kept reaching the same impasse when he mentioned what he would do in the future. Eventually he was left just looking at the golf trolley, which, like the previous gift of Newton's Balls for his desk, now seemed only to advertise the emptiness of his life.

As the speech spiralled down to silence, David Birdham took the executive decision of shouting 'Jolly good show, George', and leading a round of applause.

After that the assembly dispersed rather quickly. Groups of the younger ones adjourned to pubs, the board members went down to their drivers, and members of the Personnel Department queued for final handshakes and farewell quips. One little group of hard-core drinkers, which Graham noticed included Stella, stayed resolutely and rowdily together, while the uniformed waitresses circled, collecting plates and glasses and putting away the remaining wine bottles.

'I think I'd better go,' said George abruptly in the middle of a long-winded effusion from the internal postman, and moved unsteadily but quickly over to the anteroom where the coats had been dumped.

Goodbye, George, thought Graham. Last I'll ever see of you, you boring old fool.

Then he saw the gleaming golf trolley, abandoned and forlorn. Oh, God, last thing he wanted when he took over the reins on Monday was George stumbling in to collect his present.

With a cheery cry of 'Forgetful to the last' tossed towards the group of drinkers, Graham pushed the trolley after its owner.

He stopped in the doorway. George was fumbling on the floor. The volume of coats had pulled down a hat stand and he couldn't identify his 'British Warm'.

'I've got something of yours, George,' Graham pronounced

226

jovially.

The fuddled, sad eyes looked up at him. Then George rose and put a hand in his pocket. 'I've got something of yours, too, Graham.'

He withdrew the hand. On his palm lay Graham's gold cigarette lighter.

'Thank you. I noticed I'd lost it somewhere. Never thought I'd see it again. Did I leave it in your office?'

'No.'

'Oh. Where did you find it then?'

'That's the strange thing,' said George Brewer slowly. 'It came in the post this morning. Addressed to me. From some car-hire firm. Apparently they'd found it in one of their cars.'

CHAPTER THIRTY-ONE

Graham went down by the stairs. He waited in the shadows of the Reception area until the lift arrived. The doors opened and George stumbled out, suddenly shorter and more bent, pulling his golf trolley incongruously behind him.

Only one door was left open at that time of night and George had difficulty negotiating the trolley through it. Going down the steps to the pavement was also awkward. Graham did not emerge from the building until his quarry was moving along smoothly.

He had to find out how much George knew, or how much he had pieced together. In his fuddled state, the old man had not elaborated, simply handed the lighter over, apparently more struck by the unusual circumstances of its return than suspicious as to how it might have got into a hire-car. But he wouldn't stay drunk for ever, and there had to come a moment when he started to ask questions. Graham knew he must speak before that moment arrived, must pre-empt suspicion by some spurious explanation. He didn't know what it was yet, but he felt confident he'd think of something.

In the meantime he would follow his former boss and choose his moment to speak.

George Brewer moved automatically. His footsteps had trodden the same route every day for over thirty years and no amount of bitter reflection would allow them to deviate. He forgot about his farcical appendage, the golf trolley, until he came to the steps down to Oxford Circus Underground Station.

The almost expired season ticket was flashed at a collector deep in his newspaper and then George had to balance his trophy, his reward for all those years of service, on the unfolding escalator. That task, and the darkness of his thoughts, made him oblivious of his colleague at the ticket machine.

Graham was annoyed. He shouldn't have dawdled playing the private detective. He should have confronted George before, explained about the lighter, settled the business. Now he had to go through the rigmarole of going down on to the platform and accosting the old man there.

George lived in Haywards Heath, so caught the Victoria Line Southbound to Victoria. It was about half-past nine. The station was relatively empty; the drink-after-the-office commuters had gone, and the cinemas and restaurants had yet to disgorge their home-going crowds.

The trailing golf trolley was slowing George down, and Graham was close behind when they came off the second escalator. He could have spoken, called out, but he didn't.

George suddenly put on a spurt, an asthmatic run, as he saw the silver screen of a train across the end of the passage. But it was too late. The windows started to slide past. He had missed it. He stopped, panting, while the few unloaded passengers drifted past him. Then he moved forward on to the platform.

Graham stayed, apparently absorbed in a cinema poster. He told himself he was trying to perfect his explanation of the lighter, but he no longer believed it. A pulse of excitement throbbed inside him.

George stood with his back to the passage. He was holding the trolley handle with his right hand, while he looked from his watch to the indicator board. Graham checked no one was behind him and moved on to the platform.

A look to either side. No one but George had missed the train.

It took one quick, firm shove.

*

Graham was walking back along the passage before George hit the rails, so he didn't see the flash as the metal of the golf trolley made contact. Nor the great shudder that whiplashed through his former boss's body.

He strolled along, following the 'Way Out' signs, and dumped his ticket in front of the still-reading collector, who was never going to check why a ticket printed at Oxford Circus should be delivered there.

Up on street level, he felt the excitement breaking out, tingling like sweat all over his body. He looked at his watch. It was only seven minutes since he had left the Crasoco tower.

His mind was working very clearly. He knew exactly what he had to do. He walked briskly, but not hurriedly, back to the office.

He had been prepared to go all the way up to the conference room, but was saved the trouble. Stella and a couple of other tittering secretaries were just emerging from the lift.

He walked straight towards her.

'I waited for you,' he said.

The other two secretaries split off, giggling, armed with new gossip-fodder for the canteen. Stella gazed up at him. Her eyes were unfocused with alcohol, but full of relief and trust.

They took a cab to her flat. As soon as they were inside the door he seized her. He closed his eyes as their flesh joined, and the recollection of that one push, the image of George Brewer frozen untidily in mid-air, gave Graham Marshall's body a violent power.

CHAPTER THIRTY-TWO

The news of George Brewer's suicide, spreading round the office on the Monday morning, prompted much chattering and excitement, but compared to Robert Benham's death, it was a small sensation.

Partly, this was because it had very little surprise value. When most of the staff actually thought about it, they could see that George had been headed that way for a long time. Since the death of his wife, work had been his whole life, and he had made no secret of the dread with which he contemplated the void ahead of him. He was not the first to have done away with himself after a retirement party, and would probably not be the last.

So, though everyone was of course suitably sorry and management tutted over another half-day to be wasted at another funeral, they could recognise the logic of the death. In a way it tidied George up and absolved them from guilt. The idea of his spiralling down to alcoholism in Haywards Heath might have been a spur to recrimination; the idea of him dead made a neat close to his particular chapter of company history.

Graham moved into George's office 'for convenience', and to give Terry Sworder more room. Terry, he had decided, would, once the Head of Personnel appointment had been officially ratified, make an excellent assistant. His research capabilities, coupled with Graham's ruthless vision, would make an invincible combination.

Stella was not treated in anything more than a professional

231

way, and was kept busy through the day as Graham fired off salvoes of memos and letters under his 'Assistant Head of Personnel' title. In the afternoon she was called to Miss Pridmore's office, whence she returned in tears, but Graham didn't have the time to ask her the reason.

By the end of the week, Stella was working on the Secretarial Reserve, prior to taking up a more permanent position in another department.

And by the end of the week, too, George Brewer was, like Merrily Marshall and Robert Benham, a mere scattering of ash in a Garden of Remembrance.

Graham worked late on the Friday evening. It was to be a long weekend, with the Spring Bank Holiday on the Monday, and there were preparations he wanted to make for the next week. He also knew that David Birdham was in a management meeting, and half-expected the phone to ring with confirmation of the new Head of Personnel appointment. But it was a confident, not a desperate hope; Graham knew the job was his.

So, though there had been no message, he left the office at eight without anxiety. As he walked out of the Crasoco tower, he felt good. It was a week after George Brewer's death and Graham Marshall felt he deserved a treat. So, without going home first, he took himself out for an expensive dinner at the Grange. He felt no strangeness in being on his own, though as he looked at the pampered couples around him, he wondered if maybe, in time, he might once again look for a female escort. Have to be very glamorous, of course, to match his new status.

Tara Liston, now . . . Hmm. Perhaps he ought to send her a note of sympathy after Robert's death . . .

It was a thought. No hurry, though. He was under no pressure of any sort. He had all the time in the world.

He arrived home after eleven, pleasantly drunk, went straight to bed and slept for twelve hours. All the tensions of the last weeks had caught up with him and, as he relaxed, he felt unbelievably tired. What he needed now was a slow wind-down over the Bank Holiday weekend; he needed to cosset, to pamper himself a little.

He might have slept longer than twelve hours, if he had not been wakened by the sound of a key in the front door lock. He swayed, blinking, on the stairs and looked down into the hall to see Lilian Hinchcliffe.

She looked wizened and unkempt, and was weighed down by a large handbag.

He yawned. 'Good morning. To what do I owe this pleasure?'

She was silent as he came down the stairs and did not move until he was on the same level. Then, with surprising speed, she snatched something out of her handbag and, with a cry of 'You're not going to get away with it, Graham!' launched herself at him.

He was heavy with sleep and unprepared for the attack, but he managed to ward off the upraised knife, though it gouged through the dressing-gown fabric into his forearm. The pain stung him to action. With his right hand he gripped the knife-wrist, at the same time jerking his elbow up against Lilian's chin.

Her free hand clawed up at his face, scoring lines of pain as he snatched his head away. He leant back against the stairs, pulling her off-balance, then slammed her right wrist hard against the newel post until the knife clattered from her grasp. As he did it, he felt the heavy handbag thumping against his side and her free hand clutching on to his ear.

He shook himself painfully free and reached out his right hand to clamp round her jaw, forcing the mouth open as he pushed her away to arm's length. From there her reach was too short to do any harm to his body and she had to content herself with scratching and pinching at his hand.

'What the bloody hell's all this for?' Graham demanded.

'I'm going to kill you!' she screamed, fluttering ineffectually in his grasp.

'Why?' His tone, he knew, was one of infuriating irony.

'Because you're mad.'

Again the word stung and, before he was aware of doing it, he brought the back of his left hand hard against her mouth. She wheezed with pain and her struggling stopped. A gleam of blood showed where the lip had bruised against her teeth.

'Now come on.' Graham had control of himself again. 'What are you talking about?'

'You killed Merrily.'

He laughed aloud and, still keeping his mother-in-law at arm's length, propelled her into the sitting-room. He positioned her in front of an armchair and gave a little push. She subsided, the violence drained out of her.

Graham sat down on the sofa. 'So I killed Merrily, did I?'

'Yes.'

'If that's the case, how come the police didn't mention it at the inquest? How come that even their second investigation, prompted by your poison-pen letter, also drew a blank?'

Lilian had coloured at the mention of the letter. 'I know you hated her, Graham. Look at you, you haven't shown a moment of regret since she died. You were just delighted to get rid of her, and the children and me.'

'That is hardly a crime,' Graham drawled. 'I think you'd find a good few husbands who, offered the opportunity of painlessly shedding their families, would leap at the chance.'

'You planned it all. You knew it was going to happen. While you were in Brussels, while Merrily was looking after the house and tidying up for you, you knew she was doomed.'

'Any proof?' he asked, with a needling smile.

'I haven't any proof about the electricity. I've got proof . . . proof that . . .' She lost momentum suddenly, her bluster deflated. She tried to disguise the look but Graham had seen her eyes drop to the handbag slumped at her feet.

'What's in there, Lilian?'

She made only token resistance as he snatched the bag from her and drew out its contents.

'Well, well, well.' He separated the words with slow irony.

He held up the sherry bottle. Time had not helped to

234

dissolve its contents. Still through the green glass he could see the strange sediment of blue granules. Still over the label was stuck his own felt-penned warning: 'POISON. NOT TO BE TAKEN.'

'So where did you get this from, Lilian?'

'Merrily tidied the shed.' Her voice was sulky and resigned. 'Two days before she died. I helped her.'

Of course. Merrily's last accusatory gesture, the preparation for the scene of marital recrimination she did not survive to play.

'And you found this bottle. What did Merrily say?'

He was unworried, but intrigued. Had the discovery alerted Merrily's suspicions? He liked the idea, liked the idea of his wife's fearing him, of her last mortal thought in the loft, as the current slammed through her, being the realisation of her husband's power.

Lilian flushed. 'Merrily . . . didn't see the bottle.'

He understood. His mother-in-law, thinking it to be full, had snatched the sherry from the shelf and hidden it in her bag.

'And you only saw the "POISON" label when you got it home?'

She was too depleted to make any attempt at denial.

'Oh, Lilian.' He shook his head in mock-sympathy. Then changed his tone. 'You spoke of this as proof. Proof of what, may I ask?'

'Proof that you planned Merrily's death,' she replied, emptying her diminished arsenal of defiance.

'How does this prove that?' He held the bottle daintily between thumb and forefinger. 'Merrily died in an electrical accident due to faulty wiring in an old house.'

'This bottle proves that you planned to kill her, that you tried out poison as a first option, that you hoped you might be able to make her drink it in error, that then you realised it wouldn't work and . . .'

The words could have been worrying, so close did they come to the truth, but the tone of defeat with which they were delivered and the hopelessness in which they petered out, showed how little even their speaker was convinced by them. With a little surge of delight, Graham realised again his immunity, his invisibility from the searching eyes of suspicion.

'And this bottle proves all that?' He placed it on the mantelpiece and shook his head. 'Why now suddenly? Why didn't you produce your "evidence" when you sent off your letter to the police?'

'I hadn't worked it all out then,' she mumbled.

'And you still haven't,' he riposted harshly. 'Still haven't by a mile. Because there's nothing to work out. God knows what play this scene comes from, Lilian, but, as ever, you're all melodrama – you always have been. With you, everything gets inflated into full-scale comic opera. Whether it's how Charmian's behaved, or do your grandchildren love you, or your non-affair with the late, great, *gay* William Essex, it all –' He stopped for her to speak, but she thought better of her interruption, so he continued. 'It all gets overblown and ridiculous. Which is one of the reasons why I am glad to be shot of you. But . . .' He raised a finger to silence her. 'But it's now ceasing to be funny. Any more allegations of murder and I'll have you prosecuted. I don't think the police are going to be over-imp.essed by your sherry bottle. They might if it had been found in the shed the week after Merrily's death, but now . . . well, you could so easily have set it up to frame me. They're already suspicious of you, Lilian. I actually had to deter them from taking action after the letter. Now there's this knife attack this morning. Bother me again, Lilian, and I'll get you put away.'

She was still silent as he rose. 'I am going to get dressed. When I come down again, I would prefer not to find you here. Oh, and, incidentally, I will be watching out for further knife attacks.'

At the door he stopped, curious. 'By the way, what was the knife attack in aid of? Did you intend to kill me?'

'Yes,' she hissed. 'But not with the knife.'

'How then?'

She made a limp, disspirited gesture to the bottle on the mantelpiece.

'You were going to make me drink that?' He could hardly believe her little nod of assent. 'At knife point?'

The second small nod released his laughter. The joke still seemed good as he picked up the knife in the hall and placed it out of harm's way. And during the leisurely process of shaving and dressing, little chuckles kept bubbling through.

When he went back down to the sitting-room, Lilian was still there. She appeared not to have moved. Her face sagged, old and wretched.

'I am going out,' Graham announced. 'I'd be grateful if, when you go, you would leave my house key on the hall table. But if you don't, I am sure I can get it returned by my solicitors.'

He was at the door before she spoke.

'You killed Merrily, Graham. And I'm going to be revenged on you. If it's the last thing I do.'

'No, Lilian.' He favoured her with a condescending smile. 'Not even if it's the last thing you do.'

He walked out of the house to encounter a new problem.

It was a bright day, the green of the new leaves intensified by the sunlight. He started walking towards the river with no very clear intentions. He felt deliciously free; it didn't matter where he went, what he did.

'Graham.'

He turned at the sound of his name to see Stella hurrying towards him from a Mini parked opposite the house. He said nothing as she approached.

'Graham, I want to know what's happening.'

'Why are you here?' he asked coldly.

'I've got to see you.'

'You are seeing me. Why have you come here? Why are you stopping me in the street?'

'I was going to go to the house, but just as I got there a woman arrived.'

'My mother-in-law,' he enunciated. 'The mother of my late wife.'

'Graham . . .' Stella looked at him in a way that was meant to be appealing.

'What do you want?' He was getting annoyed. Fortunately there were few people around, but he didn't want scenes in the street.

'I want to know where we stand, Graham.'

He felt a flash of anger. Bloody women. Even someone like Stella, with her vaunted independence, Stella, the quick office fuck, wanted to immobilise him with commitment and responsibility.

'We stand apart,' he hissed.

She flinched as if he had hit her. Then, clenching back the tears, she announced quietly, 'Graham, you'll regret it. Just wait. Next time you want something from me, you're going to be disappointed.'

'I cannot envisage,' he replied, equally quietly, 'any occasion when I would ever want anything from you.'

That released the tears. 'You won't get away from me. I'll wait here for you, Graham. I'll get you!'

He walked away as she started to speak, and, though her voice came after him, it did not get any closer. He kept on walking and did not look back until he was at the end of Boileau Avenue. The Mini had not moved and he could see the hunched figure inside it.

By the time he reached Castelnau and the approach to Hammersmith Bridge, the glow of freedom had returned. With it came hunger. The morning's first interruption had kept him from his breakfast. He looked at his watch. One o'clock.

He went into a Mini-Market where he bought a couple of pork pies, an orange and two cans of beer. The Pakistani girl on the check-out did not look up as he handed over his money.

As he walked towards the bridge, there was a bubbling excitement inside his head. There was nothing to restrain him. Lilian. Stella. They were as irrelevant to his life as his dead

238

wife and his discarded children. No one was relevant but Graham Marshall.

Near the bridge he suddenly crossed the road and walked down to the tow-path. It was a little delaying tactic, a teasing foreplay before he revisited the scene of his triumph.

He walked along the towpath in front of St Paul's School Playing Fields and sat down on a bench to eat his picnic. The sun had summer force and glinted on the river before him. Must sort out a holiday, he thought, as he opened the second can of beer. Somewhere nice, abroad, luxurious.

He dawdled some of the way along the footpath towards Barnes Railway Bridge, prolonging the foreplay, but then gave in indulgently and returned to the scene of the old man's death. He lingered sentimentally by the parapet, even caressed the rail over which his first victim had plunged, already dead. He no longer feared drawing attention to himself. Graham Marshall was invisible, secure in his impenetrable aura of success.

He used his afternoon's freedom to go to the cinema in Hammersmith. The film was *Monty Python's Life of Brian*. The bits he saw he enjoyed, but the combination of his exhausted state and the lunchtime beer meant that he slept through most of it. He emerged round half-past five, feeling rested, and thought about going home.

But why should he? He had no reason to return to Boileau Avenue. There was nothing he wanted there – or, if Lilian or Stella were still around, there were things he positively didn't want there.

And he was, after all, meant to be pampering himself. For the first time in nearly fifteen years he was free to act on impulse.

An impulse decided him where he wanted to go.

He managed to get to a couple of King Street shops before they closed and bought a shirt, underwear, pyjamas and shaving tackle, together with a neat overnight case to put them in. Then, in spite of the afternoon traffic, with the luck that he knew now would never desert him, he hailed a cab and

239

told the driver to take him to Paddington Station.

He caught the next train to Oxford, and took a taxi to the Randolph Hotel. Yes, they did have a single room for two nights. Graham Marshall booked in.

He ate well, pampering himself. The credit cards could cope. Soon, after all, he would have the Head of Personnel's salary to fund him.

On the Saturday evening, as he drank through a second bottle of Chambolle Musigny, he thought about the sequence of events which had brought him to this point.

He was now where he should be. It was amusing to speculate what might have happened had he been appointed Head of Department when he first applied.

Presumably he would not have killed the old man. If they had met, Graham would not have felt the same repressed violence, and another derelict would have survived a few more years.

And if he had never inadvertently broken the taboo, presumably Merrily and Robert Benham would still be around to irritate and frustrate him. Even dear old George would be alive, drunk and lonely in Haywards Heath.

Graham Marshall couldn't regret any of it. The murders had given him strength when he needed it, identity and power when he had none.

He wondered again about Lilian's charge of madness. Certainly he had been in a tense state, yes; but not mad, no. He had been logical and efficient.

And, above all, it had worked.

Four murders. He couldn't resist a little, complacent smile at the thought.

But, with slight regret, he knew that that must be the end. His luck had been incredible, but the risk was always there. So many times he could have been seen and had proved invisible. So many times he could have been caught and hadn't. It was exhilarating, but dangerous.

Besides, he had achieved all that he had wanted.

He felt like a world motor racing champion retiring at the peak of his success. He had taken all the risks, he had survived, and could now enjoy the benefits of his achievement.

And, anyway, he reflected, if it became necessary, he could always come out of retirement.

With that comforting thought, he signed his dinner bill and retired to the delicious anonymity of his hotel room.

CHAPTER THIRTY-THREE

He pampered himself all weekend. Expensive meals, leisurely strolls around the colleges, a trip on the river. He felt he deserved it.

After a large lunch in the hotel on the Monday, he paid his bill with a credit card and had a taxi summoned to take him to the station.

He did not regret leaving. He felt rested and indulged and was keen to get back to work. The next day, whether or not the appointment was officially ratified, Graham Marshall would take over as Head of Personnel.

And he was determined that no one in the Department would be unaware of the change.

He took the Metropolitan Line from Paddington to Hammersmith and walked to Boileau Avenue.

He knew there was no one in when he put the key in the lock. Lilian must have taken her bitterness away, no doubt to plan further ineffectual gestures.

As he walked, he had been thinking. Except for another moment of homage on Hammersmith Bridge, he had concentrated on work. His mind was relaxed and well tuned, and he thought he saw a solution to an interminable dispute between Personnel Department and the Staff Association over a new grading system. The idea had grown as he walked along, and he was impatient to check its feasibility with some figures Terry Sworder had produced from the computer.

Graham rushed up to his study as soon as he got home and

pulled Terry's report out of his briefcase. He jotted a few notes as he galloped down the columns, then sat back with satisfaction. It would work. Put a few backs up, certainly, but his scheme had the required mix of appeal to greed and illusion of consultation; it couldn't fail to be accepted.

Preoccupied, he hadn't noticed until that moment the flashing light on his new Ansaphone, which registered the messages left. It had been switched on to record before he left on the Friday morning and he hadn't had time to check it since.

He was reaching to set the machine to 'Playback' when the phone rang. He switched off the recorder and picked up the receiver.

It was Charmian.

'Hello,' he responded guardedly, anticipating a new tirade about his shortcomings as a father.

'You've heard?'

'Heard what?'

'About . . . Mummy.'

'No.' What the hell had Lilian done now? But Charmian didn't give him any time for conjecture. 'She's dead.'

'Hmm?'

'She killed herself.'

'Good God.' Graham provided a conventional response while he tried to define what his real reaction was. He rather suspected it might be delight.

'I've been trying to contact you for the best part of forty-eight hours. So have the police. Where've you been?'

'Out,' he replied laconically.

'So she finally succeeded. Obviously it wasn't all talk. I should have listened, should have . . .' Charmian's voice broke. The shock had transformed her bottled-up emotion for her mother into guilt.

'Well, I suppose it was only to be expected.' He spoke with judicious authority, a detached voice of reason.

'Oh yes, "only to be expected"!' Charmian snapped. 'And I bet you're bloody over the moon about it!'

243

'Charmian, I can't pretend that—'

'Now you've got rid of everyone, haven't you? Now you can go back to being the fucking emotional eunuch you always were!'

'There's no need to—'

'I just thank God I've got Henry and Emma away from you, that's all, before you somehow managed to destroy them too!'

'Now just a minute. Lilian destroyed herself. I had nothing to do with it.'

'You drove her to it.'

'You can't shift your guilt on to me that easily, Charmian. She had been threatening it for years.'

A sob broke from the other end of the phone. 'You've got it all now, Graham, haven't you? The whole bloody lot. God, there's no justice. Everything's just random. That someone like you should be granted the kind of luck that . . . If I had any belief in a God, that'd destroy it. And to think – you'll get all the other money as well now.'

'What other money?' he asked, puzzled.

'Don't pretend you don't know. But if you've got any spark of decency in you, see that the children get some of it. Otherwise, just do one thing for me.'

'What?'

'Keep out of my life. I never want to see you again. You bastard!'

He replaced his receiver more gently than she had hers. She really was becoming more and more like her mother.

He corrected himself. Her late mother. The thought amused him. To those who have shall be given. The removal of the inconvenience of Lilian was a bonus he had not expected. But what had Charmian meant about the other money?

He switched the recording machine on and played back his messages.

The first voice he recognised as David Birdham's.

'Graham, I've just come out of the management meeting. I'd hoped to contact you at the office, but it went on a bit. Anyway, the outcome's good. Your appointment's agreed.

You are Head of Personnel – or, if you prefer it, Head of Human Resources. The announcement will be made officially on Tuesday. Congratulations, Graham. Have a nice weekend.'

He stretched back with pleasure on his swivel chair and let the tape run on.

'Graham, it's Charmian. I just missed you at the office and I've been trying all evening, but you're obviously out . . .' That identified the timing of the message as the Friday evening, when he'd treated himself to dinner at the Grange. Her voice sounded drunk and angry. 'Listen, it's about Mummy. She rang me to tell me, just to crow, the cow, but she said she hadn't told you yet. About William Essex. Apparently that affair she was always on about actually did happen, because the only will the old poof left dates from that time – and she cops the lot. Now all I'm saying is – I'm just warning you – I know she's cut me out of her will and when she goes, you'll get it all – but you've got to make some over to Henry and Emma. Got to! Do you understand that? That's all I wanted to say.'

The end of the message was almost apologetic.

She sounded sheepish, suddenly aware of her drunkenness.

But the news, the hard fact that the recording contained, was more bounty. Now Graham had the last piece of the jigsaw that his upbringing had denied him. Not only was he to have the benefits of an increased earned income; he was also now to have the unfair advantage of inherited wealth.

The random gods of chance were in munificent mood; and Graham Marshall was their chosen son.

CHAPTER THIRTY-FOUR

The doorbell rang and he answered it.

Detective-Inspector Laker stood there, holding a briefcase, looking up with his habitual expression of sadness. 'Ah, you're back, Mr. Marshall,' he said, though it was no surprise. He had watched Graham's return from the Ford Escort parked opposite.

'Yes.'

'I've come in connection with your mother-in-law, Mrs Lilian Hinchcliffe.'

'Yes, I've only just heard the news. From Charmian, my . . . sister-in-law.' Graham estimated that his voice sounded properly shocked. 'Won't you come in, Detective-Inspector?'

'Thank you.'

In the sitting-room instinctively they took the chairs they had used on their previous encounter.

'It's terrible,' said Graham. 'You know there have been a couple of previous attempts?'

'Yes, yes.' The Detective-Inspector nodded slowly. 'I've been investigating all the background.'

'She was rather unstable, I'm afraid. Prone to dramatic gestures.'

'Yes. Like sending that anonymous letter we discussed when I was last here.'

'Exactly.' Graham liked the reference; it seemed to recapture some of the sympathy of the previous occasion. He smiled wryly, before an unwelcome thought arrived. 'Surely there's nothing about my wife's death that . . .'

'No, no,' Laker reassured him. 'No, just sorting out a few details about your mother-in-law.'

'Fine.'

'Of course, after that letter, you had no reason to love her.'

Graham shrugged magnanimously. 'She was a rather foolish old woman. I'm not one to bear grudges.'

'No. Good.' There was a pause. 'She left no note.'

'No?'

'She did on the occasions of her two previous attempts.'

'Oh. Well, perhaps she thought those signalled her intentions sufficiently.'

'Perhaps. Seems strange, though, for someone as dedicated to the dramatic gesture as she was, not to leave a note.'

'People committing suicide are hardly rational.'

'That's true enough.' Laker gave a little grunt, perhaps even a laugh. 'Mr. Marshall, I think it quite possible that you were one of the last people to see Mrs. Hinchcliffe alive. Except for the ambulance and hospital staff.'

'Oh, really? I don't actually know the details of how she did it, or where or . . . My sister-in-law just told me it was suicide.'

Laker did not take his cue to fill in the background, but went on, 'We reckon Mrs. Hinchcliffe came to see you on Saturday morning.'

'Yes.'

'Can you tell me what happened?'

'You're not going to believe this, Inspector, but she attacked me with a knife.'

'Uhuh.'

'She was absolutely mad.' He took pleasure in returning the aspersion she had cast on him. He felt supremely confident and dared to continue, 'She was still going on about Merrily's death, convinced that I'd killed her. I'm afraid she really was round the twist.'

'And she attacked you with a knife?'

'Yes.' He drew back his sleeve to show the scratch on his arm. 'Did this. Would have done worse if I'd given her the chance.'

247

'So you fought her off?'

'What else did you expect me to do?'

'Thus sustaining the injuries I can see on your face.'

Graham's hand went up to the raw lines of scratches on his cheek. 'Yes.'

'What time did this attack take place?'

'I don't know. Round midday, I suppose.'

'Uhuh. And what did you do then?'

'What did I do then?'

'Yes. Your mother-in-law came round and attacked you with a knife, you fought her off . . . what did you do then?'

'Well, I got dressed.' In reply to Laker's raised eyebrow, he added, 'She had woken me up. I got dressed and went out.'

'Out where?'

'Well, first I went down by the river and had lunch.'

'Whereabouts?'

'Just by the river. A picnic.'

'With anyone?'

'No. On my own.'

'And then?'

'Then I walked over Hammersmith Bridge and went to the cinema.'

'Oh yes. What did you see?'

'*Monty Python's Life of Brian.*'

'Ah. I saw that a few weeks back. Not sure that I approve from the religious point of view, but it had some funny sequences.'

'Yes.'

'Did you like that moment after he'd been to bed with the girl . . . ?'

'Um . . .'

'You know, he opened the window and . . .'

'I'm sorry, I don't remember that bit.'

'No? One of the best moments, I thought.'

'Yes. To be quite frank, Inspector, I missed most of the film. Fell asleep.'

'Oh yes? So what did you do after that?'

'I took a train to Oxford.'

'Any particular reason?'

'No. I just needed a break. I've had a tough few weeks. I needed a little pampering.'

'I see. And what did you do when you got to Oxford?'

'I checked into a hotel.'

'Which one?'

'The Randolph.'

'Without luggage?'

'I had bought what I needed in Hammersmith. I had a case.'

'Why?'

'What do you mean – why?'

'Why did you check into a hotel?'

'I like hotels. I feel at home in hotels. When I need a treat I go to an hotel.'

The Detective-Inspector nodded very slowly. 'I see. Do you know how your mother-in-law died?'

'No. As I say, I only just heard the news that . . .'

'She was killed by paraquat.'

'Oh.'

'Very nasty death. Vomiting, diarrhoea, abdominal pains, local inflammation of the mouth and throat, leading to multi-organ failure.'

Graham winced. 'As you say, nasty.'

'And a very unusual way of committing suicide.'

Graham shrugged. 'If someone's determined to do it . . .'

'Have to be very determined to do it the way Mrs. Hinchcliffe did.'

'Oh?'

Detective-Inspector Laker didn't speak as he reached into his briefcase and produced a polythene bag. Carefully and slowly, he opened the bag and placed the familiar sherry bottle on the table by his chair.

The bottle was empty, though there was a dark sediment at the bottom.

'That was how she did it, Mr. Marshall. Dissolved in the

sherry were the contents of eight sachets of weed killer containing paraquat.'

'Oh.'

'Well, I say "dissolved". That's hardly the word. It doesn't dissolve, just sinks to the bottom really. Very difficult to swallow that lot, you know. Virtually have to crunch your way through it.'

Graham let out a little nervous laugh. 'As I said, she was very determined.'

'Unpleasant stuff to swallow, too. Can inflame the throat tissues.'

'If you're going to kill yourself, you don't fuss about a little discomfort, surely.'

'Maybe not. Why do you think she mixed the stuff with sherry?'

'To make it more palatable.'

Laker nodded, digesting this idea. 'Yes, I suppose that's reasonable.' He paused. 'On the other hand, if that were the case, why did she put a label on it, marking it as poison?'

'Well, er . . .' Graham felt he was losing ground. 'So that nobody else would drink it, thinking it was sherry . . . ?'

'Hmm.' The Detective-Inspector continued to take his time. 'Interesting things, fingerprints,' he announced suddenly.

Graham expressed surprise at the *non sequitur*.

'You see, Mr. Marshall, as you would expect, your mother-in-law's prints are all over that bottle. There are also others.'

'So?'

'The strange thing is that the fingerprints on the label are not Mrs. Hinchcliffe's. Or not many of them. It seems certain that someone else put that label on.'

Graham was silent.

'You wouldn't object to having your fingerprints taken, Mr. Marshall?'

It was time for anger. 'Now listen, Inspector, if you're accusing me of having a hand in my mother-in-law's death –'

'Not accusing you of anything, Mr. Marshall. But when a strange death like this occurs, it's my job to imagine the events

250

that could have led up to it.'

'Yes. O.K.'

'Perhaps you'd allow me to spell out a possible scenario to you, Mr. Marshall. Suppose we take the starting-point that Mrs. Hinchcliffe's death wasn't suicide, but that it was murder.'

'Pretty botched-up, messy murder, if it was.'

'Most murders are botched-up and messy, Mr. Marshall.'

Not the ones I'm involved in! It was with difficulty that Graham restrained himself from actually saying the words.

'Right, my scenario . . . Let's not just say it was murder, let's also say that you killed Lilian Hinchcliffe.'

'But I didn't.'

A hand was raised for quiet. 'Hypothesis, Mr. Marshall, just hypothesis. Right, let's start with the facts. Mrs. Hinchcliffe came staggering out of the front door of this house at about three o'clock on Saturday afternoon. She was very ill, vomiting, hardly able to stand. A passer-by phoned for an ambulance. She was taken to hospital and died there at one thirty-five yesterday morning. While she could still speak, she said the same thing to the passer-by who found her, to the ambulance man, and to the doctor at casualty. What she said was: "Graham did it".'

'She was probably talking about her insane idea that I killed Merrily.'

'Maybe, maybe. But for my hypothesis, let's read it the other way. And let's think of motive. That anonymous letter didn't endear her to you.'

'No, certainly not, but—'

'I agree. Not a sufficient motive for murder, no. On the other hand, you have had financial problems recently, Mr. Marshall. I checked yesterday with your bank manager and I gather there have been times when—'

'But that's all over.'

'I have also discovered,' Laker continued inexorably, 'that Mrs. Hinchcliffe recently changed her will, cutting out her elder daughter, and leaving everything to her younger daughter and husband. With your wife's death, Mr. Marshall, that meant that you–'

'But–'

'No, I agree. There wasn't much to gain, was there?' He stopped. 'Until the news of the actor William Essex's bequest.'

'But I didn't know about that. I only discovered this afternoon that–'

'Charmian Hinchcliffe left the message for you on Friday evening.'

'But I didn't hear it till this afternoon.'

Laker cocked his head dubiously. 'No? That seems rather strange. You spent Friday night here. Still, never mind, let's press on with my scenario. Your mother-in-law did come round here on Saturday morning, as you say, and by then you had decided to kill her. Two suicide attempts in the past, so you thought you'd make it look like suicide.'

'I don't know what makes you think–'

'You have shown interest in poison before, Mr. Marshall. Some weeks ago. The girl at the library remembered you very clearly.'

'But–'

'And the young man at the garden centre said that you were very specific about wanting a weed killer containing paraquat.' Laker smiled. 'But on with the scenario. Let's say you experimented with weed killer in sherry. First, perhaps you thought you could get Mrs. Hinchcliffe to drink the treated sherry by mistake, but then you realised that she'd never be fooled. So you had to *force* her to drink it.'

'But I didn't.'

'She put up quite a fight. Hence the scratches on your face. But you forced the bottle to her lips repeatedly until she had swallowed all of it.'

'That's not true!'

'There were bruises on her face consistent with her mouth being forced open. Her lip had been cut where the bottle was jammed against it.'

'That wasn't how it happened.'

252

'I suggest that it took you some time to make her swallow it all. I suggest that you left the house round three o'clock.'

'I left before one.'

'No one saw you.'

'Did anyone see me at three?'

'No, but then ordinary people are very bad witnesses, Mr. Marshall. They don't notice who comes and goes most of the time, unless the people's behaviour is very unusual.'

It was true. The success of all Graham's other murders had been based on that, just luck, the unobservance of ordinary people. And now the luck was working the other way.

'But at three o'clock I was in the cinema.'

'You don't seem to have a very clear recollection of the film. And suddenly buying new clothes and going off to a hotel in Oxford seems strange behaviour. Could look like running away, Mr. Marshall.'

Graham said nothing.

'Very well, I've given you my scenario. All I'm asking you to do is to offer me some proof that it isn't true. Anything you like. Go on, anything. Give me one reason why I shouldn't arrest you for this particularly unpleasant and ill-managed murder?'

Stung by the slight, he almost leapt to the defence of his murders. But he caught himself in time and had to be content with conditional justification. 'If I ever committed a murder, it wouldn't be mismanaged. It'd be good. I am good. I'm efficient, logical . . . systematic . . .' He ran out of self-praise.

'One reason, Mr. Marshall. That's all I ask.'

Graham felt the waters closing over his head. The pressure on his lungs was as real as it had been in the darkness of the sea at Bosham. Panic beat about inside him like a bird in a net. He felt sweat against his clothes. His eyes watered as he looked into the grave, unforgiving face of the Inspector.

He wondered if Lilian had worked it all out, foreseen the consequences of her last actions, or if the suicide had been born of simple desperation. Either way, witting or unwitting, she had made her suicide a weapon against her son-in-law and

253

demonstrated another transmutation of the power of death.

And for her, as for him, the circumstances had all connived for success.

Lilian was having her revenge. The old man on the bridge, Merrily, Robert Benham and George Brewer all shared in that revenge.

And Graham Marshall was powerless to stop the adverse flow of his fortunes. There was nothing he could do.

Unless . . .

The little glimmer of memory glowed into hope, then burst into confidence that filled him again with warmth and power.

'Actually, Inspector,' said Graham, 'I do have a witness to my leaving the house before one on Saturday.'

The announcement caught Laker wrong-footed. He could only gape.

'A former secretary of mine was waiting for me. She claimed to have some grievance against me. We exchanged a few words when I came out of the house. She said then she was going to wait till I returned.' He shrugged. 'When I came back an hour ago, she had gone. Her name is Stella Davies. If you care to check, here's her number.'

Laker took the proffered address-book, and Graham treasured the stunned look of frustration on the Inspector's face.

As before, the relief after a close shave (and this had been the closest yet) made Graham light-headed. The Inspector had gone into the hall to telephone, but Graham still curbed the urge to laugh. He must play his last scene of triumph with becoming dignity.

Stella. Good old Stella. The eternal alibi. For two of his real murders she had unwittingly stood surety, and now she could free him from suspicion for the one he had not committed.

It had been a nasty moment, a tease from the gods of chance, a threat of overtaking in the final lap, but Graham had survived, fought off the challenge, and nothing now could stop his victory.

He poured two large whiskies. He would recapture the previous intimacy with Detective-Inspector Laker. He would be magnanimous, forgiving the policeman's accusations. He would move the conversation on to their late wives and compare symptoms of bereavement.

He set the Inspector's whisky ready at a convenient table and sipped his own as he awaited the apology.

The door from the hall opened. He identified the Inspector's expression as one of sourness.

'Well?' Graham raised a confident eyebrow.

'I spoke to Miss Davies. She confirms that she arrived in her car about twelve on Saturday. She would have come to the house, but she saw Mrs. Hinchcliffe letting herself in.'

'As I said.'

'She stayed in her car until three when she saw Mrs. Hinchcliffe stagger out.'

'Persistent, eh?' Graham grinned and indicated the Inspector's Scotch. 'But what a useful witness.'

Laker did not move. 'Yes. What a useful witness. She saw you leave the house too, Mr. Marshall.'

Graham allowed himself a little I-told-you-so shrug. 'At about a quarter to one, right?'

There was a silence. When he finally spoke, Laker's voice was cold and dull.

'No. Miss Davies saw you run out of the house just before three.'

'What?'

'She started her car to follow you, but was then distracted by Mrs. Hinchcliffe's appearance staggering out of the front door. When she next looked, you had gone. You were running, she said, "like a man possessed".'

Graham Marshall mouthed, but no words came. The random gods of chance had changed their allegiance. For him, for so long, they had made what was false seem real; now, with savage impartiality, they were making the real seem false.

He felt himself sinking, sinking.